OCTOBER 19, 2009

MW01578510

Happy birthday Brian!

H_2S

H_2S

A novel

Craig McAdie

All rights reserved. No part of this book may be reproduced, stored in a retrieval system, or transmitted, in any form or by any means, electronic, mechanical, photocopying, recording or otherwise – other than for reviewing purposes – without prior permission from the author.

Copyright © 2005 by Craig McAdie
Cover Photo: Comstock.com

This is a work of fiction, and other than government crown corporations and historical figures mentioned, the characters are solely the creation of the author. Any resemblance to actual persons and events is purely coincidental.

For Paul and Daryl: great friends that everyone should have....

Wednesday, August 17

The grey pickup truck rumbled up, down, through, and around the twists and turns of a gravel road south of Lesser Slave Lake, kicking up dust and sand behind it. Surrounding it on either side of the backwoods trail were blankets of green pine trees that gently covered the rolling bed of hills that stretched to the horizon. Above lay a clear sheet of blue sky, broken only by a few puffs of soft white cloud and an intense summer sun that was hot enough to promote sweat and yet dry out the skin.

Inside the truck, the sharp scent of pine mingled with that of the dust, which was having little difficulty in finding its way into the cab through the open windows. As the driver, Clint Henderson, eased the truck along and over the curving road, he watched for the sudden appearance of a deer or a bear ambling onto the road in front of them, as well for another cloud of dust further down the road ahead that would signal a vehicle approaching from the opposite direction.

His passenger, Peter Keltner, sat back quietly on the right side of the bench seat with his knees propped against the dashboard. His face was hidden from the real world behind a tabloid newspaper, which he was reading with a level of concentration that allowed him to ignore the road on which they were travelling. The newspaper had a garish picture on its cover of what appeared to be a large ape cuddling a frightened prospector; a large headline across the top of the page screamed 'I Was Sasquatch's Love Slave'. The only human sound in the truck cab was the occasional quick laugh that he let out.

"Some good stuff in this issue, I take it," muttered Henderson after the last outburst; through it all, he kept his eyes on the road ahead.

Keltner looked over at him for a second and then buried his head back in the paper.

"You know, if those so-called journalists over at channel 4 ever covered this stuff on their six o'clock news, their ratings might be higher," was his muffled reply.

"Hell, I'd even consider watching it myself once in a while," he added as he turned to the next page.

They had just driven through a series of sharp turns when, seeing the road up ahead branch off to the left yet again, Henderson stepped on the brake pedal to slow the truck down. He finally stopped the vehicle so that it was sitting halfway in the ditch by the side of the trail. They were perched on the crest of a hill and after shifting the transmission into 'park', Henderson leaned forward on the steering wheel and scanned the horizon.

"Hmmmmmmmmmm...."

Keltner looked up from his newspaper.

"What's up?" he asked. "Anything wrong? Need me to save the day?"

Henderson leaned back and turned off the truck's engine. The rustling of the pine trees as they swayed in the gentle breeze now provided the background noise, while the dust that had been filling the cab began to settle.

He closed his eyes, pulled a small, rumpled box from his shirt pocket, and opened the top. His forefingers dug into the top of the box and extracted a chewy breath mint, which he popped into his mouth. After waiting for its brief heat to dissipate, he bit into it once with his back teeth, and then passed it forward with his tongue. Henderson started chewing it beaver-like with his front teeth.

"Uhm, well, to be perfectly honest," Henderson began. Still chewing on the mint, he opened his eyes and squinted through the windshield. "It suddenly occurred to me that I may not really have that much of a clue as to where we are."

He opened the lid of the briefcase that lay between them and pulled out a topographical map of the area. After unfolding it and stretching it across the truck's dash, he ran his finger along the crooked amber line that marked the road on which they had been travelling. He was hoping to find a landmark that looked even vaguely familiar to anything that he saw outside of the parked truck.

"Oh sure: great navigator," Keltner said, "Columbus had nothing on you. Here I am, stranded five hours north of home. My loved ones will never see me again if I keep on hanging around out here in the toolies with you."

He sighed.

"Well, I guess if we're going to be out here for awhile," he continued, "I'd better take a leak."

Keltner opened the side door, which let out a slight creak, and jumped down into the ditch.

Henderson, who was still concentrating on the map, swallowed the last of the breath mint.

"Don't piss on the truck," he said quietly.

"Nag, nag, nag," responded the muffled voice from behind the truck. "No wonder your wife left you."

"She left me because I had friends like you."

Henderson stabbed his finger at a point on the map that he believed to be the location of an oil production battery he had spotted from the road less than five minutes before.

"Hah," Keltner said from the ditch. "You didn't even know me when you and her split."

Henderson's fingertip slid along the thin amber curves that led from the battery site to the middle of the stretch of curves where he knew they were now. Now that he had found that, he believed, it might be easier to figure out where they were supposed to be, and with any luck, how to get there.

He pulled out a smaller piece of paper from the briefcase;

it listed the locations of the wells he had planned to inspect that day.

"That woman had a remarkable sixth sense," Henderson called back. "Look, you have whole forest of trees out there. Why do you insist on hanging around here? Get some fresh air, for crying out loud. Go off and play."

Henderson then opened his own door and climbed out to stretch his legs. The sensation of the solid, fine gravel under the hard rubber soles of his work boots felt good after being cramped in the truck for the past two hours. As he heard and felt his knees crack back into position, he breathed deeply. The fresh air that filled his lungs and the hot sun heating the back of his neck made him feel a bit drowsy.

Henderson shook his head and walked around to the back of the truck. He saw Keltner making his way through the thick grass to the edge of the woods.

"I'll bet there's spiders in here," Keltner called out. "Probably snakes too. Big ones that are just waiting for a tasty morsel such as myself to stumble into their waiting fangs."

"Don't worry. I've heard that snakes are very health conscious. They won't eat anything with high levels of cholesterol."

"Ha, ha, ha. You're a funny man, Henderson. Tell me: do you have any friends at all?"

"I'd like to do better, but Mom's behind in the cheques she sends them, so I have to make do."

"I thought so."

"Thanks for making my point. Look, if you don't hurry up, I'm going to leave you here."

Keltner disappeared into the woods. About a minute later, Henderson saw him reappear.

"Man, those thistles tickled the tip of my dick!" Keltner said gleefully.

"Yeah, well, in the wild they can grow pretty tall," replied Henderson.

Keltner threw a handful of Saskatoon berries at him.

"Have you figured out where we are, red leader?" he

asked.

"I think so," replied Henderson as he returned to the truck.

He sat in the driver's seat with his legs hanging onto the road and stretched out his map in the cab. Keltner sat on the other side of him.

"I think we're on the right track anyway," Henderson said. "There's a major compressor station about three miles down the road here. The entrance road to that continues around the station and into the bush, where it leads to a dead end. I would bet that the well is at the end of that road."

Keltner looked at the map closely.

"Are you sure that's a road? It looks more like a cut-line for a pipeline right-of-way."

"Trust me. If it isn't a road, then there's no way to get to the well, and that's that. But I have to believe that there's something there that allows the operators to get to it."

"Tell me again: just exactly what is this thing we're looking for anyway?" Keltner asked.

"It's classified as a single well gas battery. What that typically means is that the gas from the well is produced through a glycol contactor, which is a processing vessel that uses a chemical called glycol to strip water from the gas, and it's then tied directly into the Nova system to be sold."

"Uh huh. Right."

"Okay, it's a pipe that sticks out of the ground through which natural gas flows from the well that your people drilled and is now measured. The water is removed from the gas stream through a chemical reaction that takes place in a big tower. Then, through the good graces of a monthly pro-rationing system that we, the gods of the industry, dictate, the company that owns that gas can sell it to the major natural gas transmission company in the province."

"Ah. I see. So why, then, are we so determined to look at this well?"

"Nobody's inspected it in over four years. It's classified as 'suspended', which means that it hasn't been on production for a while. We still have to check it to make sure that it's properly shut-in and the wellhead is still in reasonable condition. Sometimes we come across a wellhead that hasn't been properly suspended and the thing's leaking like crazy."

"Well, now that you put it that way, it doesn't sound too complicated," Keltner said.

"I figured that I'd start you off with something relatively simple."

Keltner shook his head as Henderson closed the door and started the truck.

"On the other hand, I don't think I'll ever understand you gas inspectors at all," he muttered.

Henderson and Keltner were field inspectors with the Alberta Energy and Utilities Board, the provincial body responsible for regulating the energy industries that operate within its jurisdiction. The mandate of the EUB, or "the Board", as its employees and industry in general have come to know it, is to ensure that the energy resources of the province of Alberta are developed in an efficient and orderly manner, and to create the necessary rules and regulations to carry out its duties effectively. Although the Board was created to regulate all aspects of energy development in the province, by far the greatest amount of its attention is placed on the oil and gas industry, which is responsible for approximately 90 per cent of all such activity.

The overall administration and regulation of the oil and gas industry is centred in the Board's head office in Calgary. There are also a number of field offices scattered throughout the province, and it is the inspectors from these offices who make sure that the drilling rigs, service rigs, and all oil and gas production facilities are constructed and operated in accordance with the Board's regulations. Henderson and Keltner, who were based out of the Edmonton Area Office, both liked to believe, much like most of the other men and women based in the field offices, that they did all of the Board's real work.

Henderson turned the truck left onto a thin trail that branched off from the main gravel road. There was a large white and red sign shaped like an arrow by the side of the road and Henderson assumed, and hoped, that this sign would show them the way. A few minutes after turning onto the tightly curved road, Henderson and Keltner drove into a large clearing and stopped.

To their right was a large building: this was the actual compressor station. The hum of the huge, electrically driven machines housed inside rose above the noise of the truck engine as soon as the vehicle stopped and the crackling sound of the tires crushing gravel had subsided.

"I don't see anything else," Henderson said. "I don't think this is it."

Keltner looked out of his window toward the right.

"Looks like there's a path over there heading north," he replied. "I'll bet it's down there."

Henderson eased his foot off the brake pedal and the truck coasted slowly around the north edge of the compressor station under the power of its idling engine. He reapplied the brake after he turned the truck slightly onto the long, narrow, grass covered clearing that cut through the forest ahead. Again, he shifted the transmission into 'park', and there was a slight increase in the pitch of the engine.

"Geez, I don't know," Henderson said slowly. "It doesn't look too solid."

"Christ, you're a wus!"

Henderson looked at him. Keltner returned the look, along with a smile on his face. He batted his eyelashes.

"Well, you are," Keltner added. "And I say it only because I love you to pieces, my darling. I'm trying to save something of your dignity. Look, I've driven on hundreds of roads that were a hell of a lot worse than this one and I'm still here. You gas plant inspectors are too damn soft and that's what scares me about becoming one. Next thing you know you'll want the operators in this province to pave all of the roads to their facilities. Tell you what..."

Keltner cleared his throat and grabbed the steering wheel.

"Move over and let a real man drive," he added. "I'll get us there."

Henderson sighed.

"You know, whenever we're out in the field together, we always manage to get stuck someplace," he said. "Doesn't that frighten you? Doesn't that tell you anything at all? I mean, I never get stuck when I'm out by myself. Now, so far on this trip, we've been lucky. I like to think that one of the reasons for that is that I've made some smart decisions this time and that would include the decision not to drive on that so-called road."

"Ah, your decision sucks and just serves to reinforce the notion that you are a truly pathetic human being."

"Gosh, thanks. You're telling me that you'd go ahead on that?!"

"Well, like you, if I was by myself, probably not."

Henderson dropped his head onto his hands, which were perched on top of the steering wheel, and sighed.

"What?" he said.

Then he shook his head.

"No. Never mind. I'm not following this and I'm not sure I'd really want to even if I did."

"Look, it's quite simple, Clint," Keltner said. "We both agree that if we were by ourselves, neither one of us would risk this, right?"

"Umm...okay, now I'm really convinced that I don't want to hear this."

"Look, is it not true that together, you and I have set a new office record this year for getting stuck when we're out in the field?"

"Boy, have you got that one right."

"Is it not also true that the office expects us to get stuck when we go out in the field together?"

"Now that one's news to me, I have to admit."

"Well it's a fact. Spenser told me just last week that he

could always tell when you're trying to teach me whatever supernatural hocus-pocus it is that you pretend to know something about because our trucks are the dirtiest in the parking lot. As a matter of fact, I'd say that it's at the point where it's not only anticipated, but there'd be a lot of disappointment if it didn't happen. It's almost become an office tradition."

Henderson lifted his head.

"Oh, come on," he said. "So what you're saying is that we are going to start down this trail and that we can count on getting stuck, but we're doing it because those back in the office are not only expecting it, but are counting on it?"

Keltner looked up, performed some mental calculations, and nodded his head twice.

"Exactly: we're doing it for them. Consider it an act of unselfishness that will live forever in the hearts and minds of our colleagues. It's something dependable, a rock almost, that they can cling to when the stresses of this job are getting to them."

"That's crazy!"

"Then do it for yourself!"

"Change that. *You're* crazy. And I definitely don't want to hear this one."

"Yes you do, but it's a bit subtle, so you really have to pay attention."

Keltner cleared his throat again and held his hands up in front of him.

"Okay, when you're by yourself, nobody else is around to see you chicken out of this, right?"

"I...suppose."

"Well, right now you look like a real wussy and I'm letting you know it. I'm calling you all sorts of names and gradually destroying any sense of pride that you may have had, I mean, worse than usual. And I don't need to tell you what the rest of the office is going to hear, now do I? I mean, if the situation were reversed, you'd let me know about it; that's what friends are for. Therefore, ipso facto, QED, and I told you so, if you want to recover any trace of your masculinity on this trip, after I've called you a chicken-shit weak-kneed Norbert, you will have to drive down this trail."

"Even if it means getting stuck?"

"Especially if it means getting stuck. What's more important: a clean truck or your dignity?"

"I still don't believe this," Henderson replied while shaking his head.

"Plus, so far I haven't really learned anything on this trip that I haven't seen before. Except for this. I want to see a suspended whatever you called it. My mind is open and I'm willing, and I expect you to fill it with some of your infinite wisdom."

"Oh brother," Henderson said quietly. Then he sighed again.

"Okay, I'll do it," he added, "but only in the interest of furthering your education and getting you to shut up. Watch out for wet spots."

"At a boy, Clint. I knew you'd get some guts if you hung around me long enough."

Henderson rolled his eyes as Keltner sat up and prepared himself for the bumpy ride ahead. Henderson shifted back into 'drive' and stepped on the gas.

Compared to the roads down which they usually drove, it was relatively smooth for the first hundred feet or so.

Then they started hitting the ruts that lay buried under the thick, wild grass that covered the trail further along. The truck began bouncing like a yo-yo, but Henderson kept his foot on the gas and the truck continued to lurch forward.

It didn't take long to reach the point at which most people would have applied their brakes and tried to stop, and Henderson's experience battled with his natural instinct to do exactly that.

That instinct continued to nag at him, and got louder as the truck bounced along the trail. He sighed to himself, resigned to the fact that at some point it would win and that he would have to obey it. Right now, however, the quick glances that he made to either side of the truck told him that there was no way to turn around without stopping. That meant, of course, that he would have to keep moving until that special moment when his options would finally run out.

"Hold it!" Keltner yelled, announcing the arrival of that moment loudly.

It was too late. Henderson felt his stomach sink along with the truck's wheels into the soft ground.

He closed his eyes and dropped his head. When he looked up again, he saw that Keltner had his head out of the window. He was studying the right, rear wheel.

Henderson turned off the engine. Keltner pulled his head back into the truck and looked at him.

"Well now you've done it," he said quietly. Then he laughed.

"Well now you've done it," Henderson echoed with a nasal whine. "Nobody likes you, you know."

"I know. That's why I have no friends. Except for you, of course."

Henderson opened his door and stepped out onto the suddenly elevated ground. As he walked around the vehicle, he saw that each of the truck's four wheels was buried to the centre of its hubcap.

"Shit," he said.

Keltner walked around from his side of the truck.

"You know, you often use words like that when I'm out here with you," he said, "and I figure that they're all part of your highly educated and technical vocabulary. Then, wanting to emulate you because you're my hero and all, I use words like that at home around Kathy and she slaps me. Especially when it's in front of her family. It's no wonder I'm dysfunctional."

Henderson tried not to laugh.

"You prick," he said through clenched teeth. "I ought to kill you and leave your body here for those snakes you're so scared of."

"Well, you could," Keltner replied. He was now squatting down, surveying the half-buried wheels. "But I honestly think that you're going to need my help to get you out of this mess. Hmm. Why don't you get in and see if you can back out of here."

Henderson hopped back into the truck and started the engine. After letting it idle for a minute, he floored the gas pedal. The truck roared and reared up, but it couldn't quite break free of the mud that held it. Another roar and the truck attempted to lunge forward. Henderson tried again in reverse, but the truck still refused to leave its burrow. Keltner waved his arms and Henderson shut off the engine.

"Now what?" Keltner asked.

Henderson leaned on the edge of the window, his fingers cradling his chin. He looked toward the front of the truck, along the cut-line, and then he turned to look behind it. Then, squinting, he looked at Keltner.

"Well, I suppose we could go back to that compressor station and see if we can get some help," Henderson said. "Mills and Hudson are up here this week, but I'll bet we're too far out to get them on the radio."

"Yeah, but even if they were nearby, personally I'd be too embarrassed to share this one with anybody."

"Oh right. I guess they wouldn't understand that we did this for them." Henderson rolled his eyes skyward again as he got out of the truck.

Then they began the hike back along the cut line.

"You know, I like coming out in the field with you," Keltner announced after a few minutes.

"Well, I think I'm glad to hear that," Henderson replied.

"Yeah, the weather is usually pretty good when I'm out in the toolies with you. When I'm out in the field by myself, it always seems like Mother Nature has PMS."

"Now, I'm sorry to hear that," Henderson said. He paused for a second and then added "Hang on. Wait a minute. No, no I'm not."

"I do think, however," said Keltner, "that I'm going to ask Spenser for another instructor."

"Now why is that?"

"I'm getting tired of walking everywhere."

"We wouldn't walk if we didn't end up traveling down clearings you always mistake for inter-provincial highways."

"Yeah, but as an instructor, you're supposed to know more about these things than me."

"No, no, no, no, no. I'm supposed to be teaching you about gas plants, remember? And you're supposed to learn all that you can from me so that when things are slow in your drilling department, you can still work. See, that's what's known as justifying your paycheque. Besides, when you go out to check a rig, you travel over some pretty rotten roads. It's not like this is a novelty for you or anything."

"Yeah, but when I'm with you I always get so caught up with the sage, mature wisdom and insight that you're graciously sharing with me that, well, I guess I just get all giddy and forget about the mundane things in life, like roads and stuff."

Henderson sighed.

"So tell me then," he said. "Are you actually learning anything from me?"

"It's hard to say. I think I am, but I prefer to let my brain absorb information, kind of like osmosis. I don't believe that a person actually learns stuff by asking questions or doing things."

"Or by paying attention."

"Oh, I pay attention, in a kind of subtle way. Just because I don't jump up and down with excitement every time I learn something new doesn't mean that I don't appreciate any of this wisdom. Deep down, I'm sure I'm understanding it and storing it somewhere extra special. And at some point in my life, I'm sure that all of the knowledge that I've gleaned from you will come in very handy."

"That means we could turn Pete Keltner out on his own next week and he'd be able to inspect a gas plant by himself?"

"As easily as you could inspect a drilling rig on your own."

"So, Pete: what were you saying about the weather?"

"Poinggg. That sorta came out of left field, didn't it?"

"You know me and drilling rigs don't get along. There's no logic to them."

"Like there is with gas?"

"Well, processing gas makes some sense. At least it goes in one end and comes out the other."

"And in between it burps and coughs and gives off steam and horrible farty gas smells and makes other funny noises, and does things I'm sure nobody really understands; you know, just like when Kathy makes me eat something extra-spicy. The only things that do that on drilling rigs are the people who work on them, especially the tool-pushes. That's why we leave gas plants to whiz-bangs like you."

"Well, at least you recognize that I do have some talents."

"Yeah, but what we have to do is divert some of those talents to finding you a girlfriend."

"Uh, oh. I know this conversation."

"You know, Clint, I just don't understand it. You're what, thirty three years old . . ."

"Thirty four."

"Okay, thirty four years old. You're somewhat good looking: that's according to my wife, by the way, because I just don't see it, but she's pretty smart about these kinds of things, so I'll take her word for it. You've got a good, steady job that pays sort of not bad and has a pension. And you don't wear a baseball cap. I mean, what more could a woman want?"

"Ah yes, but you see most women in northern Alberta aren't interested in getting involved with anyone after hearing that you got married. They're all still in mourning."

"Well, you know I feel bad about that, but they have to realize that there is only one of me. Still, we've got to find someone for you before you get too old. I don't think that the Board's health plan covers Viagra."

"Gosh, Batman, it's a good thing we've arrived at the bat compressor station so we don't have to continue with this conversation anymore."

"Well, you'd better not be expecting me to drop this topic just like that."

"You will if you want to get out of here."

The large rectangular buildings that enclosed the huge electric motors stood before them, protected by a fine mesh, chain-link fence. Henderson and Keltner walked around the perimeter of the compound until they found the main gate. It was padlocked.

"Ah, Christ," Keltner muttered as he jiggled the lock. "Now what?"

Henderson was looking through the fence.

"I think I see some boards over by the main building," he replied. "I'm gonna crawl under the bottom of the gate and see what I can find. You can keep your portly little body here."

"Yeah, okay. I'll stand guard and watch out for deranged squirrels."

Henderson lay on the ground beneath the gate, grabbed its bottom edge, and pulled himself into the yard of the compressor station. When he was clear of the gate, he got up and walked over to the edge of the building where he had seen a pile of junk. Parts of five large, flat pieces of thick wood, each about three and a half feet long, were buried beneath some pieces of sheet metal and a length of fibreglass insulation. Henderson carried these boards back to the gate, two at a time, and slid them under the gate to Keltner.

The walk back to the truck was quiet. Henderson and Keltner had to continually shift the boards they carried in order to give each of the different muscles in their arms an equal opportunity to experience the load. About twenty minutes later, the huddled mass of the grey pick-up truck once again lay before them, buried indignantly in the soft ground.

Henderson scrambled into the back of the truck and unbolted the jack, which he passed out to Keltner. Then they stood silently for a minute, looking first at the truck and then at each other.

"Well," sighed Henderson, "I guess we'd better get to it."

Each cycle would begin with them jacking up each of the truck's four wheels in turn. While each wheel was suspended, they would place one of the boards under it and then they lowered the truck. When all four wheels had solid wood beneath their treads, Henderson or Keltner would climb into the driver's seat, start the truck and back it along the length of the wood until the wheels ran off the boards and settled into the ground behind with a sloppy thud. Then they repeated the procedure.

When they had successfully backed the truck out about thirty feet, Henderson looked at his watch. It had been a little bit more than three hours since they had started harvesting the truck. They had just finished jacking up the four corners of the truck for the eighth time and he was exhausted. His partner didn't look much better and, like him, was covered in mud, dirt, and sweat.

"Okay," Henderson said as he wiped his brow. He threw the jack in the bed of the pickup. "Your turn. Give it all you've got this time. It's six o'clock and I'd really like to get out of here."

Keltner was sitting in the truck with the driver's door open. He fired up the engine and put the truck into reverse. Then he thrust the gas pedal firmly to the truck's floorboard.

The truck's tires let out a terrible shriek as they spun, almost frantically, on the wood beneath them. This time the weight of the truck pushed the boards into the ground, but the traction held and the wheels were able to spin fast enough to keep the truck travelling even after it had left the boards. Mud and grass flew from the sides of the truck. Keltner, who was trying to control the vehicle while peering out from the open door, kept his foot on the gas. His forehead was wrinkled and he was concentrating on the path behind, his eyes darting from side to side of the trail.

Henderson yelled and waved at him to keep going as he jogged along with the wildly bucking truck. Still driving backwards at full throttle, Keltner looked up at Henderson for a half second.

"Go, go, go!" Henderson's arms yelled. His arms were swinging madly as he ran beside the truck. "If this doesn't work, we'll be out here all damn night!"

After it had travelled about two hundred feet, the truck found solid ground and its frantic bouncing eased. Keltner applied the brakes after backing out another hundred feet, and jumped out.

"See, I told you I'd get us out of here," he cried jubilantly.

"Yeah, and you're ugly too, but I don't hear you bragging about that. Now get your ass in the truck and let's go!"

They both jumped back into the truck. Keltner took the wheel and backed it out of the rest of the clearing. They traded places when they found themselves back at the compressor station.

As they buckled up their seatbelts, Henderson turned to Keltner.

"Explain to me again exactly why I take you anywhere," he said.

"Because I'm an exciting conversationalist with gorgeous brown eyes to die for and broad shoulders. Now shut up and drive: we both owe each other a drink."

Thursday, August 18

As a reward for their efforts the previous afternoon, Henderson and Keltner allowed themselves an extra hour of sleep that morning. The pounding on his motel room door stirred Henderson from a deep sleep. With one eye closed and squinting through the other, Henderson looked at his watch and saw that it was half past eight.

"Go away!" he called out.

"Come on, Clint," replied the muffled voice on the other side of the door. "That's not very polite. What's the magic word?"

"Hold on a minute, for Christ's sake."

"No, that's not it. Now, I know that your mother taught you better than that."

Henderson rolled over and lay on his back for a moment with his eyes closed. He took a deep breath and then threw his legs out from under the covers and sat up.

Then he stopped.

"Ooh," he exhaled slowly.

At that moment, Henderson became painfully convinced that someone had gone back to the cut-line where they had been stuck the previous afternoon, retrieved the boards they had used to get themselves out, and then sometime during the night had crept into his room and replaced the muscles in his shoulders, arms, and legs with them.

Henderson dug his fingers into the knot that now called his left shoulder home as he staggered over to the door to let Keltner in. His partner was standing in the hallway looking at the business section of the morning paper when the door opened.

"And good morning to you too, sunshine," Keltner said without looking up. "This is your eight thirty wake-up call. The sun is shining and the stock markets are up. It's a beautiful day out there, so let's get out and experience all that life has to offer."

"Oh, do shut up and close the door," replied Henderson as he grabbed his clothes and stumbled into the bathroom. He took a long shower and stood for a while with the water pouring over his aching body, letting the pounding, hot water linger on his shoulders. When he finished, he dried himself and stepped back into the bedroom of the motel room. The drapes were now open and the morning sun filled the room at an angle. His muscles seemed to be quiet for a moment and Henderson felt much better.

Keltner lay on the other bed in the room reading the closing stock market quotes from the previous day. He was totally oblivious to the television that he had turned on to listen to the morning news.

"Well, hot shot?" Henderson asked as he rubbed his hair with a towel. "Make enough money to retire yet?"

"Nah," was the reply. "Damn Dakota Industries dropped almost three bucks yesterday. Your mutual fund is up though."

"Why the hell don't you put something into it?" Henderson asked. He was brushing his hair in front of the mirror. "That was great advice you gave me."

Keltner folded the paper and dropped it into the small wastepaper basket beside the bed.

"Yeah, well, you know me," he said looking around, first at the television, and then outside. "I'm a great one for following everybody else's advice but mine. C'mon, you're gorgeous, so you can quit playing with your hair already. What's on the agenda for today?"

"Home, James. Back to Edmonton, with a brief stop at

the Western Triassic gas plant this side of Saint Albert."

"Aye, aye. Captain. But let's get some breakfast first. I'm starving."

Henderson gathered up his things and put them in his overnight bag. Then, after checking out of the motel and putting his bag in the truck, he and Keltner wandered into the motel's coffee shop.

"Look, there's Mills," Henderson said as they stood in the entrance.

"Yeah, but look who's with him," Keltner replied with a groan. "It's Hudson."

They tried to sneak to one of the booths by a window, but Mills saw them first and held up a hand in greeting. His eyes were red and he looked tired. Hudson was sitting with his back to the door.

Henderson and Keltner walked over to their table.

"Greetings, gentlemen," Keltner said. "How's it going today? Didn't see you at callisthenics and the singing of the company song this morning."

Hudson turned to face them and grunted. Keltner slid quickly onto the bench seat next to Bob Mills, forcing Henderson to sit next to Gillis Hudson.

The waitress brought breakfast plates and set them in front of Mills and Hudson. After pouring coffee for Henderson and Keltner, she took their order.

"You boys are off to a bit of a late start this morning," Keltner said to Mills after she had left the table. "Tip back a few last night?"

"Damn game went into extra innings," Mills responded quietly as he sipped his coffee. His unfinished breakfast lay before him, waiting to be picked up by the waitress.

"And he kept me up with him," Hudson mumbled, "until he fell asleep and I had to shut off the tube. Christ, I hate having a roommate."

Henderson shot a subtle glance at Keltner.

"Then why do you bother, Gillis?" Keltner asked. "The Board will spring for a room of your own."

"Stinking Board wages. Poverty pay. At least if we split a room, I can make a bit of coin if I claim for the per-diem and pay for half a room out of my own pocket."

"Ahh," said Keltner. Henderson couldn't tell if his partner was nodding his head or shaking it.

Hudson took a bite from his plate and threw down his fork.

"God, the crap they serve in these places," he said quietly. "Figure they have a captive crowd and so they can get away with anything. Excuse me, miss?"

The waitress had been passing by their table and swung around.

"Yes sir. Can I help you?"

"Yeah, you sure can," Hudson said with a sweet smile. "Does this look like something I would eat?"

The young woman looked confused as she pulled out her pad and fumbled through its pages.

"I think … I'm sure that's what you ordered, sir," she stammered. "Yes, here it is."

Hudson slid the plate across the table. The waitress barely caught it as it slipped over the edge, but a piece of bacon still fell to the floor.

"That's not what I bloody well asked now, is it? If you can't give me something edible, then I'll just have my fucking coffee."

Henderson had picked up the bacon from the floor and put it back on the plate. He smiled helplessly at the waitress before she took the plate back to the kitchen.

"Dumb slut," Gillis said under his breath.

Henderson raised his eyebrows at Keltner, who was looking at the ceiling.

"So, um, where are you two off to this morning?" Mills asked.

"We're heading back," said Henderson. "We have to stop at Western Triassic today and then home for a nice long weekend."

"Is this guy actually learning anything?" Mills jerked his

thumb towards Keltner.

"I learned how to use a jack yesterday," Keltner said with a big smile. "And to appreciate the drilling sector when it gets busy again."

Mills looked at Henderson with a puzzled expression.

"Never mind." replied Henderson, shaking his head. "It's a terribly long, boring story and I wouldn't want to embarrass anybody so early in the morning."

"Okay, whatever. Either of you going to be home on the weekend?" Mills asked. "I need someone to take on-call Sunday night. It's my anniversary and I promised my wife I'd take her out."

"Aw, isn't that just the greatest?" Keltner replied. "Some place expensive, I hope. Your wife deserves it. She's a sweetheart."

"Are you kidding? You know who I work for."

"I'd love to help you out my man, but I might be going to Kathy's brother's on Saturday for dinner."

"I'll do it," volunteered Henderson. "I don't have anything planned."

"Thanks. Well Hudson, we'd better hit the road. We've got a long day ahead of us."

Mills grabbed the bill and, after Henderson and Keltner got out of the way, he and Hudson slid out of the booth and left. Henderson watched and waited until they had left before saying anything.

"Might be?" he said.

"What?" Keltner replied, his brow furrowed.

"Might be going to your brother-in-law's for dinner?"

"Oh yeah. Some sort of family function. I don't know if I'm invited yet."

"Christ. Are you on the outs with Kathy's brother again?"

"Uhm, yeah, pretty much since the last time we had dinner there."

"Okay, I'll bite," said Henderson slowly before taking a sip of coffee. "What happened this time?"

Keltner shrugged.

"I don't know, really," he replied. "I mean, I know his wife is a bit sensitive and I know that she hates the word 'puke', but honestly, that's what her cooking tasted like."

The result of Henderson's attempt not to spit out his mouthful of coffee was that he gagged on it instead.

"I see," he said as he wiped his mouth with a napkin when he finally had his coughing fit under control, "and you thought you should tell her?"

"Well, somebody at the table had to say something. It's for her own good, for crying out loud. You know how special Larry and what's-her-name are to me."

"Are you kidding me? The guy I hear referred to on a regular basis as a festering boil on the butt of humanity?"

"Who says that?" Keltner asked indignantly.

"You do. All the time."

"Yeah, well. Anyway, Kathy's trying to smooth the waters."

"Again?" Henderson replied.

"Again," echoed Keltner, and then he added, "Mills looked a little rough this morning, don't you think?"

"Yeah, I remember those days long ago when I was his age," Henderson said. Then he shrugged. "Mills is all right, but man, I don't know how he keeps up the pace."

"Ah, he's just at that point in his life where his every instinct is guided by either his liver or his crotch," replied Keltner.

"I guess I don't get that either," Henderson said. "Like you said, his wife is such a sweetheart and I have this gut feeling that Mills isn't exactly RCA when it comes to fidelity."

Henderson sighed as he took a sip of coffee.

"Oh well," he said. "And then, of course, there's Hudson …."

"Oh yeah," Keltner replied. "Now there's an individual with some serious issues."

"Ah, he's just hard to get to know."

"Well, it's not like his attitude helps."

"Who knows?" said Henderson. "It might be that he has some problems that we don't know about. I mean, it could be that there, but for the grace of oxygen at birth, go I."

"Oh hardly. If that's the barometer, you had oxygen in spades. So how come he's with Mills this week? I mean, it's not like he enjoys Hudson's company like you enjoy mine."

"Cardinal doesn't trust Hudson to be out on his own. Too many stories coming back to the office about him."

"Such as?"

"Bunch of stuff. You didn't hear any of it from me though. Nothing concrete, well, nothing they can prove. Cardinal has it set up now so that Hudson has to travel with someone else. That's why the oil production guys have to travel in pairs."

"You mean the safety story is horseshit?"

"They really do keep you drilling guys in the dark, don't they?" said Henderson with a smile.

"Head office knows us well enough to know that we're smart enough not to hurt ourselves, so there's no need for us to be baby sat. As for the rest of you, well, it's crazy! Tying up twice the manpower because of one person?"

Henderson shrugged.

"Yeah, well, I don't understand it either," he replied.

"It's a waste if you ask me," Keltner said. "Why don't they kick him down to head office along with the rest of the dweebs?"

"Guess nobody down there wants him either. Remember, Cardinal hired him, not head office. Now he's stuck with him."

"Poor Mills."

"Maybe you'll consider yourself lucky from now on and remember that you could be out inspecting oil batteries with Hudson instead of inspecting gas plants with me. Lord, I am *so* good to you."

"Oh, come on now, Clint: why would I want to be anything other than a gas plant inspector? After all, you guys are men among men, protector of the weak and helpless, and saviours of trucks and other defenceless machinery."

Henderson took another sip of coffee.

"You just remember that."

Keltner buried his face in his hands on the table.

"Oh, I'm so, so, so terribly sorry. Can you please find

room in your more than generous heart to forgive an ungrateful wretch like me? I just can't take it. Quick: give me your butter knife so I can slash my wrists."

The waitress arrived with their breakfast when Keltner raised his head.

"More, umm, coffee?" she asked.

Keltner started laughing.

"You must be a real treat to wake up to," Henderson said to Keltner. "I swear I'm going to leave you somewhere."

They took their time over breakfast. The conversation ranged from work (on Henderson's part) to virtually everything else (on Keltner's part), with particular emphasis on the chest sizes of former girlfriends and where to find window seals for a 1938 Dodge.

The waitress who had caught Hudson's plate was at the cash register as they stepped up to pay.

"Was everything all right, sir?" she asked with a mixed smile. "I'm sorry about your friend."

Henderson shook his head as he handed her his credit card.

"You don't have anything to be sorry about. Really. Don't worry yourself about him. He's having a bad week."

"Bad decade, actually," added Keltner.

She nodded hesitantly, handed Henderson the credit slip to sign, and went over to seat some customers who had just walked in.

"Leave her a big tip, okay?" Keltner said.

"Boy, it's easy to play Rockefeller with my money, isn't it?"

"She deserves it. Plus, I saw her giving you the eye. Think of the impression you'll make."

"Too late: she saw me with you."

"Yeah, but I'm taken. She'll have to settle for you."

"Come on…"

They purchased some snacks for the trip, along with a classic car magazine for Keltner, and walked out to the parking lot to the truck.

The resonating, rumbling voice of its engine revealed nothing of the trial it had been put through the previous day, although Keltner had made a point of kicking clumps of dried mud from under the wheel wells.

"You should clean your truck more often, you know. Do you know what kind of image this presents of the Board? What are people going to say?"

Henderson threw a crumpled chocolate bar wrapper at him.

The trip from Slave Lake was quiet and smooth. It was another beautiful summer morning and Henderson drove with the window down, rather than turning on the air-conditioning. The fresh late summer air stirred up the dust that had settled in the cab like a squatter and outside the gentle hum of the truck's tires on the smooth asphalt contrasted sharply with the sound of rubber crunching on the gravel roads they had travelled on over the past week. Keltner was reading his classic car magazine and had said little since leaving.

Henderson turned on the radio and the background was filled with the voices that rose from one of the many talk shows that inhabit the airwaves during a weekday morning.

As they travelled along the highway, the signs of human population increased in frequency. The majesty of the pine forests flattened out to the broad expanse of prairie farmland. Whereas in Slave Lake, one could find himself in isolation within minutes of leaving the town, here the increasing number of farms and gas stations that lined the sides of the highway reminded Henderson that the closeness, the companionship, and the complications of other human beings were never very far away.

About three hours after leaving Slave Lake, the truck found the busy four lane highway and the quiet, gentle restriction of the winding two lane ended. Slower vehicles could now be passed with ease and Henderson sped up a bit. Morinville, the first town at which the final miles to home would begin ticking away, passed by silently on the left.

Further down the road, silent and almost completely hidden by a row of spruce trees that were dwarfed by their northern cousins, was their final stop before heading home for the weekend. Most people wouldn't have even noticed the facility from this distance, but Henderson knew it was there. Its clouded past still hung above it despite the brilliance of the sun which gleamed from its tall silver towers.

Henderson looked over at his sleeping passenger.

"Hey. Wake up over there."
Keltner's eyes fluttered open.
"Are we there yet, daddy?"
"Almost."
Keltner rubbed his eyes and yawned.
"Okay. Tell me about this one. Are the roads paved all the way to the front door or can I count on getting stuck again?"
"You've been out here before, haven't you?"
"It doesn't look familiar."
"Well, you probably don't recognize it in daylight," Henderson said. His voice then took on an official tone, somewhat like that of a tour guide's.

"The Morinville gas plant, owned and operated by Western Triassic Oil and Gas Limited. Located right in the middle of a number of rural residential subdivisions, the original application to construct the large sour gas processing and sulphur recovery plant had been met with strong opposition from the local area residents. The Board hearing to approve this son of a bitch was an ugly one."

Henderson then continued with the story using his normal voice.

"It was almost funny. You should have seen the Western Triassic people. They treated the locals like they were a bunch of dumb country hicks, which, of course, they aren't. I think they were actually quite surprised that the people didn't roll over and give in."

"But despite the public outcry, the Board still approved it. I think that even the hearing panel was apprehensive about it, but they pretty much had to, because Western Triassic had met all of the application requirements. The panel made sure that the approval was subject to a number of special conditions, all of which were intended to make the local residents more comfortable and friendly to the idea of the construction of this facility in their backyards. Regardless of all that, though, people in the area are still pretty much pissed off at us. Now, of course, our people in Calgary who approved this thing get to sleep easy every night while we baby-sit it."

"That's all very nice," Keltner said, "but I don't know. These gas plants all look the same to me. Is there going to be a test later?"

"It's also one of the few plants left in the province that still has a sulphur block. Pretty much everyone else ships the stuff out as a liquid. Western Triassic has promised to do the same at some point, but you can bet that promise has gone the way of the dodo."

"Oh yeah, the sulphur block," Keltner said. "I recognize it now. I was out here one night last winter. Odour complaint."

"And I bet you didn't find anything."

"Uh, yeah, come to think of it. It was a wasted trip. At two in the morning."

"Yep, that's it. A phantom complaint, most likely from one of the locals still ticked at the Board. I knew it would come back to you. I don't think there's anybody in our office who hasn't been out here at least once. Anyway, the one thing going in our favour is the plant foreman, Shawn Jackson. I'm sure he must be counting the hours until he retires next year."

"I'll bet he moves far away from here," said Keltner.

"No, I doubt it. Jackson lives here. It's his community. This is his home and these people are his neighbours. Jackson understands their issues with this plant. Hell, he has the same concerns."

"He wanted the plant to be built in a more remote area. He also wanted the sulphur shipped out as a liquid right from the beginning. But his bosses basically told him that his opinion was worth squat. The rest, as they say, is history. Those that make the decisions went ahead with their plans to build the plant in this particular spot anyway."

"Now Shawn has to fight with his own people all the time to get the money he needs to run this place decently. I really feel sorry for him. It's an on-going battle for him. Especially considering the royal dink, son of a bitch tyrant asshole he has to work for: William Arthur. He's a real piece of work, he is."

"Sounds like he gets a Christmas card from you every year," said Keltner.

"Oh yeah, you can count on that. William Arthur: champion of radical free enterprise who hates area residents, the Board, and anyone else who stands in his way of squeezing every dollar he can out of the ground."

"Boy, you really don't like this guy, do you?"

"He's number two in my book."

"Only number two?"

"I'm thinking in terms of bodily functions. He's like a god damn vampire when it comes to oil and royalty holidays. Geez, I still remember the smirk on the jerk's face three years ago when it fell to Spenser to tell him that the plant had been approved. Since then, that plant has been the source of more complaints, real or otherwise, than any other facility we look at. Of course, most of them come in at some ungodly hour in the middle of winter. I suppose we're lucky. We only have to go out when we're on call. Jackson always shows up. Every call, every single one of them. And he stays to the end, until it's been handled. He always says he couldn't sleep anyway. All I can say is that he must have a real understanding wife."

"It's the phantom complaints that get me," Henderson continued. "You know, like we were saying: the ones that always come in the middle of the night. Then you get up, get dressed, and come driving all the way out here to find that there's nothing wrong."

"Like the one I had." Keltner murmured.

"Exactly. And you can bet the same people out here who still hold a grudge are making them. Probably their idea of revenge. Personally, it makes me less sympathetic to any of the complaints we get from out here."

"Hey now," Keltner said. "You can't start thinking that way. There are a lot of good companies out there, run by people like Jackson, or who, at any rate, at least listen to their own Shawn Jacksons."

"Yeah, I know." Henderson sighed. "But it makes it pretty tough sometimes to maintain a perspective, you know?"

"I hear you, my man, I hear you. But we've got to be better than that. Otherwise, the next thing you know, you might as well work in Calgary for one of the bad guys, thinking like the William Arthurs of the world."

"Ugh," Henderson shuddered. "That's a scary prospect. But don't you wonder about our people in Calgary sometimes? I mean, they still approve these things, even when nobody wants them. Don't they realize what we have to put up with afterwards? God, I wish they would get it through their heads that we work for the same organization."

"Well, you know how much I like head office types," Keltner said, "but let's face it, mate. There's only so much they can do. If the company follows the rules, the Board has to approve it. And you can bet that the lawyers in Calgary who sleep with our regulations and know them inside and out, especially the loopholes, aren't exactly starving."

"Yeah, I suppose. But it pisses me off!"

"I know it does. Just keep on remembering what I said. There are the good ones, including our own. With lots of Shawn Jacksons working in the industry."

"Okay."

"There you go. Feel better now?"

"Yes, mommy. Thank you."

"You're welcome."

The truck was now approaching the plant. Henderson could see that the plant appeared to be operating normally today. A wisp of bluish-yellow flame at the top of the acid gas flare stack was barely visible. The wavy sky above the incinerator stack told him that the sulphur plant was working well, stripping the hydrogen sulphide from the raw gas and recovering over 98 per cent of the poisonous gas as elemental sulphur. The remainder was being burned in the incinerator, heated to a temperature high enough to ensure that the resulting sulphur dioxide was being adequately dispersed. Raw sulphur was being deposited onto the bright yellow block that grew slowly beside the sulphur recovery plant.

It always struck Henderson how colourful the plant was, with the silver towers and vessels of the raw gas processing plant, the tall, bright red and white incinerator stack, and the yellow sulphur block. At the extreme south end of the plant site, there was the runoff pond, which caught and held the rainwater that flowed down from the sulphur block and which reflected the slate of brilliant blue sky above.

Henderson moved to the left lane and slowed down in order to make the turn into the plant's parking lot.

"Okay," Henderson said, "we won't be here long. I just want to stop in and see how things are running today. Also, that group from Calgary is coming up next week to see some field facilities and Spenser asked me to set up a gas plant tour."

"Isn't that the job of your fearless leader?"

"You know we don't like to display Larson in public. Besides, he's on vacation for the next three weeks. I'm doing it as a favour for Al."

"Yep, you don't get lips like those from sucking on lemons."

"Uhm, perhaps, although some might refer to it more diplomatically as a sound career move. Bottom line is that I don't mind doing it for Al. He makes life bearable."

"And Larson doesn't?"

Henderson glanced at Keltner before his gaze returned to the road.

"I've noticed that you're not in a hurry to transfer downstairs," he said with half a smile.

"Well, despite your wonderful tutoring, I'm still not gas plant material."

"That's it? If you're halfway serious about joining us downstairs, I could have you running *this* plant inside of two months."

Keltner sighed.

"And Larson's a dork," he confessed. "Everyone knows that."

"You don't hear me say that," Henderson replied with the other half of the smile, "but those of us in the dungeon do wonder how he made it to supervisor, although you notice he's never gone any further. He never goes out in the field anymore and doesn't like to make waves. Hell, he doesn't even like to dip his little toe in. Spenser may be a crotchety old crustacean..."

"Oh Christ, Spenser's been around forever," said Keltner. "I think he's the only board hand who's had a posting in each of the field offices. Hell, I wouldn't be surprised to find out that he was around when oil was formed."

"Yeah, but he's not an idiot. He's onto Larson, and he knows there's nothing he can really do about him. That's why he lets us run to him when we need some pull. And if he needs to know anything about what's happening out there in the gas plants, he comes straight to us."

"Doesn't Larson have a problem with you going over his head?"

"Ah, he's little more than a year from retirement, so he's coasting. As long as it doesn't make him look bad, I don't think that he really cares."

"Besides," Henderson winked at Keltner, "I suspect that at some point, Spenser has had a little chat with him about all of that. Let him know that if he wants the authority, he'd better start taking the responsibility."

Henderson pulled into the parking lot and found a parking spot marked 'VISITOR'.

"I'll only be a few minutes," he said to Keltner. "You can stay here if you want."

"Nah, I'll come in. I might learn something"

"Okay, but be good."

"You wish."

Henderson and Keltner walked along the cast-iron grating that was the sidewalk to the main office door. In the background, they could hear the gentle roar of the gas plant. It was actually very quiet, which was a bit of a surprise considering the size of the facility; Henderson knew that this was a result of some of the restrictions and conditions that had been placed on it by the Board because of its sensitive location.

The door opened with a creak and they stepped into the main entry. An attractive young woman behind the front desk looked up from her desk and smiled at Henderson.

"Hi Clint," she said pleasantly.

"Hi Stacy. Is Shawn around?"

"Sure is. Go on in."

"Thanks. By the way, this is Peter Keltner. The nurse at the home said it was good for him to get out and get some fresh air once in awhile. Don't worry, though: he's not dangerous unless you say 'yogurt'."

Stacy giggled. Keltner stepped forward.

"Nice meeting you, Stacy," he said with his most enchanting smile. "Actually I'm out here to show Clint how to do his job properly. If you ever have any problems with him, feel free to phone me directly."

Stacy's suddenly furrowed brow contrasted with her still smiling mouth.

"Oh, you'll be the first on my list." She giggled. "It's a pleasure to meet you, Peter."

"Lord, don't tell him that," Clint replied. "It's like giving a starving kitten a saucer of milk. Now you'll never get rid of him."

"He's just jealous," Keltner winked at Stacy.

The small building was actually nothing more than a medium sized mobile home that had been converted into the plant's main office. Henderson and Keltner walked down the narrow hallway to the far end and turned into the office on the left. A portly, older man stood up from behind his desk and extended his hand.

"Clint, how are you doing today? Nice day to be out in the field."

"I'm doing fine, thanks. This is Peter Keltner, a drilling inspector from our office. Things are a little slow with the rigs right now, so he's learning the gas side of the business."

Jackson shook Keltner's hand.

"Oh, I think I've met Peter before. Didn't you come out one night when one of our neighbours had a bit of a problem with our operation?"

"Yeah, we were just talking about that actually," responded Keltner.

Jackson poured coffee into two cups and his own big mug from the machine on the table behind his desk. He handed a cup each to Keltner and Henderson, and then took a sip from his mug.

"So," Jackson said after he took his seat and motioned for Henderson and Keltner to sit down as well. "What can I do for you two gentlemen today? Are we in trouble?"

"No, no," Henderson began. "Not at all. No, we have some of our people coming up from our Calgary office next week. We're talking real pencil-pushers here. They don't get too many opportunities to get out for some fresh air or see any real live field equipment, so they're coming up to see some of the facilities in the Edmonton area. I've been asked to arrange a trip to a gas plant and was wondering if you would mind if I brought them out here to show them your plant."

"When?"

"Next Wednesday."

Jackson opened up his day-planner to the 24th of August.

"I can't see a problem with that," he shrugged. "There's nothing special planned. Sure, bring them on out; it'll be a nice change. What time?"

"Preferably right after lunch, about one. Also, could you spare an operator to help me with the tour?"

"Don't ask for much, do you?" Jackson said with a laugh as he opened his day-planner.

"I'd owe you one."

Jackson nodded as he made a note in the day-planner.

"Sure: why not? Rick's on day shift starting Monday. He's pretty good at that sort of thing. Especially if there are women in the group."

"Which there are," said Keltner.

"Pete…"

"Well, you promised."

Henderson sighed.

"As long as it makes everybody happy, yes, there will be women in the group. Are you happy now?" he asked looking at Keltner.

"Delighted."

"Shawn?"

Jackson nodded and smiled.

"Sure. It'll make my day, too."

"Great," Henderson said. "Now that that's been taken care of, how are things running out here?"

Jackson shook his head.

"Plant's running fine," he said, "but the money's really getting tight right now. Arthur came out last week and gave me advance notice of next year's budget. Part of that included a list of four men that I had to lay off immediately."

"Say what?" Henderson replied. "I don't get it. This is one of Western Triassic's biggest money makers. How can he do that?"

"Oil revenues are through the roof, so the company is going after the greasy stuff like there's no tomorrow. Arthur wants to take advantage of some government grant money before it dries up and he thinks that we can make more money here by trimming costs. The profits from this place are to be maximized and diverted into next season's drilling program."

"I don't believe it," Henderson said. "So, who got the axe?"

"Michaels, Collins, Phillips and Simpson. Simpson was strictly maintenance and one of the remaining operators is going to have to do his work. Basically, I've lost one operator per shift. And it's not like I'm running this place over-staffed as it is."

"Between you and me, I don't mind losing Michaels," he continued. "He's good at what he does, but he always was a bit of a slacker and a trouble maker. The other three were really good workers, though. And I really feel sorry for Simpson. That poor kid'll never get another job around here."

"Why not?" Keltner asked.

"Simpson's a little on the slow side," replied Jackson. "He's a good kid, but some say he's retarded. Nobody would give him a chance. I hired him to work with our maintenance people and he was doing really well. He's one hell of a hard worker, always cheerful, and eager to learn, although the guys had to learn a bit themselves at first about how to deal with him. It was good for them, though, and I think that Simpson was pretty happy because he was given a chance; he was becoming self-sufficient and good at what he was doing. We all pretty much enjoyed having him around."

"On the other hand, I always got the feeling that Arthur felt uncomfortable with Terry around. I'd bet that's why he was included on the list of those to be let go."

"That's not fair," Keltner said.

"Nope, sure isn't," replied Jackson. "I argued 'til I was blue, but Arthur was adamant that Simpson had to go."

The three men sat quietly for a moment. Finally, Keltner broke the silence.

"Well, let me talk to my dad. He owns a farm east of the city. He's getting on in years and could probably use some help. I mean, no guarantees, but let me see what I can do."

"I don't want you to feel obligated, but that would be awful decent of you," Jackson replied, "and I know it would sure be appreciated. We've been trying to find something for him around here, maybe with one of our battery operators. I'd really like to see this kid get something. He's proven that he can do some real good work if given the chance. He's really made a lot of progress working here."

"Meanwhile, you boys finalize the details of your tour and let me know if you have any problems. Barring any unforeseen difficulties, I guess that Rick and I will see you Wednesday."

Henderson and Keltner rose from their chairs and each shook Jackson's hand in turn.

"Thanks, Shawn," Henderson said. "Hang in there. I'm on call on Sunday and I'd prefer not to spend the night out here."

Jackson put up his hands.

"I'll do my best," he replied, "but with the number of men I've got now, I can't make any promises. I know I'd like a quiet weekend myself."

Henderson and Keltner said good-bye to Jackson and Stacy, and then stepped out of the office into the bright sun. Neither said another word until they got into the truck. Henderson started the engine.

"Makes you wonder, doesn't it?" Keltner said soberly. "It's

almost as if it doesn't matter to these big shots that it's real live people, just like them, who are losing their livelihood whenever the corporate profit picture looks just a little bit cloudy."

"The part that really gets me," said Henderson as he backed the truck out of the parking spot, "is that some of these companies whine and cry about how many jobs are going to be lost if they don't get millions of the taxpayers' dollars to help them make money, and then they brag about being such great corporate citizens."

Henderson checked the highway and, when it was clear of traffic, roared angrily onto the southbound lane.

"On the other hand, when oil and gas prices are setting records, they're still not happy. Personally, I don't know if I like the idea of my taxes going to those in this industry who believe that the biggest risk is treating their own people with some level of respect."

Thursday, August 18 - Evening

Henderson dropped Keltner off at his house and, after picking up a bottle of wine and the latest Clint Eastwood video at the store down the street from his apartment block, he pulled the truck into the extra space in the building's parking lot.

After he unlocked the apartment door, the first thing to greet him was the smell from the kitchen. He tossed his mail on the table and went over to the sink. There, sitting on the edge of the counter as a reminder, was the empty milk carton that he had not only forgotten to take to the garbage, but had forgotten to rinse out as well.

"Yech," he thought as he stuffed the carton into the garbage bag under the sink. "Well, let's see what sort of other surprises we have in the fridge."

He opened the refrigerator door and saw very little.

"Hmmm. Looks like it's grocery time in Henderson land," he muttered. "Well, at least there's no Chia Pet ranch this time."

He picked up two little plastic containers that contained hot sauce from a local Mexican fast food restaurant.

"Wonder how some macaroni and cheese dinner would taste with this mixed in? I guess there's always popcorn if it doesn't work out."

After mixing his dinner and putting it on the stove to heat up, Henderson went into his living room and sat down. Flashing lights on his answering machine indicated that there were three messages for him. While he waited for the tape to rewind, he opened his mail.

There was a loud click when the message tape had reached the beginning. Henderson had already sorted out the contest letters and fliers, and had just opened the first bill.

Beep. "I'm not in. Leave a message."

Beep. "Good evening, Mr. Henderson. I'm calling on behalf of your local New Democrat Party candidate and wanted to talk to you about the upcoming election. Uh, I'll phone you back next week. Good night."

That's okay; don't bother, Henderson muttered.

Henderson opened a late birthday card from an old friend who now lived down east.

Beep. Pause. There was a muffled voice in the background.

"It's that machine, John."

Hi, Mom.

"You talk, John. You know how I hate that thing."

"Hiya, boy. Just phonin' to see how you're doing. I guess you're not back yet from up north. We'll be talking to you over the weekend sometime."

Henderson smiled and leaned back in his easy chair.

Beep. Pause. Click.

"Wrong number," Henderson guessed. Or possibly the girl of my dreams.

Or both.

Henderson poured himself a glass of wine and started the movie. An hour later, with his salsa and cheese dinner finished and another glass of wine drunk, he lay down on the sofa to finish watching the movie.

He almost made it, but fifteen minutes shy of the end, Henderson was sound asleep.

Friday, August 19

The clock radio clicked on right at the end of the commercial leading into the six o'clock news. Henderson opened an eye and the bright blue numbers on the face of the radio confirmed that it was six in the morning. He groaned: please Lord, let me have major dental surgery planned today so I don't have to go into the office.

But then a weary smile crept across his face.

No you don't, he heard it say to him. It's a flex day, so you can go back to sleep.

Just like you'd want to on a real workday.

His hand wriggled its way out from under the blankets and turned off the radio. Then he rolled over and buried himself under the covers.

"Oh yes: I live for that," was his last thought before he dozed off again.

Because of the hours that they had to work without overtime pay, and in recognition of the conditions under which they worked, field staff in the area offices were entitled to have every second Friday off. For Henderson, it was one of the best things about working in one of the Board's field offices. He enjoyed having a weekday off. The streets are quiet and there was a unique feeling about being able to do what he wanted while the rest of the world was at work.

He woke up again around nine. He stretched and laid in bed for a few minutes, feeling the smooth, cool sheets against his skin. The air in the apartment was already slightly hot and stuffy, and the sun leaked brightly through the gaps in the closed blinds.

Henderson got up, took a hot shower, and shaved. Then he massaged after-shave gel into his face and felt the stinging velvet caress his face. After wiping the cloudy haze from the steamed bathroom mirror, he looked at himself and breathed deeply.

Eh. Not too bad, I suppose.

Henderson put on a light golf shirt and a pair of baggy cotton pants, which felt light and smooth on his legs compared to the hot, heavy blue jeans he wore at work all week. Feeling refreshed and relaxed, Henderson poured himself a cup of coffee and stepped onto the balcony of his apartment.

He took a deep breath and held it: another absolutely beautiful summer day, he thought.

Henderson unfolded a sun-faded fabric lawn chair and, sipping his coffee, sat down and began reading the newspaper. His peace was interrupted about ten minutes later by the ringing of the telephone. His ears heard the answering machine click on after the second ring.

"I'm not in. Leave a message."

Beep.

"Yes you are. No I won't."

Leisurely, Henderson got up from his chair and stepped into the kitchen to pick up the phone.

"Hi Pete."

"Hi mate," responded the cheerful voice. "What's up?"

"Oh, let's see, now. Birds, the clouds, minute particulate matter emanating from various industrial sources that results in odour complaints that get you and me up at night."

"Ha ha. I keep saying it. You're a funny man. So what did you get up to last night?"

"Not too much. Things got a little foggy and dark by

seven thirty. How about you and Kathy?

"Ah, just watched a movie. Alien."

"Again? Christ, you must have that video worn out by now."

"I can't help it. That scene where the creature bursts out of that guy's stomach and skedaddles across the floor always makes me laugh. It looks like somebody skinned Kermit the Frog and sent him packing."

"Ah, such culture. This from the guy who thinks that M.C. Gainey looks like a demented Gordon Lightfoot."

"He does! And it's not such a leap, if you really think about it."

Henderson heard Keltner clear his throat.

Oh no, he thought as Keltner began to sing.

"If you could twist my mind, love…"

"Okay, I get the point," Henderson interrupted. "Look, what do you want?"

"I need you to come over. I want some company while I work on my car."

Henderson rubbed his eyes.

"You're kidding," he said.

"No. I'm lonely."

Henderson looked at his watch.

"Yeah, okay. What the hell. I'll be there in five minutes."

"Make it ten, no, fifteen. You have to pick up some orange juice and fizzy water on your way over. I've been welding since seven this morning and I'm really thirsty. And make sure it's freshly squeezed, not that stuff that's made from concentrate. Trust me, I can tell the difference."

Henderson paused.

"Anything else?" he asked. "Breakfast perhaps, say some sausage and eggs? Caviar and toast? Kibbles and Bits?"

"No, just the orange juice. Kathy made breakfast this morning before she left. Oh, hold it. Yeah, get some tortilla chips, too, will ya? I've got a craving. And hurry up. I'm on the verge of complete dehydration."

Henderson laughed.

"I'll be over as soon as I can."

When Henderson pulled up to the house, Keltner was standing on his driveway. He walked over and kicked some caked mud from the truck's rear wheel well as Henderson got out.

"So what's this?" Keltner asked as he kicked off another piece of mud. "Did you join one of those religions that doesn't believe in baptizing your truck very often?"

"No time," Henderson replied. He tossed a plastic jug of orange juice to his friend. "I was going to wash it today, but someone wanted me to play delivery-man and baby-sitter. Say, I'm curious. How do you know if it's freshly squeezed?"

"Just between you and me, I can't. I used to tell Kathy that I could tell because the fresh stuff has seeds in it. Then I found out that she had collected a half dozen seeds and recycled them in the juice she gave to me in the morning. Now I rely on whatever the container says."

"What if she's recycling the container?"

"Hey. You're talking about the woman I love."

"Uh, okay. I'm sorry. How's the car coming?"

Keltner took a large drink of freshly squeezed orange juice.

"Floor pan's almost in," he said. He wiped his mouth. "Come on in and have a look."

They walked over to the garage. To some, Keltner would have been a comical figure, with his welding masked perched on his head, his old, ratty T-shirt and his permanent grin, but Henderson knew how serious Keltner was about restoring the old Dodge that sat in his garage.

"Where was I the last time you were here?"

"You'd just put the floorboards in."

"For the first or second time?"

"I think it was the first. So I take it that you had to do it again?"

"Yeah, well look in over here. See where they attach in to

the firewall? I thought that it was all one solid piece of metal, but it wasn't, and I hadn't noticed that there was a spot where it was all rusted out between the two thinner pieces. So it all had to come out again."

Henderson whistled.

"Bet you were impressed."

"Yep, but at least I got to try out some of those new words you taught me out in the field. I wish you had told me they were dirty. Kathy almost had a fit when she heard them."

"Uh huh. That's you, all right: pure as the snow driven over. Nice smooth weld you've got there, by the way."

"Actually, I'm quite surprised how easy this old metal is to work with."

"So what's next?"

"Electrical system. Hoorah. Am I ever looking forward to that."

"Ah, you'll do fine. You've done a great job so far."

"Thanks. Once the electrical's done, I'll be able to start piecing the interior back together. That's when it'll start looking like a car again. Then I'll really be excited about finishing it."

"When do you figure?"

Keltner shrugged.

"I'm hoping by next spring. I'm gonna put some heat out here so I can work in the winter."

"Geez, Pete, it really does look great."

"Yeah, well, I'm sort of proud of it."

"As well you should be too."

"Say, mate, you got time for a snack?"

"If you're making it."

"Well, come on into the house and have a seat while I wash up."

As Keltner prepared some lunch for them, Henderson sat at the kitchen table.

It was a beautiful home. Keltner had essentially ripped out the entire interior and replaced it all himself. The kitchen overlooked the family room and was separated from it by a deep brown oak railing. At the far end of the family room was the fireplace that Keltner had built himself. Henderson and Keltner had spent a number of evenings playing chess in front of a crackling fire. The overhead track lighting would dance off the gold clock that Henderson had given to Keltner and his wife Kathy on their wedding day. The room was warm and cozy, thought Henderson, all thanks to Keltner, who had done a masterful job. There seemed to be no end to the man's talents.

Right now, the room was quiet. The sun poured through the balcony doors into the kitchen, giving it a brilliance that made Henderson appreciate the relatively short Alberta summer. Keltner sat down at the table with two of his custom grilled cheese sandwiches. Henderson took a bite from his.

"Not bad," he said. "You'll make somebody a wonderful wife someday."

"I don't get too many complaints," Keltner replied. "Kathy is still holding out hope for you, though."

"Wow. It's like déjà vu all over again, except on my time. Where have I heard this conversation before?"

"No, no. I'm serious."

Henderson shook his head slowly.

"I tried it once, remember?" he said. "It wasn't a pretty sight. Besides, you know how it is: life sucks and I'm the straw."

"So you say, but still, she's convinced that there's someone out there who's looking for a cute little dickens like you. Kathy worries about you, you know. She's afraid you're lonely."

Henderson stopped chewing. He was quiet as he looked out onto the balcony into the brightness of the sun.

"And if I have to be honest about it," Keltner said in mid-bite, "so am I."

Henderson turned his head to look at Keltner, who had also turned his head to look out toward the balcony. He waited until Keltner's gaze returned indoors to the kitchen table.

"You know, that's really nice," Henderson said slowly. "It's great to know that someone cares. But sometimes I really wonder if I want to get involved with anyone again. Let's face it, is it worth the hassle? I look around at the some of the guys at work who are, supposedly, 'happily' married and I really have to wonder. I mean, we all go to Calgary for a course or something and all the married guys want to do is watch strippers at bars and cruise the stroll, gawking at the hookers. Yippee. Then, because I'm single, they tell me how lucky I am because I can take advantage of all of that because there's no chance of me being caught by my wife."

"I mean, don't get me wrong," Henderson continued. "I enjoy seeing a naked woman as much as the next guy, but you can't tell me that these guys are really happy with their lives if that's the only way they can get their thrills anymore."

"Pete, you're one of the few that are different," he added, "and yet, I can't help but think sometimes that we're the weird ones. I don't want to end up like them. I kind of like the fact that right now, I go where I want, when I want, and I don't have to lie or report to my conscience the next morning. Give me one good reason why I should get married again and end up like those other guys."

Keltner looked out at the balcony again.

"You know, Clint," Keltner replied after a pause, "I think that you're being way too hard on yourself. I don't believe for a second that you'd never end up as a hooker-ogling, peepshow fanatic if you get married again. You're too good for that."

"The difference between you and them is that you're too smart to end up like them. You're looking for more in life. I see it when you're out in the field. You're not content to just do your job; you're always looking for a way to make it better and you're not afraid to accept a challenge. Hell, you love the challenge. And I think that's what you need in a woman."

"By the way, that's also why I often wonder what you're doing out here in a field office. I mean, why the hell aren't you down in Calgary, where you could make a difference?"

Henderson started to answer, but Keltner held up his hand. Henderson closed his mouth.

"Anyway, that's where I think you've got it all over those other guys," Keltner continued. "You can make a difference because you're smart, conscientious, and most of all, you give a damn about the job and other people. I mean, do you know why

Al asks *you* to do things like this tour next week?"

"Haven't the foggiest," Henderson replied "Probably because of the large 'S' on my forehead."

"It's because you're good at it. You have a way with people, a presence."

"Uh huh."

"Look, when the rigs got slow, I didn't ask to go out in the field with you because I knew we were going to have a good time; if I had foresight like that, I'd be buying more lottery tickets. You can educate without talking down to or making your student feel small. You can do it because you can read people and somehow know what they need and how they need to receive it. Provided that you think that they're worth it, you give a damn about the other person, and that's what sets you apart from the others."

"I think you'd bring that to a relationship, and what's more, I don't think that just anybody would do. As I said, you need someone who'll offer you a challenge. You wouldn't be happy any other way: you'd get bored."

"You know," Keltner continued, "I think that the other guys are fascinated by hookers because for them, there's a thrill in the thought that there's this strange, attractive woman within a few feet of them, and knowing that for the right price, they could have sex with her. And it's pretty sad to think that that's the only way they'll ever get a thrill out of life. You don't need that. You're more interested in what people are, how they think. And you need someone who'll make you think. Somebody who isn't particularly special to you would bore the piss out of you. And in return, I think you'll be a much more exciting person to whoever is lucky enough to get you."

Henderson sighed.

"Think so?"

"You're fairly fussy and particular. Unfortunately, that's one of the downsides of having more of a brain."

"I don't know about that," Henderson replied. "Sometimes I think that you and Kathy are about the only couple who're actually happy being married. And you're both smart as hell. Is that why it's worked for you two?"

"Well, I know that when we're out in the field, I talk about women and sex an awful lot, but that's pretty much all it is. I enjoy sex and, like you, I enjoy looking at a naked woman as much as the next guy. Truth is, as far as I'm concerned, women are one of the few things in this world that evolution didn't screw up."

"Kathy is the best damn thing that ever happened to me and I love her like nothing else. What else could I ever want? She's beautiful, intelligent, independent, and she makes me feel good. She stands by me when I'm on about her idiot brother. Well, most of the time anyway. I have nothing but love and respect for that woman. And I honestly believe that somewhere out there is someone like that for you."

"Don't worry about those other guys. Settle only for making yourself, and some lucky girl who deserves you, happy and you'll do all right. Trust me. Let the other guys have their strippers and their hookers and their fantasies. You don't need, or want, them."

Henderson thought for a moment and then a slight smile managed to find its way onto his face.

"It's wonderful having morals, isn't it?" he said.

"I guess I shouldn't be so hard on the guys at work," Keltner laughed. "Most of them are actually pretty really good dudes. You just can't take them too seriously."

"You know, you're pretty smart for a senior inspector," Henderson said.

"Just don't tell that to anybody in the office," Keltner replied. "Next thing you know, they'll be trying to make me inspect gas plants. Besides, it doesn't always work in our favour."

"What do you mean?"

"Kathy was royally steamed about something this morning, and I sure bore the brunt of it."

"Oh yeah?"

"She came into the bedroom this morning to say good-bye to me. She tucked my teddy bear in with me…"

"Your teddy bear?"

"Teddy badger, actually. His name is Leopold. Anybody at the office hears about him and you're toast."

"Fair enough. But why can't I meet anybody who would do that for me?"

"Don't worry, you will. So anyway, she kisses my forehead, strokes my cheek and tells me that she loves me, and then the next thing you know, she's dumping a glass of water on me. Can you believe that?"

"It depends. Knowing Kathy, I'm sure she had a good reason. Off hand, I'd bet that there's something that you said in between."

"All I said was 'Work hard baby: Daddy likes nice things.'"

Henderson shook his head.

"You are such a charmer," he said.

"I know. That's why I don't understand the Niagara Falls treatment."

Then Keltner smiled and winked at him.

"And she'll come home to me tonight with a smile and a hug," he added. "Her sense of humour is one of the reasons why I won't give her up for anything."

A dog, a mixed breed with short hair, tan colouring with black eyes, and big enough to rest her head on the table, came up to them and nudged Keltner's elbow with her nose. Keltner looked down at the dog and began scratching her behind her right ear.

"Well, hello Alexandria," Keltner said. "Glad to see you could take a break from your daily twenty-four hour nap to come visit us."

The dog's tail began to wag in time to Keltner's voice.

"I hate you, you know," Keltner responded as he continued to scratch Alexandria. "It's a good thing that your mommy likes you because I despise you. I resent the fact that I have to breath the same air that you do, especially since you licked the butter in the butter dish on the table last Christmas in front of your uncle Lawrence."

The dog wagged her tail faster. Her eyes looked up at Keltner and they hung on every syllable that he uttered.

"Well, I suppose that you want me to interrupt whatever it is that I'm doing to get up and let you out."

Keltner rose from the table when he said 'out' and that's the point at which Alexandria snorted, bounced back a bit, and then started dancing over to the glass doors that opened onto the patio, bobbing her head continuously. She kept looking back to make sure that Keltner was still following her.

"I'm coming, I'm coming," he said, "you freeloader."

When he slid the doors open, Alexandria sprung onto the patio and ran out into the yard, sniffing the ground all along the path she took.

"And don't hang around with any of those purebreds!" Keltner called out just before he closed the doors. "They think they're too good for this family!"

He stood there for a minute and watched Alexandria in the yard.

"She's a good dog," he added with a smile before he returned to the table.

"Now, where were we? Oh yeah, why don't you get out the chessboard while I get dessert. It's been a good two weeks since I whupped you and I'm starting to get rusty."

The phone rang.

"Whoa," Keltner said as he jumped from his chair and grabbed the phone. "Hold onto your desire to lose there for a minute, mate."

"Hello?" he said into the telephone's mouthpiece.

Then his face broke into a grin.

"Hey, MRFL," he said quietly. "How's the shift going?....Oh, good: any chance you might be home on time tonight? I have a surprise for you.....Oh yeah....Me? Well, I had some company for the afternoon....No, nobody interesting."

Henderson looked up at him.

"No, it is Clint," Keltner said into the phone. "Well, some of what he's talking about is work related, so how interesting can it be?....Okay, okay. Hold on, I'll ask."

Keltner turned to Henderson.

"Kathy wants to know if you're going to curse us with your presence...."

Henderson couldn't help but smile when he heard the

muffled yell of "Pete!" from the other end of the telephone line.

"I mean, bless us," recovered Keltner, "with your presence at dinner this evening."

"Well," replied Henderson, "how can I refuse a gracious invitation like that? Sure."

"He says if he has to, he will," Pete said into the phone to Kathy. "He also said that he'd make the garlic bread....Right...I love you, too. Can't wait for you to get home. Bye."

Keltner hung up the phone and returned to the table, where Henderson had set up the chessboard. Henderson looked up at him.

"MRFL?" he asked.

"Huh? Oh. My Reason For Living. I suppose you've taken white already."

Sunday-Monday, August 21-22

The muffled ringing of the telephone from under the pillow on the nightstand jolted Henderson from his restless sleep. Grumbling a sharp curse, he opened his eyes and looked at the time: a quarter to one.

"Shit. Shit, shit, shit, shit, shit."

On-call is a duty that no Board inspector enjoys or really appreciates; an inspector spends one week at a time on a rotating schedule when he or she has to be available to take phone calls requiring Board assistance during the hours in which the area office is closed. These phone calls can range from requests from drilling rig engineers for approvals to abandon dry wells, to the odour complaints being made by residents who lived around facilities like the Western Triassic gas plant, to full scale emergencies such as well blowouts.

Because a phone call could come at any hour of the day or night, a week on call can be a gruelling stretch. For Henderson, just anticipating the phone screeching at him at any time during the night made it impossible for him to have one decent night's sleep out of the seven. Because he was filling in for Mills this evening, Henderson figured that it wouldn't be too bad to miss sleep for one night. However, he also knew that if he were to be cranked out of bed because of some major disaster at a rig or gas plant somewhere, tonight would be the night.

The phone rang again and Henderson's right arm lashed out from under the covers to knock the pillow off the nightstand. Henderson usually covered the telephone with a pillow to soften the blow of the phone's clattering in the middle of the night. He knew, however, that ten pillows would have had little effect when that horrible little beast decided to start nagging him at one in the morning, and the first ring always startled Henderson awake.

Henderson sat up on the edge of the bed and picked up the receiver.

"Yeello," he muttered groggily.

"Good evening, Mr. Henderson," responded the sweet, tired voice of the on-call operator. "I'm sorry to disturb you, but I have someone from - it sounds like - Mitec Explorations, I believe. He needs an approval for a well abandonment. I have to warn you, though: it's a very bad connection."

Henderson rubbed his closed eyes with the thumb and forefinger of his left hand. Mitec Explorations? He'd never heard of them.

"Okay," he sighed. A bad connection usually meant a long phone call. "Put him through."

He ran his hand through his tussled hair and then reached for the briefcase that he kept by the bed when he was on call.

"Go ahead, sir," the operator said.

A loud rasping filled the earphone and Henderson pulled the receiver away from his ear. A disembodied voice came on the line.

"Hallo?" it said. "Hallo? Who am I speaking to, please?"

"My name is Clint Henderson," he replied. "Who is this?"

"Oh, my name is . . ." The rasping on the line cut out the rest.

That's when that little thing that raises big suspicions planted itself in the back of Henderson's mind.

"I'm sorry," he said loudly. "I didn't catch your name. Could you please repeat it?"

The rasping subsided somewhat.

"My name is Frederick Montague," the voice said.

There it was, the first clue: was that accent sounding somewhat forced?

"I would like to abandon a well up here in the Lariat Field, please."

"Okay, hang on for a minute."

"What? I can barely hear you."

"Just wait a minute!"

Henderson fumbled through the papers in the briefcase.

That's strange, he thought. Drilling rig activity was down overall and Keltner himself had mentioned that there were no active rigs in that region of the province right now . . .

Keltner.

Suddenly everything became quite clear.

"Mr. Montague," Henderson said calmly. "I'm sorry, but I'm entertaining a young lady right now and I can't take your call. Please call back during regular office hours. And for Christ's sake, stop crumpling that paper by the phone: it makes a horrible racket!"

The line cleared and Henderson heard the familiar sound of Keltner's laugh on the other end.

"You dog, Henderson," Keltner said. "Who have you got there with you?"

"Nobody," Henderson replied. "I said that to trap you. I knew you'd bite at it and I was right. Now go away."

"I just wanted to liven up your evening. It's pretty slow out there right now. Think of how disappointed you would have been waiting for the phone to ring and nobody calling you."

"It would have been just like high school," Henderson replied. "I'm forever in your debt. I owe you one and believe me, I will repay you for this."

Keltner laughed.

"I'll be looking forward to it."

Henderson paused for a moment. If anyone else had pulled a stunt like this...

Henderson smiled and shook his head.

"By the way, did you end up getting an invite tonight?" he

asked.

"Sure did. Just got in as a matter of fact. Lawrence of Dumbrabia was in fine form this evening, too, droning on and on and on and on and on and…"

"Okay, I get the point. The important thing is did you behave yourself?"

"I did. I tell you, you would have been so proud of me. Even Kathy says that she was. In fact, I've promised the love of my life that I'm going to do my very best from now on to patch things up with the little weasel and his significant bother."

"Hmm. Sounds like you're off to a good start."

"Sure am. Good night, Clint."

"Good night, Pete. See you in the morning."

Henderson replaced the receiver in its cradle and covered it again with the pillow. Then he fell back into bed and drifted slowly back to sleep.

Monday, August 22

As usual after a Sunday night spent on-call, Monday morning arrived far too early for Henderson. He leaned back in his chair in the conference room on the second floor of the Board's Edmonton area office and leafed aimlessly through the pages of the morning newspaper as he waited for the others to assemble for the regular Monday morning meeting. As he scanned its pages, his brain slowly caught up with the rest of his body, which had started the week, somewhat grudgingly, less than two hours before.

Al Spenser came into the room and the rest of the staff settled down into the chairs spread around the rectangular tables that had been assembled into a larger U-shaped table.

Henderson looked at his watch. It was five minutes past eight and Keltner was nowhere to be seen yet. He sighed and shook his head.

"Figures," he muttered to himself, and that's when Keltner raced into the room and grabbed the vacant chair next to Henderson. He tossed a crinkled yellow bag onto the table in front of Henderson.

Spenser was looking through some papers that he had taken out of his briefcase and didn't appear to notice.

"You're late," Henderson whispered from the corner of his mouth as he opened the bag. There were three doughnuts inside and he reached in for one.

"You can't rush quality," replied Keltner as he stared straight ahead in an attempt to look attentive. "Hey, don't take the last maple-glazed!"

"If we may begin, gentlemen," Spenser began. "What 'appened on-call during the weekend? Anything we should all know about?"

"A few abandonments," Mills said, "and an odour complaint on Saturday afternoon. Turned out to be a screwed-up vapour recovery unit on that old sour Gypsum Petroleum battery west of the city. I shut it in, which didn't impress the operator too much, but I told him he's going to have to operate that facility at reduced rates until they can get the vapour unit repaired."

Spenser shook his head.

"That old battery 'as been a pain in our ass for what, the past three years now?" he said. "I do believe it's time for some permanent action to get that piece of crap fixed once and for all. Anyway, you did the right thing. Jesse, could you and Mr. Mills see me later and we'll put together a letter to Gypsum. Anything else?"

"Not as far as I'm concerned," Mills replied. "Clint took the calls for me last night."

"It was pretty quiet," Henderson said. "I had a crank call about midnight. Real weirdo. I suspect impotence, combined with a touch of alcohol."

Spenser smiled and nodded, and then put a check mark next to that item on the agenda in front of him.

"Right. Well, then, moving on to the next subject. . ."

"I resent that," Keltner whispered.

"Yeah, right," Henderson whispered back. "I'll make a note of it and ensure that action is taken to heal your feelings. Here:"

He threw the almost empty bag at him.

"Have a doughnut."

"There's that lot coming up from Calgary on Wednesday,"

Spenser continued. "Clint, were you able to arrange a tour of a gas plant?"

"Yep. Shawn Jackson at the Western Triassic gas plant north of town has agreed to show them that plant on Wednesday afternoon. I understand that some of the people who are coming up on Wednesday worked on the original application and hearing, so I thought that might be interesting for them."

"Aye, that's an excellent idea, Clint," Spenser said. He looked up at Henderson. "I really do appreciate the effort you're putting into all of this, you know. Now, does anybody 'ave any idea what we might do with these people in the morning?"

"Well, while we were up north last week, Peter said that he'd find a rig to show them," Henderson volunteered.

Keltner's face remained emotionless, but under the table, his right foot shot out and kicked Henderson's chair.

"Why, thank you, Peter," Spenser said. "That would be great, it would."

"Uh, sure. No problem," Keltner replied.

He tried to kick Henderson again, who, as before, was able to get his leg out of the way in time.

"I'll get you for this, Henderson," Keltner said through clenched teeth.

Henderson smiled.

"Right, if that's it then," Spenser concluded, "I'd say that the meeting is adjourned for today. Oh, wait. There is just one more thing. I'd like to see Jesse and Gillis in my office right now."

The rest of the staff stood up from their chairs and left the room to collect their phone messages and prepare for the rest of the day. Henderson remained in his seat and watched Gillis Hudson walk out the door toward Spenser's office.

"Well, thanks loads," Keltner said to him. "Do you have any idea how hard it's going to be to try and find a rig that's working in this area?"

"Shh, shh, shh." Henderson held up his hand.

Keltner followed his gaze out the door toward Spenser's office.

"What do you think that's all about?" Henderson muttered

quietly.

Spenser was sitting behind his desk when Hudson arrived at his office. Jesse Cardinal was leaning against the filing cabinets on the wall opposite the desk. Hudson knocked on the wall next to the open door.

"Come in," Spenser replied.

Hudson stepped into the room. Spenser stood up, walked around the desk, and motioned Hudson toward a chair across from his desk.

"Sit down, lad," Spenser said as Hudson entered. Spenser closed the door behind him.

Hudson sat in the chair on the opposite side of the desk.

Spenser returned to his seat, sat down, and lit a cigarette. He inhaled deeply.

"I know I'm not supposed to be doing this, what with the smoking rules and all," he said as he exhaled the thin blue smoke slowly toward the ceiling, "but sod it."

His head dropped and then, after a couple of seconds, he looked up again. When he did, he was looking straight at Hudson.

"I must admit that this is extremely difficult for me, Gillis," Spenser said. He looked around for an ashtray and, not finding one, stubbed out the half-smoked cigarette on the side of his coffee mug. He then moved the mug to the side and stroked his chin with his hand.

"First off, I want you to know that before it goes any further than this room, you'll be given a chance, right now in fact, to give me your side of the story. But you 'ave to be straight with me; don't even think about trying any bullshit."

Hudson sat up in the chair and began to fidget slightly. He licked his lips and wiped his hand across his forehead, brushing the wispy brown hair up onto the side of his head.

"Wha, what are you talking about?" he asked.

Spenser opened the top drawer on the right hand side of his desk and pulled out a tan cardboard folder. Wordlessly, he tossed it onto the desk in front of Hudson, who took it cautiously and, after looking at both Spenser and Cardinal for a second, opened it to read the contents.

For a few seconds, he scanned the pages contained in the folder. During that time, Spenser lit another cigarette. Then, with almost a hint of nervous irreverence, Hudson tossed the entire package back on the desk.

"What about it?" he said.

Spenser took a deep drag from his cigarette and exhaled.

"I want to know if it's true," he said quietly.

"I don't know anything about any of that crap," Hudson said. "It's all lies as far as I'm concerned."

Spenser leaned forward, picked up the folder and opened it. He stubbed out his cigarette and cleared his throat. Then he sighed.

"I'm really sorry that you can't do any better than that, lad," Spenser said. "These charges seem pretty bloody solid to me. As you can see, they've been brought by the president of the company that operates that battery you did the production audit on last month. Now, 'e says that you approached him and claimed that you 'ad discovered an oil theft scam, in which some crude oil production was being transported from the battery to a middleman, 'oo disposed of the crude without asking any questions. None of this oil was ever reported and, as a result, no royalties were paid to the government; any money made from the sale was pure gravy. 'e said that you approached 'is production foreman and offered to ignore what you 'ad found for a percentage."

Hudson sat silent for a moment.

"You don't believe that, do you?" he asked.

"Believe me, lad, I don't want to," Spenser replied, "'onestly, I really don't, but I must admit that the evidence against you is pretty tough."

"We had one of the other inspectors go over the facility's records when this was brought to our attention," Cardinal said from behind Hudson, where he had been standing. "We also went over your audit report. It confirms that a sizeable portion of the oil production from this battery was not being reported. It's also clear that you must have either missed it or overlooked it. That much is true. What we want to know is: was this all intentional or just a mistake? In other words, did you attempt to extort the company or are you just incompetent?"

Hudson mouth dropped open, and then it closed again. He jumped out of his seat and began pacing the room. Sweat had made the hair on the back of his neck begin to curl.

"I don't believe this," he cried. "I just can't believe that you're going to accept the word of some crook?"

Spenser sat back in his chair.

"'e's not a crook," he said. "The fact is, son, that the scam was being run by a group that's not the slightest bit connected to that company. They came in at night and pumped the oil straight from the tanks into their trucks. 'e wasn't trying to hide anything. The company was being ripped off as well. They didn't receive a single cent from the stolen production. As it turns out, their morning operator thought that 'e was screwing up in 'is math and was a wee bit scared shitless for his job."

Hudson stopped. He was facing the wall with his eyes closed.

"You see, Gillis," Cardinal said, "your big mistake was attempting to blackmail the wrong people. You just didn't think this through enough before you decided to pull this stunt."

Hudson's head dropped forward, and it began to move back and forth slowly.

"I still don't believe this," he whispered.

Hudson stopped shaking his head and took a deep breath. Then he turned around.

"Okay, so now what?" he said slowly. "What happens now?"

Spenser put the folder back on his desk and lit another cigarette.

"The president of the company 'as agreed not to press charges against you," he said. "The people involved 'ave been arrested, but they don't 'ave a clue 'oo you are. Now, 'e and I 'ave agreed that it wouldn't really serve the best interests of either the

Board or the company to 'ave a messy trial and expose all of this to the public. Personally, I think it's quite generous of 'im. To be honest, this whole thing is one 'ell of an embarrassment and it could make us all look real bad. 'e has every right to press charges, but 'e isn't going to."

"'owever," Spenser continued, "you must realize that your employment with the Board is over, as of right now. I want you to leave this building and I want you to be quiet about it. Jesse will see to it that your desk is cleaned out and your things are forwarded to your home."

Hudson snorted.

"I could sue you for wrongful dismissal," he said.

Spenser nodded at Cardinal, who stepped in toward the desk and held forward an envelope. He gestured for Hudson to take it.

"What's this?" Hudson asked.

Spenser got up, walked around the desk, and sat on its edge across from Hudson.

"Inside is a description of your severance package. I must admit that if I 'ad my way, though, it would be empty."

Hudson took the envelope

"I don't care what's in it," he said slowly. "I'll still sue you."

Spenser smiled for a minute.

"Oh aye, you think so, do you? Look, I know 'ow you're feeling, son, I really do. You're in a difficult situation, and you're angry and more than a bit embarrassed."

Spenser then turned and slammed his hand on his desk, the loud bang echoing through the room. He shot his finger out at Hudson.

"But you just try it, mister, you just bloody well try it! We'll press charges so fast that it'll make your goddamn teeth fall out of your mouth! Don't you get it? You don't 'ave any room to bargain 'ere! You accept what we've given you or god damn it, I'll personally see you in jail!"

Hudson leaned toward him. His eyes were bright and wild.

"The hell with you! All these goddamn corporations get all

the breaks, while I worked my ass off and got nothing for it! I can't stand the way you and the rest of this fucking loser organization suck up to them!"

Spenser looked at him for a moment. His chest was heaving and now he was sweating.

"Get out," he said instead, quietly but distinctly. "Get the 'ell out of 'ere now before I 'ave your ass thrown out."

Hudson stood, turned, and stepped toward the door. He swung it open and then stopped. He turned to face Spenser; a smile had returned to his face.

"You're not done with me," he said. "I'll never forgive you for this. I swear, I'm gonna hurt you! Somehow, I'll hurt you all real bad, especially you, you ignorant old geezer!"

Hudson kicked the pane of glass in the door as he left. It shattered and shards of glass flew into the hallway. As he stomped out of the office, Henderson had been coming down the hall. Hudson pushed him roughly out of the way. There was a loud bang as Hudson slammed the door when he left the building.

Henderson rubbed his shoulder and stood there for a minute, silent and surprised. Spenser and Cardinal had stepped into the hallway and looked at the shattered pane of glass in the office door.

"Are you okay, lad?" Spenser asked Henderson.

"Uh, yeah. No problem."

Spenser and Cardinal waited until Henderson left the hallway.

"What do you think?" Cardinal asked.

"About what?" replied Spenser.

"He sounded pretty serious with that threat. He's pretty pissed, you know."

"Aye, 'e did, didn't 'e," replied Spenser.

Then he shook his head and flicked his hand at the door.

"Ah, I doubt 'e means anything. I mean, what could 'e do? 'e's just pissed off at 'imself for getting caught, that's all. We nailed 'im dead to rights, we did, and 'e bloody well knows it. Nothing 'e can do about it now."

Hudson took another long, deliberate drag from his cigarette. As he exhaled, he looked at its tip. He had really tried to get his mind onto something else, but in the meantime, he saw that he had left an impression of his bite in the filter. Above him, the haze of cigarette smoke hung under the fluorescent lights like frosty blue scud. Hudson sat quietly and, while staring into his beer, was able to consider for a minute how useless the fans were in the designated smoking section.

Just behind him, under the dull, cellophane red of the overhead spotlights, a tall, slightly skinny, naked blonde tried to stifle a yawn as she twirled around a pole mounted in the middle of the makeshift stage. In the background, the distorted sound of some unrecognizable rap song blasted through the thin speakers mounted in the ceiling.

When the girl finished her act, the sparse crowd clapped apathetically and Hudson swallowed the rest of his beer.

"Assholes," he muttered.

He stubbed out his cigarette and signalled to the bartender for another drink. Then he glanced over his shoulder to see the next act. She was sauntering out from the dressing room, dressed in a cheap, garish blue and silver miniskirt. Hudson sneered and turned back to the bar as his fourth beer arrived.

When the music started again, the far door opened, letting in a bright blast of sunshine. It overwhelmed the girl's act and stunned her audience for a moment. When the darkness returned and Hudson's eyes had readjusted to the dinginess of the room, he heard a sharp, leering whistle. He turned around.

The man who had just entered the bar looked familiar, but at that moment, with the world around him spinning slightly, Hudson couldn't place the face. The man sat down at a table by the stage and put his hand up.

"Hey, buddy, how about a beer!" he called out.

The bartender nodded as he picked up a wet mug. Then he pulled the lever that poured draft into the glass.

"Who's that guy?" Hudson asked him. "The one that just came in?"

"Oh, he's been coming in here practically every day for a while now," the bartender replied. "Used to work at that big plant north of here."

He put the full glass on the counter top and opened the small gate leading from behind the bar in order to make his delivery.

Hudson pulled a twenty-dollar bill from his shirt pocket and put it on the bar.

"That's okay," he said, "I'll take it to him."

The bartender looked pensive, but he shrugged, took the money, and put the change back on the counter. Hudson took most of it, leaving the rest as a tip, picked up the beer and walked over to the table.

The man who had ordered the beer was moving along with the beat of the music and yelling encouragement to the stripper. Hudson pulled up a chair and placed the beer in front of the other man.

He looked at Hudson with some hesitation before he took the mug.

"Uh, thanks, bud," he said. He stared for a moment at Hudson.

"This isn't that type of place, you know," he said and then took a drink. Then he wiped his mouth with a Kleenex that he had pulled out of his pocket.

"And even if it was," he added, "I doubt I'd be interested in you."

Hudson put his hand out.

"Gillis Hudson."

The music almost drowned out his voice, so he repeated it, this time somewhat louder.

"Uh, Warren Michaels," was the reply that came with the uncertain handshake. Then he pointed at Hudson.

"Hey, wait a minute. I recognize you. Aren't you one of those Board fucks?"

"If you mean did I work for the Board, then yeah, I did," was Hudson's reply. "Well, used to anyway. Bastards let me go this morning."

Michaels looked at him with a grin and held up his glass. Hudson clinked it with the rim of his.

"Welcome to the club," Michaels drawled. "I didn't think that the Board let anyone go, unlike the pigs I used to work for. Man, you guys are rumoured to have 'job security'. That was supposed to make up for the chicken-shit wages."

Hudson looked up at the girl, smiled at her, and then turned back towards Michaels and shrugged.

"They're all the same, I guess," he replied.

Michaels laughed. Then the smile left his face.

"Yeah, you're right," he said slowly, "they're all the same. All those big shots with their expensive suits and silk ties, sitting in their plush offices, doing nothing but making big bucks and porking their secretaries. Their only responsibility is to decide which of us underpaid working stiffs have to bite the bullet when the cash flow dries up. It's enough to make a guy want to puke."

Hudson nodded in sullen agreement.

"Then when a guy tries to make a few bucks on the side so that he can get some enjoyment out of life, he gets crucified," he added quietly.

"Now, she," Michaels said, pointing at the dancer in front of him, "could make my cash, and other things, flow like a fuckin' river!"

Michaels watched her for a minute. Then he turned back to Hudson and pounded his fist on the table.

"It's not fair!" he yelled. "You know they laid off four guys at our plant? Three guys with families to feed and another who'll never, ever, get another job anywhere. I'd like to see some of those fat ass bastards get canned and see how they like it."

Michaels held his near empty glass with a tight grip. Hudson thought that it would shatter in his hand.

Michaels's eyes were glassy.

"God I want to get them," he hissed, almost inaudibly. "I'd like to really screw them bad."

Hudson leaned back and looked at the girl gyrating on the stage.

"Amen," he spat.

Michaels took another drink.

"So what," he asked, "did I do to deserve all this personal attention from you?"

Hudson looked at the floor for a second and then into Michaels's eyes.

"It just seemed to me that you might like to vent a bit," he said quietly, and then he ordered two more beers.

Michaels looked wary.

"Say what?"

"You know," replied Hudson. "Share your bitching with somebody."

He smiled and clinked Michaels's glass with his own.

"Like me," he said with a smile.

The day before, some may have considered Hudson and Michaels to be adversaries. Their relationship was strained at first, but as Hudson and Michaels spent the afternoon drinking, talking, and commiserating in the smoky, dingy room, they realized that they had more in common than they both might have originally thought. When they finally left the bar, dusk had begun to fall.

"Well, I'll see you again some time," Hudson said.

Michaels was already walking way.

"Whatever," he mumbled as he rolled his eyes.

Hudson fumbled with his car keys and dropped them on the parking lot gravel twice before he was able to hold them steady enough to unlock his car door. He fell into the driver's seat and tried to start the car with his trunk key.

Finally, he found the ignition key on the key ring, and loud music blasted on as soon as the motor started; Hudson punched the stereo's power button off. He put the car in gear, and it lurched forward a couple of times as his foot slipped on the clutch. He drove ahead slowly, and stopped when he got to the parking lot exit. Hudson flicked on the right signal light and squinted first off in the distance to the right, and then to the left.

"Shit," he muttered. "It would just finish the day off nicely to get nailed by a road check, wouldn't it? Son of a bitch."

He opened the window to get some fresh air into the car. Then he hit the signal light stalk to the left and shot onto the highway, the rear wheels of the car kicking up gravel and dust when he planted his foot on the gas pedal.

Hudson drove along the highway for a few minutes, his fingers crossed to ward off the chance that flashing blue and red lights would appear ahead, accompanied by a set of barricades and a group of policemen just waiting for him. He decided that to increase the odds in his favour, he'd better take the back roads home. There was one road in particular that he was coming up to that should not only be empty, he reasoned, but might even get him home sooner.

He slowed to a crawl on the highway. Another car, which had originally been a couple of miles back when Hudson had pulled onto the highway, had closed the distance between them and the driver blew the horn as he swerved into the other lane to pass.

Hudson shot his hand out of the window and flipped his middle finger at the other car.

"Piss off, you impotent paedophile!" he screamed.

He crept along the highway for a few more minutes, mumbling about the various losers that seemed to inhabit his world, until he found the road he had been looking for and turned right onto it.

Off the highway, the road and surrounding fields were pitch black. The road itself was fairly straight and flat. The next major street it would meet up with would be that which ran behind his home on the northern end of the city.

He drove through a gentle gully and across a creek bridge. As he crested the bank on the other side, he noticed a glow that hung just above the horizon on the left. He knew that the light came from the Western Triassic gas plant at which Michaels had worked.

Hudson slowed to a stop at the next crossroad, the one that ran in along side of the plant, and from there he could see the plant. Its incandescent lights shone like a brilliant crystal in the night sky.

He shut off the motor and the night's silence filled the car. With the driver's side window down, cool night air crept into the car. Mixed with it was the low rumble of the plant's compressors.

He ripped the plastic wrapper off a fresh pack of cigarettes, pulled one out, and lit it. Inhaling deeply, Hudson stared at the gas plant.

Hmm, he thought. It does just kind of sit out there alone.

And unprotected, he realized.

With that thought, one corner of Hudson's mouth started to form a smile, but it developed into a sneer instead.

He knew the plant was a moneymaker for Western Triassic. He also knew that the profits that rolled out of it were all that the company's brass in Calgary really cared about. Michaels had reaffirmed that to him that very afternoon. All the empty statements the company had made about wanting to help the local economy, and operating it safely and cleanly, were just hollow promises to help it get its permit.

So Michaels had said.

Hudson wiped his face with the palm of his hand and rubbed his eyes, trying to get his mind a bit clearer. The effects of the beer were subsiding somewhat, he thought.

And what about the Board?

Hudson sneered again as he remembered the decision report justifying the approval of the plant because 'approving the plant was in the best interests of the province as a whole.'

"Yeah, right," he muttered. The jerks in Calgary who approved this thing didn't have to leave their warm beds at night to answer the complaints of the area residents.

Ah, yes, the area residents: the fools who actually thought they could stop the plant from being built, he thought. They would have been better off saving their money and moving the hell out of there. After all, when a corporate giant decides that it's moving into an area, all the ants had better scatter before they're stepped on and crushed.

All that fuss, Hudson reflected. And now, there it sat: the subject of so much controversy, so lonely, so quiet, yet at the same time, so open and unprotected...

He sat forward, so that his arms were resting on the top of the steering wheel. He slowly scratched his top lip with the nail of his thumb.

"You know," he said softly to himself, "if one had a half a mind to, one could do a hell of a lot of damage with this place."

He looked back over his right shoulder and saw the city lights.

The prevailing winds were usually from the west, sometimes the southwest, and the city was to his southeast, so it would be out of danger. He looked into the dark ahead of him to the right and he raised his eyebrows.

"But what about all of that lovely farmland, eh?" he muttered, which was followed by a quick chuckle.

He stubbed out his cigarette and lit another. After taking a deep drag, he sat back and cradled his chin in his left hand.

It's unprotected, but then why shouldn't it be? This wasn't the old wild west of the United States. There may have been anger on the part of the area residents when the plant was built, but really, what could they do but accept it? This was Canada, for Christ's sake: even if the opposition were extreme, the people would shrug their shoulders and shrink away once the plant was built.

Hudson started the car and turned down the road that ran along the plant site. Slowly, he drove past the plant itself and made mental notes of the location of the control and process buildings, and, most importantly of all, that of the huge sulphur block.

Hudson stopped the car briefly when he reached the main access gate. Leaving the car running, he opened the door and stepped out onto the gravel driveway. With its annoying chime seeming somewhat louder in the night air, the car nagged at him about the keys still in the ignition.

"Shut up," he muttered quietly and slammed the door shut.

He walked up to the gate and peered through to the main control room. He could see that the lights were on inside, but no one had responded to the sound of a car that had driven up to the entrance to the plant.

Looks like the night shift is on full alert, Hudson thought to himself.

He looked around at the process buildings. There was a cloud of steam rising from behind the silver towers that poked through its roof. In the back of the yard, behind the control and process buildings was the sulphur block. The illumination of the yard lights did not quite extend to the sulphur block, however, and as a result, it lay there quietly in a dim light, covered with weird shadows.

Providing the only noise from the plant were the compressors, not loud enough to be distinctive, but there all the same, and their sound mixed with the background of the night air.

From within the ambient consistency of the hum of the compressors, a buzzing slowly emerged and circled Hudson's ear for a couple of seconds. Then there was a brief silence, which was followed by a burning, ticklish pinprick into the right side of his neck.

"Son of a bitch," Hudson mumbled as he slapped his neck.

He wiped his hand against his shirt and swept away the crushed remains of the mosquito. Then he was bitten again on his left cheek. This time, though, the mosquito had left a bit of

Hudson's own blood on his cheek when it was squashed.

"Liable to get eaten alive in this god forsaken country."

Hudson got back into the car and backed onto the road. He paused for a minute and had one more look at the gas plant before he put the transmission back into drive and put his foot on the gas peddle.

"Yep," he thought as he lit another cigarette. "A lot of damage indeed."

Tuesday, August 23

Hudson returned to the bar at about the same time as he had the day before. Michaels was already there, as he had expected, sitting in the front row. He was too busy ogling the semi-naked woman with red and blue hair cavorting and writhing in front of him to notice Hudson when he first came in.

Michaels groaned when he realized that it was Hudson who had sat down in the chair next to his.

"Christ," he said loudly over the blaring music. "You again? Why the hell don't you leave me alone? You give me the fucking creeps!"

Michaels gaze returned to the girl and he tried to ignore Hudson. His smile came back and he began to pound the table with the palm of his hand. His attempt to keep in time with the beat of the music was off by about one quarter note.

"I want to talk to you," Hudson yelled above the noise, trying to attract Michaels's attention. After he had repeated himself twice, getting louder each time, Michaels turned to look at him.

"Look, man!" Michaels yelled back. "I talked to you yesterday. The fact that I was half cut helped me overlook the fact that you are something far less important in my life than the company I used to work for. It was fun while it lasted and it let me get a few things off my chest, but don't think that it means we're best friends now, you understand? I'm trying to forget about the plant and the Board, and I don't need you to remind me of them, okay? So, piss off already!"

Hudson's arm shot across the table and he grabbed Michaels's jacket collar with a tight fist.

"Look it, asshole," he said with an angry calm, his face within inches of Michaels's. "I thought you said that you wanted to get back at them, to hurt them real bad. I've come up with an idea that I thought you might be interested in that would not only do just that, but also make us a shit load of money. But it looks like you're just another god damn useless quitter! Is that what it is? Do you really want to get back at them and maybe get rich, or are you just going to sit here for the rest of your life, whining and moaning about how life took a dump on you? 'Boo hoo hoo: this is my life now. I can't do anything else. I am so useless. Give me some TLC, take off your clothes, and make the big bad world go away'. Oh yeah, I'm sure that will really impress toots here. Do you really think that this slut really gives a shit that you're down here in gynaecological row, whining about your life?"

Michaels looked into Hudson's eyes and what he saw there scared him a bit. Michaels grabbed the arm holding the coat and when Hudson relaxed his grip, Michaels sat back in his chair.

"Okay, okay," he said as he exhaled a lung full of smoke, "let's hear all about this wonderful idea of yours."

"That's better," replied Hudson. "Now, what I need to know first is if the other guys that were laid off think the same way you do and, if so, could we count on them joining us."

Michaels thought for a moment and then shrugged.

"Damned if I know. I haven't spoken to them in a while."

"Give them a call, Warren, my man," Hudson said, "and let's find out if they want to make a whole lot of money to supplement their severance pay."

Wednesday, August 24

The sun had risen above the horizon and Henderson sat with his eyes closed, facing directly at it, absorbing its heat. The air had a slight crisp edge to it and, apart from the occasional car that passed along the road next to the field office building where they sat, the only sound came from a few birds that sounded like they were having a tough time getting going this morning. He took a deep breath.

"So," said the voice from Keltner, who was sitting next to him. "Here we are."

"Yep," Henderson replied, "here we are. Both of us."

"Do I look okay?"

"You look adorable. How many times are you going to ask me? You are a man among men, and champion of the weak and downtrodden."

"Yeah, but do I look the part?"

"Absolutely. Stop worrying about it."

"I've never done anything like this before."

"You're making it sound like it's your wedding night. Did you bleat like that then, too?"

"No, my protests were a fair bit louder. And I was able to fend Kathy off for almost half an hour. Ah, I guess you're right. I mean, how tough is it going to be? All we have to do is play wet nurse to a bunch of head office geeks."

Henderson lifted the sunglasses from his face and looked disdainfully at Keltner.

"Have you no respect?" he asked. "These people are the ones who help develop and form the policy by which the citizens of this province are protected from the oil industry. Or something like that anyway."

"These people are nothing more than a bunch of pencil pushing nerds who have nothing better to do today than follow us around and then go home to their friends and say 'see, I told you those field animals don't know anything.'"

"You're so cynical."

"One of us has to be. Besides, I had a nice, easy field trip planned for today and you had to ruin it."

"Oh, stop crying. I don't know why you volunteered for this in the first place if all you're going to do is bitch about it all day."

Now Keltner raised his own sunglasses and looked at Henderson.

"You're kidding, right?" He looked at his watch. "Oh, look. It's quarter to nine. They were supposed to be here forty-five minutes ago. I guess this means that they're not going to show up. See ya."

He rose from the picnic bench where they had been sitting. Henderson grabbed his arm

"Sit down," he said.

Keltner complied.

"You're not going anywhere," Henderson said. "They're only fifteen minutes late."

"You told me that they'd be here at eight."

"I told you that because I figured you might try to get out of this by being fashionably late. The extra thirty minutes gave me some breathing room."

"Oh, so now you're saying that you don't trust me. I am aghast, nay, shocked and hurt. I was even here right at eight."

"Actually I'm quite surprised about that. I'm sorry. I really thought you'd try something."

"Well, I probably would have if I'd thought of it. Anyway, your apology is accepted and I will again consider you to be a member of my immediate circle of friends."

"Imagine my relief to know that my world is yet again complete and sane. Here comes the bus."

Henderson stood up from the picnic bench as the bus pulled into the main parking lot. Keltner stood up beside him.

"Are there any cute girls on that thing?" he asked.

"What would Kathy say if she heard you talking like that?"

"She'd probably appreciate the fact that I'm still a growing boy with active glands. Besides, with any luck: she'll - never - know - now - will - she?"

"Uh, huh. Maybe. We'll see."

Henderson and Keltner walked over to the bus. The driver opened up the door and Henderson stepped into the bus, followed closely by Keltner. Henderson took of his sunglasses. Keltner left his on.

"Good morning, ladies and gentlemen," Henderson began. "Uh, my name is Clint Henderson. I'm a senior gas plant inspector out of the Edmonton field office and my lovely assistant here is Peter Keltner, star of stage, screen, and the occasional Broadway musical. Say hello, Pete."

Keltner waved weakly and muttered a barely audible "hello".

"Okay. Now, despite the fact that he's trying to give you the impression that he's nothing more than my less than overly enthusiastic bodyguard, Pete is actually a drilling rig inspector and you have the pleasure of having the two of us escort you on your field trip. The itinerary includes a trip to a drilling rig, which my friend here is chomping at the bit to show you. After lunch, we'll be going to the Western Triassic sour gas plant for a tour. By any chance, are any of you, uh, familiar with what we're about to see today?"

One hand went up. Henderson looked at the owner, who was seated in the back of the bus, and saw that it belonged to a woman who, to him anyway, seemed a little out of place with the rest of the group.

"And who might you be?" he asked.

"I might be Renee Wilson," she replied with a bit of a chuckle. "I work in the Gas Department in Calgary. I actually work on the team that processed the application and attended the hearing for the Western Triassic plant."

"Oh wow. Well, Renee, welcome aboard. Now, have any of you ever been to a drilling rig before?"

This time, no one replied.

"Hah! Well, Clint," Keltner said, slapping a hand on Henderson's back, "it looks like you have to be fairly careful with what you say, whereas I can tell them anything and get away with it."

There was a murmur of laughter. Henderson went to sit down on the seat behind the driver but Keltner dove onto it first.

"I call 'shotgun'," he said. "I want the window."

Henderson stared at him. Keltner smiled and batted his eyelashes at him in return.

Henderson turned to the driver.

"Are you familiar with the Barrhead area?"

"Vaguely."

"Okay. Let's head north on highway 2. My friend here will guide you to the rig site when we get to Morinville."

The driver nodded and then closed the doors. Then, with the dull roaring groan that distinguishes school buses attempting to accelerate, the bus pulled out of the parking lot.

Because it was the tail end of summer, there were very few rigs operating close to the city. Adding to the problem was the fact that Keltner wanted to be sure that the group saw a rig that was normally in excellent condition. The last thing he wanted to show these people was a piece of junk that had somehow managed to find its way into his jurisdiction. It took almost an hour to reach the rig that Keltner had selected.

Keltner was an expert when it came to drilling rigs and Henderson had decided that he would stay out of Keltner's way while he conducted his portion of the tour.

Despite all his talk and faintly disguised protests, Keltner turned out to be a very informative and entertaining host. The toolpush on the rig had not been told about the tour and appeared somewhat surprised by the busload of Board people that had pulled onto his lease site from out of the blue. The look on his face seemed to show fear of imminent invasion, but he knew Keltner from previous inspections and seemed very amenable to having the group look at his rig. Henderson knew that this was one of the better rigs that operated in the province. That's why Keltner had chosen it, and Henderson wasn't sure if the toolpush's acceptance of the tour was the result of the pride he took in his unit's operation or the fact that the majority of the group were women, a gender rarely seen on most drilling rigs. He hoped for the former, but could understand the latter.

After all, he thought: how much different would that make him from Pete?

Throughout the tour of the drilling rig, Henderson was amazed at the way his friend handled the group and the ease with which he interacted with them. Keltner explained how the rig operated in simple, straightforward terms, and yet he was unpatronizing throughout. Henderson admired the patience Keltner exhibited when he answered the questions that the group asked, even though Henderson knew that the answers to those questions were, for the most part, obvious to anyone who worked closely with the rigs. Keltner also knew that most of those on this tour were not familiar with drilling rigs, which encouraged him even more.

The tour of the drilling rig concluded about an hour and a half after it had started. Henderson suspected that most of the people in the group had learned a great deal from Keltner and his humorous, informative manner would not be forgotten soon. As a bonus, Henderson found that he learned things that he did not know, even though he had inspected a number of rigs himself during his time at the Board.

Feeling like a teacher at the zoo with a class from elementary school, Henderson collected the hard hats and conducted a head count. Satisfied that everyone was aboard, Henderson again stood at the front of the bus to inform his charges of the remainder of the schedule. Keltner stood behind him, presenting the image of the faithful bodyguard he had tried to convey earlier. His grin indicated that he seemed to be enjoying his role as instructor.

"Okay," Henderson announced, "it's now eleven thirty. We're going to a restaurant in Westlock for lunch."

"Where the hell is Westlock?" an unidentified voice asked, which was followed by laughter.

"Westlock is a little town about fifteen minutes east of here."

"Is the restaurant licensed?" asked another voice.

"Pete, is the restaurant licensed?"

"Why are you asking me? You know I don't drink. Much."

"Yeah, right. Okay, yes, I do believe that the restaurant is licensed."

This was greeted with a round of applause.

"However," he continued, "we have to be at the gas plant by about one o'clock, so we should be on the road by about twelve thirty. That doesn't give us much time for lunch, so unfortunately, you're not going to have a chance to linger over a cool one, let alone three. You're going to have to save it for dinner. The good news is that Mr. Keltner is buying."

"Say what?" exclaimed Keltner.

"Put it on your Board credit card. You've demonstrated that a man of your influence must have a pretty high limit."

The bus started up and Henderson and Keltner took their places. Henderson turned to his partner.

"Good job. It really looked like you enjoyed that."

"All an act, I can assure you."

Henderson reached over and grabbed Keltner's cheek between his thumb and forefinger.

"You know I don't believe that, you big softy!"

Henderson had made reservations at the restaurant, which was a favourite of the staff from the Edmonton office. He and

Keltner were regulars and the manager had arranged everything pretty much to perfection. Henderson discussed the time problem with him while the others were being seated and he assured Henderson that the service would be prompt.

As Henderson walked over to the area where the others were sitting, he noticed that Keltner had located himself strategically in the middle of a group of the younger employees. He appeared to be elaborating on some aspect of the rig tour. His audience seemed impressed by Keltner's knowledge and sense of humour, and appeared fascinated with whatever it was he was telling them.

The rest of the staff had broken up into small groups and were discussing what they had seen so far with each other. Henderson noticed Renee Wilson sitting by herself at the far corner of the table. She was looking over the menu.

Henderson sat down across from her. She looked up and smiled.

"Mind if I join you?" he asked.

"Sure," she replied as she returned to the menu. "Be my guest."

"So how come you're not engaged in frank discussion and exciting repartee with the others?" he asked her.

Without raising her head, she looked over the top of the menu at him. She laughed when she saw the smile on his face.

"I guess I'm not really a part of their group," she replied. "I don't really know any of them. Most of them are new to the Board and this trip is part of their basic training course."

"And you?"

"Me? I'm a ten year veteran with the Board."

"So then how did you come to be here on our little tour?"

"Hmm. Where do I begin? Well, I've been handling gas plant applications with the Gas Department for almost a decade now and you know, in all that time, I've never really been out to see one. I can tell you what they should look like on paper and I can pretty much tell you what's required to build one so that it conforms to our rules and guidelines, but I have no idea what they look like once they are built. I mean, I've seen them from the highway, but I've never seen one close-up. When I heard about this trip, I asked my supervisor if I could go along."

She looked back at the menu.

"You must think that's pretty goofy," she added.

"Now why would you say that?" he asked.

"Hey, I know what you guys out in the field think of us in head office. You think that we don't have a clue about what actually happens out here."

Henderson shrugged.

"Not necessarily," he said.

"Oh, come on."

"Well, okay, yeah, come to think of it, I think I've heard that said around the office. I may even be guilty of it myself once or twice. But tell me that those of us who work out here in the field don't have a somewhat, how shall I put it, rustic reputation down in head office."

Renee's cheeks turned a slight red.

"I wouldn't say that," she said.

"Really? Now you don't expect me to believe that, do you?"

"Well, okay," she replied slowly. "I'd probably have to agree a little bit with that."

"So I think it's safe to assume that from this we can also agree on something else," Henderson said. "There's no doubt about it, stereotypes can be nasty things and can be quite inaccurate."

Henderson looked over at Keltner, who stuck his tongue out at him.

"Except for those about drilling rig inspectors, of course," he added.

"And maybe a big part of the problem," Henderson continued, "comes from the fact that some of the people we've run into from head office, not all of them mind you, but some of them, don't seem to have any idea of what it's like to be out here on the front lines. I'll give you an example: the Western Triassic plant we're going to. Now, I'll be honest with you. A lot of us out here have wondered how the hell the thing ever got approved in the first place."

"So I suppose that the result is that I, or at the very least, my department, get the blame for that?" Renee asked.

"Well, I don't know if I'd say that...," Henderson said with a nervous smile.

Renee sat forward and put her arms on the table.

"Come on," she said. "Be honest with me. I hate liars, especially those who do it to avoid hurting my feelings."

"Yeah, okay then. Yes. At one time, perhaps."

"But we do send the applications out to the appropriate field office for an initial assessment," Renee said.

"Unfortunately, in our office, the person who provides you with those assessments is my supervisor who..."

"Fred Larson?" Renee interrupted.

"Uh, yeah. That's him. Anyway, you didn't hear it from me, but I don't think he's set foot in a gas plant for years. I know I shouldn't say this, but for your own sake, and that of the Edmonton area, I wouldn't be putting too much weight in what he has to say."

"So how do we get the opinion of you guys out in the field? We can't read minds, you know."

"Ah. Touché."

"So then how," Renee added with a sly smile, "do we get rid of the stereotypes that we have of each other?"

"Hmm," Henderson said. "Well, now I can say that I've met you in person. I can see that you're an intelligent person who has a job to do and who, I'm sure, did your damnedest to ensure that, as you said, the application conformed to our regulations. Now here you are, out in the field, away from your office, and you've at least gone to the trouble to come out and see what's going on. I think that what would really help is for all of us, you in head office, we in the field, to get to know each other better. Open the communication channels a bit more so that we can get more respect for each other's views."

"Agreed," Renee replied. She took a sip of water. "Okay, here's a slightly different solution. My boss would kill to get someone from the field transferred into our group."

She put the glass down and looked into his eyes.

"Would you be interested?" she asked.

Henderson covered his mouth with his hand.

"Well," he said as he sat back in his chair. He smiled at her. "You never know."

"See, there you go," she replied with a wink. "We're on our way to getting rid of stereotypes already."

"Well, anyway," he added as he sat forward again and picked up the menu, "I'm glad that you made the effort to come out with us today. As far as I'm concerned, that right there sets you apart from the others."

"After ten years, I think it was about time," Renee said.

"Better late than never," Henderson replied. "Besides, if this trip serves merely to nip in the bud the perception that some head office staff have about us out here in the field, then it will have been worth it."

Renee returned his smile. Henderson got the impression that it wasn't something she gave away readily. He scanned the finger on her left hand. It was empty.

"So, tell me about the rest of the group," Henderson said.

"Oh, not too much to say. Most of them have come right out of high school or college. A lot of them are here only because it's part of their training and they're treating this trip like a couple of days off. You may have noticed that some of them are suffering from pretty wicked hangovers."

"Sounds like they're grooming themselves for a job in the field."

Renee laughed again.

"Well, they're young," she said, "and I can't keep up with them anymore, so I don't even try. When we're at the hotel this evening, they'll go their own way, and I'll go mine."

"Which is?"

"Typically, it's a quiet supper by myself and then I retire to my room with a good book."

Henderson paused for a minute. He swallowed hard.

"Uh, would you, uh, maybe like some company tonight?" he asked. "Maybe for dinner?"

"Well, I wouldn't want to be an imposition," she replied. "I'm sure that showing us around today can't be a lot of fun for you, and I wouldn't want you to tie up an evening as well."

"To be perfectly honest," he said, "it really wouldn't be that much of a burden. I have absolutely no plans for tonight and besides, it would give me a good excuse to get out of my apartment. And just maybe, it would go a long way to opening up those communication channels."

Renee thought for a couple of minutes and then she smiled again.

"Yeah, okay," she said, "I'd like that, but only as long as you're sure you don't mind now."

"I wouldn't. Not a bit."

"Well, there's a pretty good restaurant at my hotel, if that's okay with you."

"That's the hotel that everyone from the Board stays at when they come to Edmonton?"

"Yeah, the Capital Garden Inn. It's just down the road from the field office."

"I know the restaurant," Henderson said. "It's excellent. There's a lounge there as well, called 'The Sand Bar'."

"Sounds like you've been there before."

"Oh, maybe once or twice. Why don't you meet me there about six thirty?"

"Six thirty it is. I'll be there."

"I might even wear a tie."

"What? A field inspector in a tie? My goodness, how ever will I recognize you?"

"I could wear my hard hat. It has my name on it."

Renee laughed and then winked at him again.

"No, that's okay. I'm sure I'll figure out a way to pick you out of the crowd. Consider it part of my effort to destroy those nasty stereotypes we were talking about."

"Are you ready to order?" asked the waitress, who had a hint of a smile. She had actually arrived at their table a few minutes before.

Michaels and the other employees who had been laid off at the Western Triassic gas plant had arranged to meet in the basement of Michaels's home and were now sitting as a group around the glass coffee table on the middle of the room. The man sitting to the right of Michaels threw down the magazine that he had picked up only few minutes earlier. Originally intending to be read, the magazine had spent most of its time in the man's possession being drummed against the palm of his left hand.

"Where the hell is he?" he yelled. "You told us he'd be here an hour ago."

Michaels took a swig from his bottle of beer and then looked at his watch.

"Calm down, would ya?" he sighed. He wiped his mouth with the back of his shirtsleeve. "I know he promised he'd be here by now. He must have a good reason for being late."

One of the others finished the beer that he had opened just a few minutes before. He put the empty bottle onto the coffee table, opened the cooler that was next to the couch upon which he was sitting, pulled out another bottle, and opened it. He took a drink.

"Why do have the feeling that I'm wasting my time here?" he asked. "I'll bet this guy was just shittin' ya anyway."

Michaels turned to him and then looked down for a few seconds while he rolled his eyes, shook his head, and sighed again. Then he looked up and grabbed the collar of his colleague's shirt.

"Steve, would it be possible for you to just try to shut up for a few minutes?" he spat. "When Hudson gets here, you'll see that the wait was well worth it. I thought he was full of crap at first, too, but he managed to convince me."

Steve Collins looked over Michaels's shoulder at one of the others, who was sitting in an easy chair behind Michaels. That man shrugged and shook his head.

"Okay, whatever you say, Michaels," Collins replied with his hands up. "As long as you're providing the beer, who am I to question you. My useless fate is in your hands."

The rest of the group spent a bit of time trying to figure out if they should laugh. A couple of them decided that it might be all right and were able to let out a slight chuckle before they all heard the slam of a door and then footsteps tumbling down the stairs, which announced Hudson's arrival. Hudson had just entered the room when Michaels was on to him.

"Where the hell were you, man?" Michaels yelled. "You said you'd be here over an hour ago!"

Hudson looked around at the others.

"Relax. I had to check on a couple of things, all right? Just back off. Everything's cool. Jesus."

Michaels held up his hands and sat down. He twisted the lid from another bottle of beer.

"And take it easy on that stuff," Hudson added. "In order for this thing to work, I need everyone to be somewhat clear-headed. I won't be able to count on anyone who's half-whacked."

Hudson fell into one of the empty chairs and clapped his hands together.

"So," he continued, "are you going to introduce me to all of your little friends?"

Michaels nodded.

"These are all the guys that were laid off last week, just like you asked."

He started with the man seated to his left and moved

around the room.

"Gillis Hudson, this is Steve Collins..."

Hudson stood and shook hands with the man who had wondered if he had been wasting his time. Collins was a clean-shaven young man with a strong grip. Wedding band. Faded, old blue jeans. Family man. Probably kids too, guessed Hudson.

"Gordon Phillips..."

The man sitting in the easy chair behind Michaels rose to shake Hudson's hand. One-day growth of beard and oily jeans. Not only was he not wearing a ring, but there was no pale patch on his ring finger.

"And Terry Simpson."

The young man jumped from his seat and wiped his hands frantically on his jeans before shaking Hudson's hand eagerly. His smile had appeared as soon as his name was mentioned and although there was enthusiasm in that smile, Hudson noticed that there was a slight dullness in his eyes. Hudson suspected that the smile was there in part because Simpson had been recognized by someone, and in part to impress him.

Hmmm, thought Hudson as he returned the smile and shook Simpson's hand: I don't know.

"Did you bring them up to speed about what we talked about?" Hudson asked Michaels after he had sat down again.

"Ah, a bit," Michaels replied. "I told them that they had a chance to get back at Western Triassic and make a little money at the same time. I also told them that there was a little risk."

Hudson looked around and snorted a laugh.

"Actually, if we want to be absolutely honest" he said as he drilled into Collins's eyes with his own, "there's one hell of a lot of risk. What I'm thinking of is, to be truthful, really, really illegal."

"But if we're successful," he continued with a wry smile, "then we'll have kicked in the nuts of both Western Triassic and the Board and, on top of all that, walk away with a whole shit load of money. If any of you don't want to participate, then get the hell out of here now. If you even think about telling anybody else, I'll not only deny it, I'll track down where you live and make your life extremely painful. I've got nothing to lose, anymore. I hope I'm clear on that."

"We discussed it before we came over," Collins said, looking at the others, "and first thing Warren did was pound in the fact that what you have in mind is against the law. I have to admit that I was pretty scared when I heard that. But my savings account's almost gone and with the wife unable to work, I need money bad. Warren told us that when everything was said and done, we'd be able to get out with no one knowing who we were. Is that right?"

"If everything goes according to plan and everyone holds up their end," Hudson said. He was looking at Simpson when he uttered the last bit. "We go in at night and come out at night. No one will see us enter or leave."

Collins nodded.

"Well," he said finally, "let's hear what you have in mind."

"Spenser's going to have a fit when he sees this," Keltner said as he tucked the charge card receipt into his wallet.

"Do you whine like this at home or am I just special?" asked Henderson.

"I can't help it. Being out in the field with you brings out the muse in me."

They were walking across the parking lot to the waiting bus, where the members of their tour group were waiting for them.

"Man, he's going to wonder why I'm screwing up his budget when these people are all on expenses anyway."

"What did you do? Take a course?" Henderson continued. "Look at it this way: it's a small price to pay for an hour of conversation with four women."

Keltner stopped Henderson.

"Hey, now, speaking of conversation with attractive ladies," he said, "I noticed that you pretty much monopolized the attention of one particularly attractive little staff member. Care to tell me about it?"

Henderson felt his face flush.

"Nope."

"Aw, come on, Clint. Okay, don't tell me for me. Tell me

so I can let Kathy know that there's still some hope for you yet. Do it for her."

"Okay," Henderson sighed. "Let's just say that I won't be eating alone tonight. It's just dinner. That's it. There's no more to it. End of discussion."

Keltner laughed quietly.

"You smooth little rascal you. Kathy's going to be tickled pink."

"Just be careful what you say. It's not like we're getting married or anything. Now let's go. We have minds to mould waiting for us."

"Aye-aye, mon capitaner," Keltner saluted. "First comes love, then comes marriage..."

"If you keep this up," Henderson began. He was trying to keep a straight face, but it wasn't working, "you're not going to have to wait until you get home to get a slap. Now get on the bus."

"I love it when you threaten me," Keltner replied as he quick-stepped to the bus. "It gets my adrenaline running and I feel so alive."

The bus pulled into the plant's parking lot at one thirty five. Henderson saw Shawn Jackson waiting by the main doors of the office. Standing next to him was a taller, brawny man whom Henderson recognised from previous inspections of the facility.

Henderson was the first one off the bus after it had stopped. He shook Jackson's hand.

"Sorry we're late, Shawn," he said. "Hope you haven't been waiting long. Service at the restaurant was a touch on the slow side today."

"No problem," Jackson replied. "Just trying to take in a little of what's left of summer. Clint Henderson, this is Rick Mastogne: he'll be your escort today."

Henderson shook Mastogne's hand.

"If you don't need me for anything else right now, Clint,"

Jackson said, "I'll let you boys handle this. As much as I would like to join you, I, unfortunately, have paper work to get out."

"Thanks, Shawn," Henderson replied, "I'll talk to you later."

"How do you want to handle this?" asked Mastogne while he watched the stream of people getting off the bus.

"If you don't mind, I'd like to use your meeting room to explain how the plant operates first," Henderson replied. Keltner was handing out the hard hats. "Then we can split them into two groups and take them through the plant."

Mastogne agreed and within a few minutes, the tour group was crowded into a room that, although the largest in the main office building, was not intended to hold so many people. While everyone was either finding a place to sit or somewhere to stand, Henderson picked up a piece of chalk and began drawing large blocks on the blackboard. When he had finished drawing the blocks, he drew lines to connect them and wrote the names of the individual plant processes in the appropriate blocks. Mastogne brought in a schematic of the plant and pinned it to the wall next to the blackboard.

When Henderson was finished drawing, he put the chalk down and the room hushed.

"Okay. First of all, this is Rick Mastogne," Henderson began. "After I'm finished explaining how this particular plant operates, he'll be taking some of you through the plant site and, with any luck, the two explanations should match."

This was followed by some laughter, although Henderson noticed that one of the staff in the back rolled his eyes and two others looked at each other and shook their heads slightly.

Henderson then described the processing of natural gas through the plant. He started with a description of the oil batteries in the area and how their solution gas, the gas that is produced along with the oil, was gathered and transported to the plant through its own separate pipeline system. He also showed on a map the gas wells that were drilled in the fields to the north that provided the second source of the plant's feed.

Using the schematic, along with diagrams he drew on the

black board, Henderson showed how the two gas streams entered the plant in two different streams and were combined after being brought to equal pressure through a set of compressors located in a building at the plant inlet.

"When we get outside," he explained, "you'll see this compressor station sitting off by itself on the north side of the yard."

Henderson then went on to describe how the gas was put through inlet separation, where water and the heavier hydrocarbons drop out of the gas stream as liquids.

"The water, which is extremely salty, is usually more of a nuisance than anything else, although sometimes there is some value in injecting it back into the formations from which the oil is produced. This helps maintain pressure in those formations."

"The liquids are sent to an additional process train," Henderson continued. "A liquid product called condensate, which can be considered to be a very light, and very valuable, oil is removed from the gas stream. The gas stream is subjected to further processing in the refrigeration plant."

He described the details of the refrigeration plant, which is used to chill the gas and extract lighter hydrocarbon liquids.

"Now, at this plant, the refrigeration plant extracts propane and butane, which are stored in the large bullet shaped tanks that you'll see on the east side of the plant site."

"So, at this point, we have a fairly dry gas stream," he added. "However, you have to remember that the natural gas that comes into this plant is extremely sour. That is, it contains hydrogen sulphide and carbon dioxide, both of which must be removed from the gas before any processing can occur."

He explained how a chemical called amine is used to render the gas sweet. In a vessel called a contactor, this chemical reacts chemically with the hydrogen sulphide and the carbon dioxide, and strips these two gases from the remainder of the gas stream.

"Which is all really wonderful and all, but that leads to a fairly major problem: what do we do with the hydrogen sulphide and carbon dioxide now?"

"Carbon dioxide, while a greenhouse gas, is not in itself poisonous. Hydrogen sulphide, on the other hand, is a completely different story. In small concentrations, it has a smell like rotten eggs; at higher concentrations, it quickly destroys the sense of smell. It can cause instant death at a concentration of less than 1000 parts per million, which is less than 0.1 per cent. If you consider that the sour gas stream leaving the contactor at this plant has a hydrogen sulphide concentration of almost 75 per cent, you can see that this stuff can become a headache in a real hurry."

"Now, in small amounts, hydrogen sulphide can be burned and converted into sulphur dioxide. This is also a poisonous gas, but it is not as odorous and if burned in a tall enough flare stack, it will disperse quite readily into the atmosphere."

"This is okay for small amounts of hydrogen sulphide, but when larger volumes are involved, as they are at this plant, we at the Board require the operator of the plant to remove it from the gas stream and convert it to elemental sulphur."

Henderson went on to describe the sulphur plant, in which the most complex process in the entire facility is performed.

"The acid gas stream is separated into two parts," he said. "One third of the stream is burned with a precise volume of air and this results in the conversion of the hydrogen sulphide to sulphur dioxide and water. This is almost exactly the same reaction that occurs in the flare stacks at other, smaller gas plants except that in this case, the sulphur dioxide is not dispersed into the atmosphere. Instead, it is re-combined with the other two thirds of the acid gas stream. The sulphur dioxide and the remaining hydrogen sulphide now react in a vessel containing a catalyst, and this results in the formation of elemental sulphur and water."

"Both of these reactions give off a great deal of heat and water, which is used to carry away the heat. The water is converted to steam and is used in other areas of the plant. The sulphur is condensed and in this particular facility, it is added to the large block that is located at the extreme south end of the facility."

"However, because there's carbon dioxide in the acid gas stream and it's not really possible to control the air-gas ratio precisely, this reaction isn't 100 per cent efficient. Therefore, during the course of your tour, you will notice that the conversion process is repeated three times. The small volume of acid gas that remains after the third conversion process is incinerated in the tall red and white stack."

Henderson turned away from the blackboard and looked at his audience.

"Whew, I didn't know I knew all that," he concluded. "They don't pay me nearly enough. Anyway, that's basically how the plant operates. I realise that it may be a little confusing, but hopefully the tour will help clarify my explanation. Does anyone have any questions?"

Two hands went up. One of them belonged to Keltner; Henderson nodded at the owner of the other.

"How much sulphur does this plant recover on any given day?"

"Ummmm," Henderson looked at Mastogne, who had been sitting at the back with Keltner. Mastogne walked up to the front of the room.

"Our plant is designed to process a maximum of approximately 100 million cubic feet per day of raw gas," Mastogne replied, "or as we are now conditioned to think, about 2820 thousand cubic meters. It is designed to handle a gas stream containing ten per cent hydrogen sulphide, or approximately 382 metric tonnes. Provincial regulations, your regulations, require us to recover at least 98.5 per cent of that inlet sulphur. Right now, we have approximately 250 metric tonnes per day coming into the plant and on a good day, we'll get about 247 tonnes, or 99 per cent of the total inlet, being recovered and put onto the block."

"Any other questions?" Henderson asked.

Again, two hands were raised. One of them belonged to Renee, while the other belonged yet again to Keltner.

"Yes, Renee?" Henderson said.

"Most of the other sour plants in the province disposed of their sulphur blocks years ago and now ship their sulphur out to market as a liquid through a pipeline. Does Western Triassic have any plans to get rid of their block?" she asked. Henderson noticed that she had a slight smile.

Mastogne looked down at the ground. He also had a slight smile on his face, although his seemed a bit more sheepish.

"Well, I'm probably not the one who can give you a definitive answer to that," he said. "I'm not high enough on the food chain to make those kinds of decisions. Off the record, though, you can rest assured that we operators would love to see that block gone. I believe that there are plans to transition from the block to a pipeline, but I couldn't say for sure right now."

"Fair enough," Renee nodded and sat back. She made a couple of notes.

"Anything else?"

Keltner raised his hand again. Henderson sighed.

"Yes, Pete?"

Keltner stood up.

"Where do them numbers go when you wipe them off the blackboard?"

The group, including Mastogne, broke into laughter.

"Into the brush, I suppose," replied Henderson. He threw a piece of chalk at Keltner, who caught it. "Okay, on that note, let's split up the group. One half can go with Rick and the other half can come with me."

"So to make this work, we'll need explosives and flares," Hudson said. "Anybody have any ideas?"

"I have a friend who works for an oilfield supply company," Michaels said. "They cater to the seismic outfits, so they should have some in stock. Let me see what I can do."

"Can you get on it now? We need them this afternoon if we're going in tonight. Be discreet. What about guns?"

"Me and Gord like to hunt," Collins said. "We both have a collection of rifles."

"Okay, great, Hudson said. "Bring them along, with lots of ammo. I don't plan on using them, but you never know."

"Man, I don't know about this," Collins said. "It sounds pretty goddamn risky."

"There's risk," Hudson said, "but if everything goes according to plan, we go in, make our demands, and walk out with the money."

"What if the cops get involved?" Phillips asked. "I mean, this isn't jay walkin' we're talking about here. This is really serious shit! I don't want to spend the rest of my life in jail!"

"Yeah, I guess there's a chance of that," Michaels replied, nodding his head, "but I don't see it happening. I mean, Christ, everybody in the area hates that plant. Western Triassic won't call in the cops. They'll want to keep it real quiet. And they'll be glad to pay us off just to get rid of us and keep our mouths shut."

"And this is our chance to really stick it to them," added Hudson. "Look, I need to know. Are you guys in or out?"

Collins looked at Phillips.

"Wow. I don't know man," he said. "You sure make it sound easy."

"There are no guarantees," replied Hudson with a straight face, "but I'm prepared to go in. Hell, I'm the one who gets to handle all the risky shit. I'll be doing all the talking while you guys just have to sit there."

Collins looked at Phillips again. Their eyes agreed.

"Yeah, okay," Phillips said. "Count me in."

"Me too," said Collins.

"How about you, Simpson?" Michaels asked.

"Simpson's out," Collins said. "Don't get him involved with this."

"He's old to enough to make up his own mind," Michaels snapped. "Besides, you have to remember one thing: no one else is going to hire him. Come on. Give him some credit."

Simpson turned to Collins. He had a confused look on his face, but smiled when he saw his friend nod. He also nodded.

"Okay," he said slowly, still nodding his head.

"But he stays with me," Collins added quickly. "I want to look out for him."

"Yeah, yeah," Hudson replied. "Sure, whatever. Okay, that should be about it. You all know what you have to do. We'll meet back here around six."

The tour of the plant concluded, the group filed back onto the bus. Henderson thanked Mastogne, and then he and Keltner boarded the bus.

Henderson had to admit that the tour went well, even if a couple of individuals in the group, those he'd noticed earlier, didn't seem that enthusiastic or impressed. The weather had co-operated and the plant had put on quite a show, with the tall processing towers shining in the sun, the whistling roar of gas flowing under high pressure through the pipes, and the huge clouds of steam emanating from the sulphur plant.

"So," Henderson said to the group as the bus pulled out of the plant's parking lot. "What did you think?"

"Sure is different than what I was expecting," said one of the staff. "A lot bigger."

"Yeah, not at all like what it looks like on paper," said another.

The group was still buzzing when they arrived back at the office thirty minutes later.

Henderson looked at his watch. It was now after five and the building was closed. As the bus came to a stop in the parking lot, he stood up again.

"Well, on behalf of Peter and myself, I'd like to thank you for the opportunity to show you what we in the field do. When you get back to Calgary, if you have any questions about the rig or the plant you saw today, please feel free to phone either Peter or myself. Have a good trip back, okay?"

Henderson looked in the back and saw Renee. He winked, and she smiled and mouthed the words "six thirty". Henderson nodded almost imperceptibly.

After getting off, he and Keltner watched the bus pull out of the parking lot.

"What time's your date?" Keltner asked.

"I've got about an hour and a half before I meet her at the hotel."

"Are you planning on wearing a tie?"

"I was thinking about it."

"Do you remember how to tie one?"

"Sure. I imagine that it's your neck and tie a noose."

Keltner sighed.

"Well come on then, lover boy, we'd better get home so you can get ready."

The fingers of Henderson's right hand drummed triplets on the dash of the truck.

"C'mon, already, c'mon."

The digital clock in the radio told him that if he had been walking into the hotel lobby at that instant, he would only be six minutes late.

He watched the traffic lights at right angles, those that controlled the traffic travelling in front of him. Why is it that the length of time that a light is against you is directly proportional to the urgency to get somewhere on time, Henderson wondered. This seems to be especially true when your destination, and the lovely lady that's waiting there, are in sight. On the other hand, you always get the green lights when you're driving to work on a Monday morning.

Finally, the light for the other traffic turned red, and Henderson stomped his foot down on the accelerator pedal. It's not as if it really mattered that much. The engine treated the truck's weight as a burden rather than a minor parasite, and Henderson felt the drive train work at bringing the truck up to a reasonable speed.

Immediately after driving through the intersection, he signalled right, shoulder-checked, and drove the truck into the lane that led into the hotel's parking lot. Once in the parking lot, Henderson didn't waste any time looking for a spot close to the entrance. Rather, he pulled into the first empty space he saw, figuring that it would take him less time to walk the distance to the main doors than it would take to find a place fifty feet closer.

Before getting out of the truck, he checked himself in the truck's skinny rear view mirror. Not too bad, he thought, but he ran a brush through his hair one more time and made his tie just a little bit straighter.

"Ahh! Leave it alone, already," he muttered. "You're not that bad. It's not like you have to look at you."

He walked across the parking lot to the main doors of the hotel, which slid open automatically. To the left was 'The Sand Bar'.

She was sitting at a table next to the lounge fountain. Her light pink blouse and grey slacks and blazer accentuated her dark blonde hair, and the soft spot lights from the ceiling, along with the flicker from the small candle on the table in front of her, cast a light glow over her delicate features. She was holding a glass of red wine and was looking into the pool at the base of the fountain.

My God, Henderson thought: she's really pretty.

He walked over to her. The clicking of the leather soles of his shoes on the marble floor were masked by the trickling fountain. Renee saw him from the corner of her eye and turned to face him. Her smile was the most beautiful he had ever seen.

"Sorry I'm late," he said a little sheepishly.

She looked him up and down.

"Well, he really is wearing a tie. Mmm, mmm, will wonders never cease? I suppose I could forgive a good looking boy like you just this once."

"Uh, thanks," Henderson said as he sat down. "You know you're going to make me blush."

"Oh, that's okay," she replied as she took a sip from her glass. "The colour of your face will go well with the colour of this wine."

The waitress walked up to their table. She did a double take when she saw Clint.

"Well," she said, "look at you. The usual?"

Henderson sat back in his chair and looked up at her.

"Why…you say that as if I've been here before."

The waitress laughed.

"I almost didn't recognize you in that suit," she said. "You look great."

"Thanks, Amanda," said Henderson. "Oh, Amanda, Renee. Renee, Amanda. Between the two of you, I just might meet my self-esteem quota for the year."

"We've sort of met already," Renee said. "Amanda recommended this red. Excellent suggestion, by the way."

"Thank you, Renee," Amanda replied. She looked at Clint.

"It's from B.C.," she said. "Cabernet Merlot from Trepanier Cellars. Would like to try that or stick to the usual?"

"You have me convinced. I'll try the Cab-Merlot."

"A glass of red before the first day of autumn," Amanda said. "My, my, this must be a very special evening."

She winked at him and went to get his drink. Renee watched her walk back to the bar and turned to Henderson with a smile.

"She's very friendly," she said. "I take it that this is one of the regular spots for the Edmonton office staff?"

"For a couple of the field staff," Henderson replied. "Specifically, Pete and me. It's not like either of us like to get plastered, so we try to avoid the so-called regular Board office hangouts. I like the atmosphere here. It's quiet and classy, and a great place to relax. Plus they actually have a decent wine list."

"And Amanda?"

"A great waitress."

Renee looked at him suspiciously.

"Is that all?" she asked.

"Honest," he said. "She's very young and very taken. She's also a delight to talk to at the end of the day."

"I'm sorry," Renee said with a laugh, "I'm just being awfully nosy. So what's your 'usual'?"

"Once spring rolls around, I generally stick to their house Sauvignon Blanc. I generally don't start drinking red wine until the weather gets cooler. I guess I'm what you might call a seasonal wine drinker."

"Summer's also a good time for beer?"

"No beer. Can't stand it."

"What? Well, there's another bit of the image shot to hell," Renee said with a grin as she took another sip of wine. "You realize that nobody in Calgary is going to believe me when I tell them about a guy from the field wearing a tie and having a dislike of beer. They'll think I was drunk all the time I was up here."

Amanda arrived at their table with Henderson's wine.

"Thanks, Amanda," he said. "Well, fighting stereotypes is a tough job, but I get the feeling that you're up to the task."

Henderson picked up his glass and held it forward.

"Here's to this evening," he said.

Renee leaned forward and tapped his glass with her own. Henderson then took a drink from his glass.

"Mmm, that is nice," he said.

Renee took a sip and looked at him.

"So what's it like being a field inspector?" she asked.

"Well," he replied, "there's so much to it. Where should I begin?"

"How about you tell me a story about how you dealt with something nasty that we approved."

"Oh my," Henderson said as he sat back and his eyes turned to the ceiling. Then he smiled a bit, and leaned forward toward Renee.

"Okay," Henderson began, "there's this gas gathering system that feeds the Western Triassic Morinville plant, the one that you were at today. It picks up gas from some wells northwest of the plant and its approval was included as part of the plant's approval. Anyway, I was on-call, about four months ago, when I received a noise complaint from this farmer. This guy is getting up there. I mean, he has to be somewhere between sixty-five and four hundred years old, and he starts into me on the phone about how he's been on that piece of farmland for pretty much all of his life, and that he never had any hearing problems until this compressor station that sat just to the north of his property was built, and so on, and so forth."

"I let him rant for a bit," continued Henderson, "not that I could get a word in edgewise anyway, and then when he stopped to take a breath, I told him that I'm on my way. It took me about half an hour to get there and find his place, and when I arrived, he was already outside in his yard, waiting for me. I pull into the yard and as soon as I'm out of the truck, he's lighting into me. He's on about the noise mostly, but he's also into me about the truck traffic, and the snotty individuals that he has to deal with at the plant, and how the Board is in cahoots with Western Triassic."

"And he just keeps going on and on. Finally, right about the point where I'm convinced that he's going to stroke out on me, he points his finger at me, shakes it wildly, and says 'furthermore, you can take that god damn plant and shove it up your ass'."

"Oh my." Renee's eyes were wide. "Well, what, what did you do?"

Henderson took a drink and looked into the wine again.

"All I could think of doing," he said, "honestly, was to put my hand on his shoulder…"

Henderson looked up at Renee.

"And say 'Sir, I'm here to help you: not entertain you.'"

Renee burst out laughing.

"And what did he do?" she was finally able to blurt out.

"Well, he looked like he'd just stuck his finger in an electrical socket. He was basically speechless. He followed me around while I took some readings, and I found that, yes, the noise levels from the compressor station were slightly higher than that allowed."

"So what happened?"

"I knew from his comment about the 'snotty plant people' that there had to be a communication problem. I mean, Shawn Jackson, the plant manager out there, just isn't like that. I spoke to Shawn the next day and it turns out that there was indeed a communication problem. Shawn had tried to tell this gentleman that he empathized with him because his own hearing was sensitive to these types of noises, but this guy thought that Shawn was making fun of him. Shawn was desperate to come up with a solution."

"And did you come up with one?"

"We did together, and it's probably not the most elegant solution, but it worked. Another operator had built a barrier around one of their stations that was made from wood and Styrofoam. Shawn built something similar and voila, problem solved."

"So is that pretty typical of the type of thing you run into out here?" asked Renee.

Henderson shrugged as he took a sip from his glass.

"Oh, you see all sorts of things out here," he said. "You also meet all kinds of people, under all sorts of circumstances. Some of these people are great. They understand what we're up against sometimes, and appreciate what we do. Others, well they'd test the diplomacy skills of my grandfather."

"Oh yeah? Patient man is he?"

"He is now that he's dead."

Renee laughed again. This time, she almost lost the mouthful of wine she had just taken.

"I'm sorry," she said as she covered her mouth, "that was not very sensitive of me."

As he swirled the wine in his own glass and looked into its deep colour, Henderson realized that he liked getting that reaction from her. It had been some time.

Maybe for both of them, he thought.

He looked up and saw that Renee was looking at him as her laughing began to subside. Henderson noticed that her brow was bit furrowed. He sat back in his chair and took a drink from his glass.

"What?" he said with a smile.

"Mmm, just the old stereotype coming back to haunt me," she replied. "I really get this sense that you're not quite like most of the others that work in the field."

Henderson smiled slightly.

"I don't know about that."

"Oh, please."

Henderson looked up at her and saw a reflection in her left eye of the glow from the flickering candle.

"You appreciate places, atmosphere, like this," she continued. "You don't like beer. You look great in a tie. Tell me: what kind of music do you listen to?"

"Well, um, actually I like a lot of different types of music."

"Okay, let's put it this way. If I went out to your truck right now and hit the eject button on the stereo, what would I get popping into my hand?"

Henderson looked up at the ceiling.

"A CD," he replied after a few seconds. "Alcamedes's Electromagnetic Contract."

"Who?"

Henderson put his glass on the table.

"Exactly," he said.

"Well, just because I've never heard of them doesn't mean that I wouldn't like them. Tell me about them."

"No words, just music. Electronic music, but with melody, unlike a lot of electronic stuff that's out there today. Actually, I think you might like them."

"I'd like to hear them," Renee replied. "Maybe you could share them with me sometime."

Henderson picked up his glass, took a drink, and then looked into her eyes again. He liked the softness of the candle's reflection that was still there.

"That could be arranged," he said. "Just remember our deal about stereotypes."

"Deal."

Amanda appeared at their table.

"This is looking awfully cozy," she said. "Would we like another?"

"I don't know," replied Henderson, looking at his watch, "I believe that we're supposed to be going for dinner shortly."

Renee looked at her watch.

"Oh my," she said as she sat upright, "our reservations were for five minutes ago."

Henderson pulled out his wallet and gave Amanda a

twenty-dollar bill.

"That's good, my dear. We'll be back. Possibly not tonight, but you know me."

"I trust you," replied Amanda with a smile and a wink. She walked back to the bar.

They stood up from the table. Renee took him by the arm and he followed willingly.

"Come on, you," she said. "I've made reservations at the Courtyard Inn. I'm starved."

"And how was your dinner?" the waitress asked.

"Excellent, thank you," Renee replied.

"Umm hmm!" added Henderson putting his linen napkin on the table.

"I'm glad to hear it. Now, can I interest you in dessert or an after dinner liqueur?"

"Gran Marnier and coffee for me," said Renee.

"Straight up or in a snifter glass?"

"In a snifter, please."

"Sir?"

"Make it two," replied Henderson. "Although you'd better make mine decaf."

"Okay. I'll be back in a moment."

"That was excellent, Renee. You can tell your boss that his steak Oscar recommendation was right on the mark."

"Jerry doesn't get out much, but when he does, he knows what he likes."

The waitress brought their drinks.

Renee ran a finger around the rim of her snifter glass. The flame from the enclosed candle on the table highlighted the twinkle in her eyes.

"So tell me, Mr. Board Inspector," she said as she looked up at him, "how come none of the girls in this city have been able to get a ring on your left hand yet?"

"Umm, one did once," he replied with a shrug, "but it

only lasted a couple of years."

He looked at the finger on his left hand.

"I'm surprised that the scar isn't still visible," he added.

"Oh, I'm sorry," said Renee. "I had no idea. There I am, being nosy again."

"Ah, I like to think that we were too young," Henderson replied. "At least I know I was. And I guess we'd never decided what we had wanted to do with each of our lives. When we did decide, it turned out that it didn't really include the other and that was sort of that."

He looked at the wall behind her, then down at the table. He straightened the coffee spoon on the napkin three or four times and then left it alone.

"In a lot of ways, I'm really sorry about what happened," he said quietly, "but it did happen. I can't get away from that. I like to think that it was better to call it quits early than for both of us to stay unhappy. I also have to admit that I probably wasn't the nicest person in the world at the time and I've had a lot of growing up to do."

Renee took a deep breath and her finger resumed its circling around the rim of the glass, this time with more intensity.

"I'm going through the same thing right now," she said quietly.

She looked off to the right, closed her eyes, and then went completely quiet for a few seconds. When she opened her eyes again, Henderson noticed that they looked slightly fuller and were a touch damp.

"Are you okay?" he asked.

Renee nodded and looked at the glass in front of her. She swirled it a couple of times and took a drink.

"Yeah, I guess I should have seen it coming," she said. "I just can't believe that I stayed with him for so long."

"How long?"

"We were married for three years, lived together for two before that. Five years with an alcoholic with a wandering eye. I can't believe that I put up with it for so long."

"Why did you?"

Renee sighed and shook her head.

"I'm sorry," Henderson stammered, "now I'm being nosy. I suppose that's the wine talking. I didn't mean…"

"No, no, that's okay. Who knows? I suppose I always thought, hoped perhaps, that he would change, that I would be the one who he'd change for," she said slowly, gazing into the flame of the candle. "It seems like it was right from when I met him that people were telling me to smarten up, that he wouldn't change. Finally, even I had to admit that he wouldn't."

"He was supposed to be baby-sitting our son while I went out of town for a hearing. It finished early and when I got home, Sean was at the neighbours and my husband was in bed with some tramp that he had picked up at his favourite bar."

She shook her head and wiped her eyes with the corner of the napkin.

"Look at me. I always said I wouldn't do this."

"Man, I'm sorry," Henderson said, "you don't have to tell me if you don't want to…"

"No, don't be. Really, it's all right. I'm more pissed off at myself for being blind for so long to his drinking and fooling around. I also keep thinking that there was more I could have done to save it."

"You can't blame yourself," he said. "There's no way that you can have that sort of control over him."

She looked up.

"I can't help it. I just think that…"

"I've been there, Renee. Shelly thought she could change me, calm me down, make me less angry. But she couldn't, no matter how hard she tried. There was nothing she could have done to change me at that point in my life. So I doubt that there's anything you could do, if that's the way he is."

"Oh, I know," Renee replied. "That's what all my friends keep telling me."

She stared at her drink.

"Told me for some time, actually. It's just that, right now, I'm so damned mad, and angry,…"

She looked into Henderson's eyes.

"And more than a bit scared."

The background buzz of conversation in the restaurant seemed to recede. The clinking of cutlery, the babbling of drinks being poured and served, and of meals being delivered to tables and eaten, had almost disappeared.

"You know, I don't know if it helps at all," Henderson said after a moment, "but I'm still scared at times, maybe all the time. Despite all the unhappiness and anger that we had toward the end of our marriage, it really hit hard when we finally split. All of a sudden, when she was gone, it's like there was nothing. We may have been fighting constantly, but at least that was something I could count on. But then she wasn't there, and the place was empty, and it was like being alone, frightened, in the dark again. Sort of like when I was a kid."

"What do you do about it?"

"What can you do? You learn to live with it. And you work at beating it, I guess. I don't know; I'm still working at it. I've become more protective about me, and sometimes I just want to be by myself. It may not be easy, but I don't know what else you can do."

"But don't you feel like you'll be that way for the rest of your life? Like, you're going to be…alone forever?"

"Sure. You know, Renee, I remember reading once that the most wonderful thing about getting married is that in the entire world, you're the one being selected to be special in another person's life; the terrible thing about divorce is that in that same world, you're the only one being rejected by that same person."

Henderson took a sip of his Gran Marnier.

"Brother, did I find out that was true," he continued. "I was a wreck. I thought, still do sometimes, that the whole thing was my fault, that everyone else in the world knew that it was my fault, and that basically, I was no good."

"You don't seem that way at all, you know," Renee said quietly.

There was a pause.

"Sometimes I really wonder…There's a lot of things I said and did that I'm not real proud of," Henderson continued.

"Things that I will never, ever be able to apologize for. But they happened. And I can't change that and never will. I just have to work at not being like that again."

"I lived with that after we split. To top it all off, I was unemployed. I was convinced that nobody wanted me for anything. Hell, I didn't even like myself that much."

"You look like you're doing quite well now," Renee said. "You seem to have found some peace with yourself."

"More like a ceasefire. I was a wreck and sometimes, when I'm feeling down, I still am. My parents give me a lot of support. I'll never be able to thank them enough. But I also had to decide for myself that it was up to me to control my own life. If I wanted to change, I had to do it; I couldn't count on anyone else to do that for me. That included changing the way I treated people, including myself."

"I stopped getting wasted every day, I started sending out my resume, and did some volunteer work while I waited. Eventually, I got on with the Board. It's a pretty good job for the most part and I've met some really good people who have made me feel that maybe I'm not such a rotten creature after all."

Renee smiled.

"You and Mr. Keltner seem to get along fairly well," she said.

Henderson laughed.

"Pete's the best," he added. "After my parents, he's my biggest pillar of support. He doesn't preach or lecture, and he doesn't tell me what to do. He's so down to earth and I think he's really interested in what I think or do. We really get along well, and he can always seem to give me an ego boost when I need it the most."

Henderson told her about getting stuck near Slave Lake the week before.

"Pete really believes in the positive," he continued while Renee was still laughing into her napkin. "He's got an absolutely wonderful wife, who he loves deeply. You know, your own parents can do wonders, but let's face it, they're parents. I think it's a law that they have to love you, no matter what. It's a great feeling to know that people who don't have to be emotionally involved in your life decide to do so, and Pete and Kathy are two of the greatest people in the world to me."

Henderson took a drink. He rolled the stem of the glass between his thumb and forefinger and stared at the swirling, deep-orange liquid it held.

"I really don't know what I would have done without him. As much as I believe that a person can only change himself, it sure helps to have someone else there, who believes in you even when you don't. Sort of keeps things in perspective."

"It's great to have friend like that," Renee said quietly, "and I could see today that you both think a great deal of each other."

"I'm pretty lucky all right," Henderson concluded. "He's seen me when I've been at my worst. And I've seen him at his."

"That's hard to imagine. He seems so up."

"Like I said, Pete believes in the positive. I don't know how he and Kathy do it sometimes. You see, two years ago, Kathy was expecting their first child. Man, you should have seen him. You would have thought that he was the first man in history to be a father. At the very least, he was determined that he was going to be the best dad ever."

He paused for a few seconds and looked into his glass. Then he looked up and back into Renee's eyes.

"Then they lost it. That was the first, and only, time I have ever seen him cry. And I looked at that, and how they handled it and wondered what right I had feeling sorry for myself. They mourned, but they're moving on. They've inspired me to do the same."

Henderson cleared his throat and sat up.

"You said you had a son?"

Renee nodded and pulled out a small snapshot from her wallet. She handed it over to Henderson.

Henderson laughed at the picture of the little boy shielding his eyes from the sun with one hand and pointing to the camera with the other.

"He's a cute kid," he said. He passed the picture back to

Renee.

    She looked at the picture and smiled.

    "Two years old and he can already whip the world," she said. She lingered over the picture for a moment and smiled. "The little beggar."

    "You're more than a bit proud of him, aren't you?" Henderson said quietly with a smile as he took a sip of coffee.

    "Embarrassingly so," she beamed. The colour had returned to her cheeks, "and he sure loves his mommy."

    Henderson leaned forward and rested his hand on hers.

    "I envy you, you know," he said with a soft firmness. "It sounds like you have yourself a pretty sturdy anchor. He thinks you're great and I think that's all that should matter. I wouldn't worry about anyone else."

    Renee finished her drink.

    "Still, sometimes I just wonder what else I could have done to save it."

    "You'll probably feel that way for awhile, sure, but, well, for what it's worth, I think he's crazy."

    Two sets of cheeks flushed as they finished their coffee.

    "Say, are you up for another glass of wine in the lounge?" she asked. "I understand that they have a fire and a pianist."

    "Sure," Henderson replied. "Just let me get the bill."

    "Don't worry about it. It's been taken care of."

    "Ummm, okay..."

    Renee laughed.

    "Before I met you in the lounge earlier, I stopped in here and gave them my credit card."

    "Oh, well," he stammered. "Uh, thank you very much. I must admit that's a first for me."

    "Well, you're very welcome."

    "Whoa," Henderson said as he fell back into the bench seat. "I'm so sorry. I think I've had a bit too much to drink."

    Henderson had attempted to stand after Renee invited

him into the hotel courtyard for a walk, but he found that the tendency was more for him to wobble.

"Looks to me like you could use some fresh air," she said.

They were walking through the garden courtyard of the hotel, Henderson somewhat unsteadily, when he felt the softness of Renee's hand as it caressed his. He returned the touch, stroked her fingers with his, and then took the full warmth of her hand into his. He felt her draw closer toward him. As they walked past the fountain in the lobby, Henderson could smell the subtle spicy, floral scent of her perfume.

They stepped out of one of the hotel's side doors into the open courtyard. The sun was beginning to set behind the tall centre section of the building that held the rooms of the guests. Even at this time of the year, the early evening air was still warm and there were children playing and splashing in the hotel's swimming pool. Floodlights located in the bushes and hedges along the path added a magical touch to the path marked by the sidewalk.

"Oops," Renee said after she tripped over a crack between two of the small cement sidewalk blocks, "I'm starting to feel the wine as well, I think. Maybe we'd could sit down for a bit, if you don't mind."

They found a swinging lounge chair and sat down. As they watched and listened to the children play in the water, Henderson leaned his head back and breathed in deeply. He didn't know whether it was the wine, the gentle swinging of the lounge, Renee's company, or the combination of all three, but whatever it was, he hadn't felt this good in a long time.

"I love this time of year," he said with his eyes closed. "I wish it would stay like this."

"If it wasn't for winter, you wouldn't appreciate the summer."

Henderson looked at her and smiled.

"That's very true," he said; he knew that his words were slurring together. "I never really thought of it that way."

"I don't think you should be driving home tonight," Renee said.

"Yeah, you're probably right about that," he said. "It's not a pretty picture when an inspector gets an impaired. I'm sorry. I don't normally get like this."

"Uhm hm," she replied with a smile. "I have a feeling that you needed it, though. We probably both did."

"I'll take a cab home."

"What about your truck? You'll need it tomorrow for work, won't you? I really think that you should stay here tonight."

"Well, I don't know. I could get a cab back in the morning, or get Pete to give me a lift."

"What if I told you that I'd like you to stay here tonight," Renee said softly.

"Oh wow," he stammered. "Uhm, I don't have a toothbrush with me."

"You can use mine."

He turned and looked into her eyes.

"That's very generous of you, but do you really want to do that? I mean, you could catch some of my germs."

She put her hand around his neck and pulled his face towards hers. She kissed him delicately at first and then, as the kiss intensified, Henderson found her completely within his arms.

"There," she whispered when she lifted her head from his, "any other issues that we need to deal with?"

"I should warn you," he replied, "I'm not really any good, performance wise, when I'm like this."

Renee smiled.

"Give us something to look forward to then, won't it. Right now, though, I think that both of us could use a good cuddle."

He was still holding her when he awoke. Her gentle, rhythmic breathing and the feel of her skin against his was exciting and different, and at the same time, relaxing and reassuring. And yet, there was something that gnawed at him.

Henderson gave her a hug and she snuggled even closer

against him. He turned over and checked the clock radio: it was 11:30 p.m.

His throat was dry and his tongue felt crusty and swollen. His head was still spinning a bit. Gently, to avoid waking her, he slid out from under the blankets and stepped onto the thick carpet of the hotel room. He went into the bathroom and drank two glasses of water in quick succession. When he returned to the main room, he stepped quietly over to the window, opened the curtains slightly, and leaned against the frame.

The night was still clear and warm. Below him, the cars running along the main road formed a steady stream of headlights flowing through the stationary streetlights of the adjacent residential districts.

He was startled by the silky grace of her cool fingers on his back, which was followed by a gentle kiss between his shoulder blades that sent tingles up his spine.

"Dollar for your thoughts," she said quietly.

"A dollar?" he responded gently. "That's pretty generous."

"I'm sure that they'd be worth it to me."

Henderson raised his right arm and Renee slid under it. As his arm dropped to her waist, she put her hands around his hips. He returned her gentle squeeze and kissed her head. She looked out at the traffic with him.

"What are you thinking about?" she repeated. Her head was leaning on his chest.

"Nothing in particular. A lot in general."

Henderson heard a soft laugh.

"That's very cryptic. Details would be nice."

Henderson returned her laugh. He kissed her again.

"Well, first of all, I want to assure you that I don't usually stay overnight like this on a first date."

"That's okay: you're the first man I've ever invited to stay," was her quiet response.

He squeezed her a bit tighter.

"I was also thinking, as cheesy as it sounds, about life," he said, "and how it always seems to throw a curve at you when you least expect it. Here I was, living my life alone, taking each day as it comes, not really aware that I was giving it much thought. There weren't many days in which I felt ecstatic. The bonus in that, I guess, is that there weren't many days in which I was hurt either. And then bang: here you are."

"You seem to be the best thing that's happened to me in a long time and I'm scared that you're going to disappear as suddenly as you appeared. It seems like my life has been filled with those types of nasty surprises. Right now, I'm feeling things, really good things, that I didn't think I'd ever feel again. And I guess I'm worried that if the good feelings can come back, then the shitty ones can come back too."

"Christ," he added, his gaze turned to the sky outside of the window, "can I analyse things to death or what? I wonder sometimes what's the matter with me."

"Listen to me, Clint," Renee replied softly. She now stood in front of him and she had put her hands on his chest. "I'm not trying to trick you. Like I told you earlier, I'm scared too, and that's the truth. It's been a long time since I felt like this, since I've felt. . ."

She paused.

". . . like I was, I don't know, interesting to someone."

"I'm not looking for promises," she continued, "and I really don't know if I can make any myself. But you've given me a wonderful evening and made me feel like I could have many more, and, if you're willing, I'd really like to see you again. As far as I'm concerned, I've found someone who's, well, sensitive and caring, and I want you for as long as I can have you, whether it's just for tonight or whatever."

"I don't know what will happen, but the last thing in the world I want to do is hurt you. I promise you that. The only thing that I ask in return is that you not give up on us right now because you're scared of what might or might not happen. It would mean a lot to me if you'd think about taking a risk again."

Henderson put his arms around her and held her tight. He felt dampness on his shoulder.

"Okay," he said gently, "you've got it."

They kissed, deeply and passionately.

"Come on," she said when their kiss broke. A smile had joined the tear on her face and she tightened her hold on Henderson. "I'm getting cold standing here. Let's go back to bed."

At some point shortly after they went back to bed, the headlights of a full size Chevrolet appeared within the river of cars that flowed beneath the hotel window. Inside of that car, the occupants were silent.

Hudson was smoking as he drove and he was going over the plan in his head. It was perfect, he thought with pride. It was just so damn perfect!

Unlike the city streets, the highway that led north was almost deserted. Hudson checked his watch as the lights of their target came into view over the hill. It was almost exactly forty-eight hours since the last time he had travelled along this same stretch of road, when the fragments of his idea first began to come together.

He looked over at Michaels, who was dozing in the front passenger seat next to him. Then Hudson glanced in the rear view mirror at the other three. Each was lost in his thoughts, he realized, which was just the way he wanted them to be right now.

The saps, Hudson thought. He knew the money would get them, especially Michaels. But if these jerks think they could get something out of it, then so much the better.

Hudson slowed the car down and pulled onto the shoulder, as he had the night before last. Michaels awoke with a start.

"What's happening?" he asked with a stretch. "Are we here already?"

Hudson ignored him and turned to face the others.

"Everybody ready?" Hudson looked at the faces of his four partners.

They were fidgeting, glancing around at each other. The car's air-conditioning was on slightly, but Hudson noticed that they were all sweating.

"Relax guys," he reassured them. "We're gonna go in, get some easy money, and leave. No problems."

Hudson pulled a pistol from his jacket and checked the firing chamber. It contained a live round.

"Just like making a withdrawal from the bank," he added.

Hudson drove the car into the parking area of the plant. As they got out of the car, each of the men, except Hudson, took a deep breath. Their heads and eyes were darting around the lot; their breathing was short, quick, and shallow. Hudson remained steady. His eyes were moving evenly around the plant site, re-evaluating the target.

Hudson and Michaels ran over to the main office building. It was dark and locked. Taking out a tube of epoxy glue that they each carried in their jacket pockets, Hudson and Michaels made sure that it would stay that way by squirting a glob of glue into each of the building's locks. When they were finished, they went back to the car, where the other three were waiting by its open trunk. They were unloading the sports bags and their rifles.

Phillips handed a bag to Hudson, who threw the straps across his shoulders. He checked his pistol again.

"Let's go," he ordered in a harsh whisper.

They moved from the parking lot to the western edge of the plant boundary, the gravel crackling under their feet in the silent night. Their target lay before them. They were drawn to the bright lights of the control room like moths.

It had been agreed that Michaels would go in first: the operators on duty would know him.

The lead operator was sitting in a high back chair leaning

over a console when the door opened. He turned around and saw Michaels come through the door. His initial reaction was one of pleasant surprise, but that turned quickly to horror when he saw that the rifle his former colleague was carrying was pointed at his chest.

"Warren, what the hell. . . ?"

"Evening, Mark," Michaels replied. He cocked the rifle. "How are you doing tonight?"

Hudson and the other three came in quickly behind him.

"Tie him up," Hudson ordered abruptly.

Michaels pulled out a plastic strap and tied the lead operator's hands behind his back.

"Where's the rest of them?" Hudson barked.

As if on cue, they heard the laughter of the other two operators as they came in through the rear door that led to the process area. Their laughter cut off abruptly when they saw their unexpected, and armed, visitors. Phillips and Collins had them subdued quickly and their hands tied as well. When he was sure that the operators would cause them no problems, Hudson moved on to the next step.

"Collins, you look after these guys. Phillips, you and Simpson get out there and start filling in the dike around the sulphur block. Come right back here when you're done. Me and Michaels will install the explosives."

"What the hell are you guys doing?" the lead operator yelled.

Hudson stopped and sighed.

"Oh dear," he said. "They're going to get mouthy on us."

He took an oily rag from the pocket of one of the other operators and forced it into the lead's mouth. Then Hudson kicked the legs out from under him and he fell painfully onto the hard tile floor. Hudson followed through by kicking him hard in the ribs.

"Shut up, okay?" he said calmly.

The combination of the sickeningly sweet oil in the rag and the pain from the fall and kick to his ribs almost caused the operator to vomit.

"Gag the other two," Hudson said to Collins, and then to the others, he added, "You have work to do. Get on with it."

Half an hour later, Phillips and Simpson returned to the control room sweating heavily, still carrying their shovels. Hudson was sitting in the lead operator's chair when they came in. He and Michaels were both smoking a cigarette.

"Now what?" Phillips asked breathlessly.

Hudson stubbed out his cigarette on the edge of the leather chair's armrest.

"I want you, Collins, and Simpson to run a hose from the condensate tanks to the sulphur block."

Hudson picked up his sports bag and threw it to Michaels.

"But first, you know where to put these," he said.

Michaels, Collins and Simpson left the room to complete their assigned tasks. Hudson was now alone with the three subdued operators.

He was smiling when he first turned to look at them, but that smile disappeared within seconds. Then Hudson thought for a minute about what the others were doing, and the smile reappeared.

"Well, how about if we make a phone call?" he said.

Hudson spun around in the chair and put his fingers next to the first name on the list of phone numbers that he had found. He picked up the telephone and when he had a dial tone, he punched in the numbers for a long distance call. It was answered on the third ring by a sleepy voice.

"Hello?" was the groggy reply.

"Hello, is this Mr. Arthur, Mr. William Arthur?" Hudson asked pleasantly.

"Uh, yes, it is. Who the hell is this?"

"This is a really bad nightmare calling," Hudson replied. "Is it convenient for you to talk right now?"

Thursday, August 25

Henderson lay in bed for a while after he awoke and held Renee for a little while longer as she slept. When he finally thought that he should look at his watch, he saw that it was five minutes before eight.

"Shit," he muttered and rolled out of bed.

He was running late. He showered quickly, wrote a note to Renee, and ran out to the hotel's parking lot. Almost twenty-five minutes had passed between the time he got out of bed and was getting into his truck.

The office was only a short distance from the hotel. The voices of his colleagues were already buzzing on the mobile radio when he turned it on. As he drove, he heard urgency in those voices, to which he listened with half an ear as he navigated through the early morning traffic.

Then he heard Al Spenser ask if anybody had heard from him yet.

Clint snatched the hand held receiver from its bracket.

"Henderson here," he said. He was concentrating on the radio. His other hand held a tight grip on the steering wheel as he changed lanes.

"Clint, where the bloody 'ell have you been?" snapped

Spenser. "We've been trying to get 'old of you all night!"

"Sorry, Al. I wasn't home last night. What's up?"

There was a silent pause. Then Henderson heard the commotion of a busy office in the background when Spenser depressed the transmit button at his end.

"I don't want to discuss it on an open channel, lad" was the terse reply. "'ow soon can you be here?"

"Five minutes," Henderson answered. "I'm almost there now."

Keltner was there to meet him at the office's back door.

"Not the best morning to pick to be late, my man," he said as he handed Henderson a cup of coffee. "Here. You're going to need this."

"Of course," Henderson replied taking the cup without stopping, "that seems to be the way my bloody life works. Nothing happens for years, and then when it does.... "

He took a sip from the cup.

"Wow," he said. "Yep. I needed that. Okay: what's going on?"

"Can't say for sure," was Keltner's reply, "but there's some sort of serious shit happening. I've never, ever, seen Spenser this uptight. Where the hell were you last night anyway?"

He and Keltner were walking down the hallway.

"I was out. I'll tell you about it sometime."

Keltner stopped.

"You devil," he said with a grin. "I want to hear about it."

Then more seriously, he added, "but it'll have to wait. Spenser's waiting for you in his office."

Henderson ran down the hallway. Spenser was on the phone when Henderson got to his office and he motioned for Henderson to enter. Henderson noticed that Spenser had an unlit cigarette in his mouth.

"Okay, Frank, my man just got 'ere, all right?" Spenser said suddenly into the phone. "I'll get 'im out to the plant right away and I'll let you know what 'e finds . . . okay . . .yeah, I'll talk to you later, bye."

He hung up the phone, wiped his mouth with his hand, and then looked over at Henderson and rolled his eyes.

"That was Frank Sears," he said.

Sears was the manager of the Field Operations Department and was based in Calgary. He was responsible for directing the operation of the Board's field offices that were scattered across the province.

"Clint," Spenser said as he ran his right hand through his thin hair, "we think we might 'ave a wee problem out at the Western Triassic plant."

He fumbled through his pockets for his lighter and finally found it in his shirt pocket. He lit his cigarette and inhaled sharply.

"Mills was still on-call last night when William Arthur of Western Triassic phoned 'im late," Spenser continued. Then he exhaled a cloud of smoke. "'e says that someone called him at 'ome and claimed 'e was holding the plant and the operators on shift as hostages."

Henderson dropped into a chair, stunned.

"What?" he muttered quietly. "This is a joke, right? Somebody playing a prank."

Spenser sat down behind his desk and shrugged.

"I'd like to say so lad, but unfortunately, we can't treat it that way. Arthur said this guy sounded pretty serious. We tried getting a 'old of you right away, but we couldn't. Mills is out there right now, but 'e's not all that familiar with that plant. Right now, you're the only man we've got 'oo knows the facility. I'd like you to get out there and assess the situation."

"Sure," replied Henderson. He exhaled loudly. "No problem. Do we know who it is?"

Spenser shook his head.

"No idea at all. The guy 'oo phoned Arthur told 'im not to contact anyone else and that 'e would phone back later with his demands. True to form, Arthur, not being the type of prat 'oo likes to be pushed around, promptly phoned both the R.C.M.P. and us. We 'aven't heard anything since."

Henderson nodded and stood up, as did Spenser, who walked with him down the hall to the rear door.

"The R.C.M.P. are on alert and 'ave a couple of cars out there," Spenser added. "They're ready to block all of the roads leading to the plant, including the main 'ighway, at a moment's notice, but right now, they're just watching. As well, we're making arrangements with our phone company to secure one of the mobile channels for our exclusive use."

Spenser stopped Henderson when as they reached the doors and put his hand on Henderson's shoulder.

"Look, son," he said grimly, "we don't know what we've got out there. Go out, 'ave a look, and let us know what you find, but for God's sake, don't take any chances. Just be careful."

Henderson nodded silently.

"I'll be in touch," he replied.

He opened the door and walked across the parking lot to his truck. Just before he got in, Henderson looked up at the second story window and saw Keltner there, speaking on the phone. Keltner looked down at him and gave him a thumbs-up.

The plant seemed quiet as Henderson drove toward it on the highway. Parked off to the right on the last secondary road before he actually reached the plant was one of the R.C.M.P. ghost cars. It was hidden behind a long row of thick shrub and tall poplar trees. Henderson turned his truck to the right and it rumbled along the gravel road. He pulled in behind the police car.

As Henderson got out of the truck, an R.C.M.P. constable stepped out of his car as well. Henderson showed him his Board identification card and the constable held out his hand.

The constable was a distinguished looking man in his early forties, with a hint of grey starting to show at the temples. He had the type of face to which Henderson felt he could warm immediately. Henderson also guessed that he was a favourite with kids.

"Sergeant Randy Breukart," the constable said as he shook hands with Henderson.

"Hi, Randy. Clint Henderson. What's happening?"

"Nothing so far that we can see. The plant's day shift has been told to stay home until this is all sorted out. Apparently, the night shift is still in there."

From the east came another ghost car, followed closely by another car that Henderson recognized instantly as belonging to the Board. It was Mills and he had Shawn Jackson with him. Both vehicles came to a stop on the other side of the secondary road. Their occupants walked over to Henderson and Breukart. Mills and Jackson both looked exhausted.

Henderson also noticed the look on Jackson's face that made him look at least ten years older.

"Glad you could join us, Clint," Mills said wearily.

"See anything?" Breukart asked.

The other constable shook his head.

"Not a thing," he replied, "but we didn't get too close either."

"The plant appears to be operating normally," Mills said to Henderson, "so whoever's in there seems to know what he's doing."

"You mean like the night shift," Henderson replied.

The others stared at him.

"Sorry," Henderson said. "Has anyone tried calling whoever's in there?"

"Spenser wanted to wait until someone who's more familiar with the plant got here," Mills replied as he stretched. "Looks like you get the honour."

"Oh wow, lucky me," he said. "Okay, you go home and get some rest, Bob. I'll take it from here. You too, Shawn."

Mills turned and began walking back to his car. Breukart ordered the other constable to return to his position on the other side of the plant.

"No, I think I'll stay here, thanks," Jackson said quietly, his eyes cast downward toward the ground.

Henderson put his hand on Jackson's back.

"Look, Shawn," he said softly, "there's nothing you can do here, and to be honest, you don't look that good. Do me a favour and go get some rest, okay? I may need you and when I do, you have to be healthy. I'll let you know what happens."

Jackson's grey eyes stared at him.

"My boys are in there, Clint. I gotta stay here."

"Yeah, okay," Henderson sighed. "Will you at least go and wait with this officer? Get a couple of hours shut-eye in his car, okay?"

Jackson nodded. Henderson patted him on the back and he watched him walk over to the other police car.

"He doesn't deserve this," Henderson muttered, "he really doesn't."

Henderson and Breukart watched the two cars drive off. When the vehicles reached the highway, they watched Mills turn left toward the city and the ghost car turn right. Both were out of sight within a minute.

Henderson turned to Breukart.

"I'd like to go for a drive around the plant site," he said.

"I wouldn't recommend it right now," replied Breukart, shaking his head. "Too many vehicles driving around might spook them. Let's wait a little while. Wait. Hold on for just a minute, okay?"

Breukart went to his car and returned with a set of binoculars.

"Use these. You can see the plant fairly well from here."

Henderson and Breukart crept across the road and crouched behind the clump of trees that hid their vehicles. As Breukart pulled aside the shrub, Henderson aimed the binoculars at the plant, which jumped at him through the lenses.

The morning was overcast and although the towers were a dull shade of silver in that light, the rising clouds of steam from the facility were familiar. Henderson scanned the plant with the binoculars.

Everything seemed normal and he was beginning to think that the whole thing was just a prank. He smiled a bit as he pictured the night shift operators inside the control room, furious as they waited to be relieved. But then they hadn't phoned anybody to express their displeasure either, he realized, and his smile disappeared.

Then he looked at the sulphur block.

"Hold it," he muttered.

That caught Breukart's attention and he also peered through the bush at the plant.

"See something?"

Henderson handed him the binoculars.

"Have a look at the sulphur block," he said evenly.

Breukart took the binoculars and trained them on the huge yellow pile.

"Okay, but you'll have to tell me what I'm looking at."

"It's a bit hard to see from this angle," Henderson said. "Scan along the sulphur block, right at the top of the dike wall. Is there anything that jumps out at you?"

Breukart lowered his view and concentrated on the interface between the yellow of the sulphur and the dirty brown of the dike's clay. It was then that he noticed the small, black, rectangular boxes that were attached to the sulphur, spaced evenly along the line.

"Uh huh. I see them. What are they?" asked Breukart.

"I don't know, but they shouldn't be there."

Henderson wasn't sure what he should do next. There was something wrong, he knew, something definitely wrong.

A white SUV turned off the main highway and came rumbling down the road toward them. Both Henderson and Breukart recognized the bright logo of one of the local television stations painted across the hood.

"Oh, shit!" Breukart exclaimed.

Henderson buried his face in his hands. The circus is about to begin now, he thought.

Breukart rushed over to his car and grabbed the microphone to his radio through the window. Henderson heard him order his colleagues to start putting up roadblocks on the access roads and begin detouring traffic away from the plant site. The SUV pulled up to them and when it stopped, a young, well-dressed woman carrying a tape recorder and a fat man wearing jeans holding a video camera leapt from it. The couple ran over to Breukart, who was already holding up his hands.

"Before you even ask," he said to them, "we don't know anything at this point. So you might as well get right back into your car and get back to the main road."

The woman then saw Henderson, who had just stood up. She ran toward him, with the cameraman close behind her, trying to get the Henderson in focus.

"Who are you?" she asked abruptly as she turned on her tape recorder. She thrust the microphone into his face and her companion began to shoot him with the camera. "Can you tell us what's going on?"

Henderson stared at her for a minute.

"Clint Henderson. A.E.U.B. Who are you?"

"Toni Richmond. CJVX news."

"Okay, Toni," he said firmly, "why don't you listen to Constable Breukart and go back to your vehicle? As soon as we know something, we'll pass it along. Right now, we're assessing the situation and we want to keep this as quiet as possible. Chances are that this whole thing is nothing more than a joke and we're all wasting our time out here. Now, you can either cooperate with us, in which case we'll return the favour later, or you and I can start pissing each other off right now. It's your choice."

The woman lowered her tape recorder and sighed.

"You promise you'll talk to us later?" she asked with resignation.

"As soon as we know something ourselves, we'll pass it along to you."

"Come on, Burt," she said to her partner as she walked back to their SUV, "it looks like we're going to have to wait awhile on this one."

Henderson and Breukart watched them get into their vehicle, turn it around, and head back to the highway where other members of the police force were now erecting sawhorse barricades.

"I'd better get back to the main road and keep an eye on things," Breukart said. "Do you want to come with me?"

"I'd better call in first," Henderson replied, "and I don't want that reporter to hear me. I'll meet you there when I'm finished."

"Okay. See you in a bit."

Henderson climbed into his truck and picked up the radio handset.

"QJ3379 to base," he called. There was an instant of static

before the squelch cut in. The response came a few seconds later.

"Go ahead, Clint." Spenser said.

"I've had a look at the plant and I can tell that there is definitely something wrong over there, although I don't know exactly what it is yet. Have you heard anything?"

"Sod all, Clint. Not a bloody thing. We're still making calls, though."

Henderson paused for a moment.

"Do you think that maybe it's time to phone whoever's in there, Al?"

His original pause was echoed from the other end.

"I don't know, lad. Would that really be a wise move right now?"

"Well," Henderson said slowly, "the media is starting to show up. We've had one camera crew out here already. The R.C.M.P. are setting up roadblocks as we speak. I'm sure that whoever's in there has probably got a pretty good idea that we're out here too."

"Bloody 'ell," Henderson heard Spenser mumble.

Then he heard Spenser mutter to someone at the other end, "What do you think?"

There was no vocal response, but a few seconds later, Spenser came back on the line.

"Okay, Clint. Give 'em a call. You're in the best position to do it."

Henderson sighed. He felt his stomach begin to twist and burn.

"Did we get a secure channel?"

"Channel 2. They've also given us one of their operators. 'er name is Helen."

"Okay, I'll make the call now."

"Good luck, son. Let me know what 'appens. Channel clear."

"Right, channel clear."

He waited a moment before rotating the tuning dial on the radio set to channel 2. He pressed the transmit switch to call the operator. After two rings, a woman's voice answered.

"Edmonton mobile."

"Hi. Is this Helen?"

"Yes it is."

"Hi Helen. My name is Clint Henderson. I'm with the Board. It looks like we're going to be working together for a little while."

"Good morning, Clint. What can I do for you?"

Henderson opened his briefcase and leafed quickly through its pages until he found the right binder. He opened that and went through the pages until he found his gas plant contact list. He repeated the phone number of the control room of Western Triassic's plant to her and then waited for the phone in the control room to ring. In the meantime, the knot in his stomach pulled tighter.

Then the phone rang.

His throat began to burn. In the distance, he heard a bird call out. It sounded like a thrush, or maybe a starling.

Hell, what am I thinking, he thought to himself. I don't know anything about bloody birds.

The phone rang again.

Oh man, do I have to go to the bathroom, Henderson thought.

In the middle of the third ring, there was a click. An empty echo followed this, and there was a hum in the background.

This is it, Henderson thought.

"What?" The voice was cold and even.

Henderson froze. The response ran the marathon up and down his spine, raising pinpricks as it went. His knees became weak when he realized that he recognized the voice.

"Answer or fuck off," the voice said again.

No, it's not possible, Henderson thought. What the hell is happening here?

"I'm giving you one more chance, asshole."

"Gillis?" Henderson asked with a shaky voice. "Gillis, is that you?"

"Henderson?"

Henderson swallowed hard.

"Yeah, Gillis, it's me. What, what are you doing in there?"

A chuckle formed part of the answer.

"Clint, my friend," formed the rest, "this really is a small world, isn't it? But then, I guess I should have expected it. After all, who else would the Board have sent?"

Henderson's stomach began to boil. The nervousness was gone; its heat had been replaced by anger.

"Hudson, what the hell are you doing in there?" he demanded. "Who else is in there with you? What the hell is going on?"

"I have to say, Clint," Hudson interrupted, "that people like William Arthur, who claims to be a gentleman, really piss me off, you know that? I asked him very nicely to not mention this to anyone else and then he turns around and blabs his fool head off to the Board. And discretion is so important in the business world. He really needs to learn how to be discreet."

"Gillis, listen to me," Henderson said slowly and distinctly. "I want you to tell me what you're doing in there. What's going on?"

"You know, I would have to think that it would seem so bloody obvious. Well, to me anyway. Shows how thick you and the clots you work for are. Okay, here it is: me and a few of my friends have decided to claim this plant as our own for a while, at least until Western Triassic offers us suitable compensation to leave it. It's really that simple."

"You can't do this, Gillis. You won't get away with it."

"Look it, asshole, don't tell me what I can or can't do. We've done it. And if we don't get what we want, we're going to cause you and Western Triassic, and all of the plant's jerk-off neighbours, a whole lot of trouble. We're in the process of deciding right now how much it's going to cost to get us to leave."

"In the meantime, let me tell you what we've done to ensure that our demands will be met and to make sure that you people don't try anything to get us out early. We've planted a few explosives all over this plant. I might add that we paid particular attention to the LPG tanks. That should result in a pretty impressive display if we ever have to blow them up, don't you think?"

Henderson planted his head in his free hand. He began massaging his forehead.

How the hell do you reply to something like that?

"Hey, asshole," he heard Gillis say, "are you still with me out there?"

Henderson looked up and cradled his chin with his hand. His eyes were closed.

"Yeah, I'm still here, Gillis," he said. "Look, walk out now, before anyone gets hurt."

"Oh Christ, Henderson, give me a break. No one's going to get hurt if they do what they're told. Besides, you didn't even give me a chance to tell you about our masterpiece."

"I don't know if you can see it from wherever you may be right now, Clint, but you might have noticed that we filled in the open end of the containment wall around the sulphur block. Then we noticed all those tanks filled with that lovely, flammable condensate and, you know, they were just kind of sitting there. So we got to thinking: what if we pumped the condensate into the block area, around the sulphur. You know, like kind of a moat."

Henderson heard Hudson start to giggle again.

"Oh, and here's the best part, Clint. Before we filled up that moat, we planted a few incendiary devices along the edge of the sulphur block at about the level of the condensate. You see, Clint, if our demands aren't met, or if you or anyone else that we don't like tries to come in here to get us out, we'll blow this whole place sky high and set that sulphur block on fire. And you know as well as I do that if that block goes up with all that condensate around it, you'll never put it out. There'll be sulphur dioxide poisoning from here to the Saskatchewan border. And probably beyond, with any luck."

"Oh my God," Henderson said quietly.

"Oh, I don't think that He can help you, Clint. By the way, don't even think of shutting this plant in. If we see the inlet pressure to the plant drop by as much as a pound, this place will become one big fireball. And Western Triassic had better not even think about invoking their emergency response plan. That would really piss me off."

"All right, Gillis, I understand."

Think, damn it, think! Henderson's brain ordered at the same time it instructed his lungs to take a deep breath.

"Okay, uh, who's in there with you?"

"No names, Clint, I promised. But don't worry. These guys know what they're doing. The plant will continue to purr along as it has since it was built, just as long as no one tries to screw around with us."

"I see," Henderson said. "So what happens now? What do you want me to do?"

"Well, we're going to finalize what we want. Now, being the suck that you are, I'm sure that you're going to contact Spenser and tell him everything that I've told you. Tell you what: phone me back at noon, which I see is about three hours from now, and we'll have some demands for you, okay? Have a nice day, dick-breath."

A loud rattle told Henderson that Hudson had hung up the phone. He sat there for a minute, alternating between putting his head in his hands and applying lip balm to his lips, which he realized he had been licking non-stop throughout the conversation with Hudson. Finally, he started up his truck, turned it around, and drove back to the main highway.

The highway had been completely blocked off. Members of the R.C.M.P., wearing bright, fluorescent orange smocks, were manning barricades and rerouting the oncoming traffic. Henderson noticed that the original news crew had been joined by a number of colleagues from other television and radio stations. He also recognized a reporter from one of the larger Edmonton newspapers.

Henderson parked his truck in the middle of the now deserted highway, next to Breukart's ghost car. Breukart was talking on his own radio set when Henderson pulled up, but when he saw the Board truck, he put the microphone down and walked over to Henderson.

"Good news?" he asked Henderson.

Henderson looked up at him and sighed.

"I guess not," replied Breukart.

Henderson repeated the details of his conversation with Hudson.

"Okay," Breukart said after Henderson had finished, "so I'm, like, a really dumb cop, Clint, and I'm not going to pretend that I understand all of the technicalities. But I'm taking it that it's safe to assume that we're in really, really deep trouble here."

"Oh yeah," Henderson replied grimly. "Blowing up the plant would be bad enough, but if they ignite that pool of condensate around the sulphur block, well, I don't even want to think about the results. The sulphur dioxide cloud would poison everybody in its path and wipe out farmland for miles to the east. The worst part is that once it's ignited, it would be damn near impossible to put the fire out, so it would just keep burning until there was no more sulphur. And that's a really big block."

Breukart whistled.

"Wow. Any ideas as to what we can do?" he asked.

Henderson shrugged.

"Well," he said, "I just keep hoping that it's all going to go away, but it's not going to I suppose. . ."

Henderson cleared his throat and straightened up.

"First of all, I guess I'd better contact my bosses," he added. "I have to let them know what's happening. With any luck, they'll have an idea or two. Then we'll all have to take it from there."

Breukart gestured to the throng of reporters behind the barricades.

"What about them? They're starting to get restless."

"I'll try to quell their curiosity for awhile," Henderson replied, "at least until I can get someone else out here to handle them. I'd like to keep them subdued; no sense in having them blow this thing out of proportion right now. Let me call my office first and see if I can get them to send somebody out to talk to them. In the meantime, I expect that our office will want me to give them something to keep them happy. You can tell them that I'll be making a statement in about ten minutes."

"Okay," Breukart said and walked over to the crowd.

Henderson tuned his mobile set to the two-way radio setting.

"QJ3379 to base. Al, are you there?"

"Aye, go ahead, son."

"Al, you're not going to believe this. I know I don't. It's Gillis Hudson."

"Hudson?"

"Yep. He says that he and some 'friends' have rigged the plant up with explosives. He also claims that he's filled in the sulphur block containment area with condensate and he's threatening to ignite it."

There was a pause. When the voice came back, it was surprisingly calm.

"'oo's in there with 'im?"

"I don't know, Al. Hudson said that they knew what they're doing, so my bet is that they're in the industry. It also sounded like they know this plant, so maybe the company knows them. Could you contact Western Triassic and see if they can help us with that?"

"Aye, will do. Anything else you can think of?"

"You might want to start giving some thought to evacuating the area residents."

"Already being discussed, son. We 'ave people from the municipal district in the office right now."

"One condition that Hudson gave me was that he didn't want the plant's emergency response plan invoked, so we'd better be careful."

"Good point. Now what about you? Is there anything you need?"

"Well, since you asked," Henderson said, "I would sure appreciate someone from the Communications Group out here to deal with the media. I've got reporters out here like ravens on road-killed gophers."

"Right, lad. I'll see what I can do at this end. Listen, a couple of Board members and the manager of Field Ops are waiting for some information. I'd like to set up a conference call so that you can fill them in."

Henderson looked at his watch: it was already 9:30 a.m.

"Give me about ten minutes, okay Al?" he said. "I promised the press that I'd get them a statement. What should I do? Should I wait until our Communications guy gets here?"

"Somebody will have to come from Calgary, so it may be a while. No, I think it would be a good idea if you told them something."

"I'd like to tell them to piss off."

"I know, lad, I know. But right now, we need them on our side. When the locals get wind of this, they'll be turning on their TVs and radios for information. They'll be concerned about what's going on. But it's a wee, fine line between concern and fear, son. Right now, they're willing to listen. If they're frightened, and you know 'ow well the media can do that, nobody'll give a damn what we 'ave to say, and we'll 'ave panic. We can't afford that right now, Clint. We need the people in the area to know what's going on and make sure that they stay calm. Okay?"

"Sure, Al. I understand."

"Clint, you've just received, in ten seconds, over twenty years of experience in dealing with the press. I have faith in you, son: you can do it. No matter what you say, I'm behind you. Good luck. Phone us back at quarter to ten."

"Thanks, Al. Channel clear."

Henderson climbed down from his truck and walked over to the sawhorse barricades. Toni Richmond spotted him and ran toward him. The rest of the pack was close behind. Only the police and the barricades stopped them from overwhelming Henderson completely. Then it seemed as though a thousand microphones were shoved in front of him at once and he took a step backwards.

They looked at him expectantly. In a way, they reminded Henderson of starving puppies at the animal shelter looking at their new owner.

"Okay, uh, the information we have right now is sketchy," he began. Christ, I'd better choose these words carefully, he thought, and with any luck I won't look like a complete ass.

"But what we believe we have here, uh, is a situation

involving the illegal entry of unauthorized personnel into the control room of the Western Triassic Morinville sour gas plant. We're in the process of trying to confirm the identity of one of these persons and we're also attempting to get a handle on that of the others. Uh, right now, the plant appears to be operating normally and we believe that there is no danger to the local population at this time."

"What do they want?" a reporter asked.

"We don't know. They haven't made any specific demands yet."

"Are there any plans to evacuate the area?"

"I believe that, uh, at the present time, that particular option is, in fact, being considered by the Board and representatives from the local municipal district, but only as a last resort. I will let you know the results of those discussions as soon as I receive them myself."

"What happens next?"

Henderson frowned.

"In terms of?" he asked.

"What does the Board plan to do next? Do they have a contingency plan for this type of situation?"

"Well," Henderson replied, "basically, right now, it's, uh, wait and see. We're trying to get a better handle on what's going on in there and determine if there is, in fact, a situation to be concerned about. For now, that's all I can tell you."

A battery of voices assaulted him. Henderson held up his hands.

"Come on, people," he said pleadingly, "give me a break, okay? I've told you all we know right now. We'll pass along more information as it becomes available."

Henderson turned and walked back to his truck with Breukart, leaving the crowd behind.

"Are you okay?" Breukart asked him.

"I'm tired, I'm hung over, and I really didn't need this today," Henderson replied. He looked at the police officer. "Coffee, Randy. I could really go for a coffee right now."

"Christ, I should have known better than to trust you."

Collins was peering through the drapes that covered the control room's side window. In the distance, he could see the flashing blue and red lights of the police cars that controlled access to and from the highway.

"You know, your whining is really starting to piss me off," Hudson said quietly.

He was sitting back in one of the high-backed leather chairs that were provided for the plant operators in the control room. His hands were clenched behind his head, but he brought one down to pull the small remainder of his cigarette from his mouth, stub it out in the armrest next to the other burn holes he had created, and exhale the last blue cloud of smoke from his lungs. Then he sat up in the chair, which creaked as it pitched forward, and strained to look through the same window as Collins. Seeing little, he got up and walked over to the window.

Standing next to Collins, he pulled back the edge of the thin plastic curtain and looked across the grain as it swayed in the field between the plant and the highway.

"I wish you'd relax," he said gently, but with a cold firmness. "They don't know who's in here with me. Once we have the money, you and your partners can leave at night through the back. No one will ever know."

Collins nodded toward the trussed up operators who were lying quietly on the floor along the far wall.

"What about them?" he asked. "They know who we are."

"Don't you worry about that," Hudson replied, still gazing through the window. "They'll be my concern, not yours."

For a few seconds, Collins looked at Hudson. He cleared his throat.

"You're joking, right?" Collins chuckled nervously.

Hudson remained expressionless.

A shiver ran through Collins's body.

"You can't. . . ," he stammered. "Not in cold blood!"

Hudson's face snapped around. His eyes shot at Collins, who took a step back.

"Just what the hell do you suggest then?" he spat. "You know, you really can't have it both ways. They know who you are and they'll tell the cops, sure as shit, when this is all done. You wouldn't be home more than five minutes, counting your money with your precious wife and kids, before the cops'll be pounding on your door. These guys have to be taken care of."

"I didn't agree to murder! That wasn't part of this!"

"If you'd thought about it just a little bit, you would have realized that there would have to be some sort of cost to this!" Hudson yelled.

Then he sighed and put a hand on Collins's shoulder.

"Look, Collins, really you don't have anything to worry about."

A calm had returned to his voice.

"It's not like you'll have to be here for it. I wouldn't want you to get your hands bloodied. Once you and your friends get the money, you can get the hell out of here. I'll look after the rest."

"What about you, though?" Collins asked. "They know who you are. How are you going to get out of here afterwards?"

Hudson's gaze returned to the fields outside the window. He smiled for a second, as though he had remembered something pleasant.

"There's nothing out there for me," he said quietly. "No

job, no family, no friends. I want to show those bastards just who they've been screwing around for all these years. Who they've all laughed at and called names. To my face, they all acted like they were my friends, but I heard them talking about me behind my back. I heard them call me crazy, looking for any excuse to make fun of me and try to get rid of me."

He reached into his shirt pocket, pulled out his pack of cigarettes and shook one out. He put the cigarette into his mouth and lit it with a match.

"Well, you know what? I just don't care anymore," he said as he shook the match until it emitted a tiny plume of smoke.

"I'll finally show them that I'm someone they shouldn't have ignored," he said as he exhaled a cloud of blue smoke, "that I'm important too."

He looked at Collins.

"I'm here to hurt them. That's all. Honestly, I really don't care about the money."

Collins swallowed. His heart was racing, and he felt faint.

"You're going to do it anyway, you sick bastard, aren't you? You're going to blow up this plant even if they come through with the money. And you're planning on going to go up with it."

Hudson looked down at his hands, which had been balled up together in a tight fist. Slowly, gracefully, they opened, and his fingers stretched out as they waved through the air in front of him.

Again, he looked up at Collins and a sad, lonely smile returned to his face.

"Boom," he whispered.

"Clint, lad, are you there?"

Henderson grabbed the hand mike on his radio.

"Go ahead, Al," he replied.

"I 'ave Simon Rosenthal and Frank Sears on the line. They'd appreciate an update on the situation."

Simon Rosenthal was one of the Board members.

"Morning, Clint. How are you holding up out there?"

Rosenthal's voice was calm, and reassuring.

"I'm okay, so far. I think."

"You're doing fine, Clint. Al tells me that we've got the best out there and from what I've heard, I think I'd have to agree with him."

Henderson felt his cheeks flush ever so lightly.

"So tell me what's happening," Rosenthal added.

"The situation is still a little confusing. Hudson says that he's booby-trapped the plant. We still don't know what he wants, but I'm supposed to phone him again at noon to find out. Other than the plant's night shift crew, we don't know who else is in there with him, or how many."

"Do you think he's alone?"

"That's a good question. He hasn't got the background to run a plant of that size on his own."

"So the plant's still running then?" Sears asked.

"Nothing seems wrong so far," Henderson replied, "but if the plant was running smoothly before Hudson got in there, it could still be running on its own."

"Or there are others in there with 'im who know 'ow to operate a gas plant," Spenser volunteered.

"I guess we have to consider that possibility as well," Rosenthal said. "What do you recommend we do now, Frank?"

"I think Clint should stay out there and keep an eye on things," Sears replied. "He's talked to Hudson and is supposed to again in a couple of hours to find out what he wants. It may be to our advantage to keep Hudson guessing at our reaction, so the fewer people we have in contact with him, the better."

"What do you think, Clint?" Rosenthal asked.

"Well, I think I have to agree with Frank," replied Henderson. "Hudson doesn't seem to be in much of a hurry, so right now, we might want to consider waiting him out. I have no problem staying out here. I can handle it."

"Is there anything you need?"

"I did ask for someone to handle the media," Henderson said.

"He's on his way," Spenser replied. "As well, we've set up a control centre in the office here and we've requested that the media outlets contact us here for further information. So far, they've been fairly cooperative and so they shouldn't be bothering you out there anymore. If they do, just give me a call and I'll take care of it."

"What about evacuating the locals?" Henderson asked.

"We're still discussing that with the county officials," Spenser said. "We've dug up a copy of Western Triassic's emergency response plan and it looks like we may proceed down that road at some point, but we want to do it slowly. In addition to the fact that Hudson would be watching for it, the last thing we need right now is panic."

"Frank and I will be flying up to Edmonton later on today, Clint," Rosenthal said. "In the meantime, if you need anything else, let Al know."

"While we're talking about it, if I'm going to be out here for awhile, maybe you could arrange to have someone bring me some lunch."

There was some light laughter on the mobile radio's speaker.

"If I have to, I'll deliver it personally," Rosenthal replied. "In the meantime, you just hang tight and for god's sake, be careful."

"Will do. Thanks. Channel clear."

Henderson waited for the acknowledgement and replaced the handset. Breukart walked over to his truck.

"Well?" he asked.

"A couple of our big shots are on their way up from Calgary," Henderson replied.

His elbows were resting on his knees, his feet planted on the bottom edge of the truck's doorframe.

"They've set up a command post at our office in Edmonton, so those television reporters should be out of our hair any time now."

"I just saw a bunch of them pile into their car and leave."

Henderson nodded.

"Right now, then, I guess we just wait."

A grey, late model Ford pulled up to the police cordon. Henderson's heart sank when he saw the driver, who was wearing a navy-blue suit with a bright orange golf shirt, open his door and get out.

"Oh Lord," he moaned and buried his head in his hands. "Randy, give me your gun."

"What is it?" Breukart replied, giving Clint a puzzled look.

"The last person I really wanted to see today: the bloody owner of the plant. And he looks like he's in a somewhat less than receptive mood."

Breukart turned in time to see William Arthur, whose face was bloated red, march past the police officers manning the barricades and head straight toward him and Henderson. Breukart stepped forward to intercept the man before he got to Henderson's truck and he managed to block the man's stride just ten feet from his target.

"Can I help you, sir?" he asked firmly.

"Damn right you can help me," was the reply. "I'm William Arthur. I'm the president of the company that owns that plant. Some crackpot phones me up in the middle of the night and tells me that he's holding my facility hostage. I want to know just what the hell is going on out here!"

"Someone is indeed holding your plant hostage," Henderson replied, his head still buried in his hands.

Arthur stormed over to the truck.

"And just who the hell might you be?"

Henderson looked up. Arthur's face was now crimson and contorted, and he was sweating profusely. Henderson sighed.

At least a stroke would shut him up for a while, he thought.

"My name is Clint Henderson. I'm with the Energy and Utilities Board."

"Well tell me, Henderson," Arthur asked angrily, "just what the hell are you talking about?"

"There is at least one individual in there right now, likely more, who are probably armed. They're holding your employees hostage and there has been a threat to blow up the plant unless certain demands are met."

"And?"

"And what?"

"What are the bloody demands?" Arthur screamed. "What the hell do they want?"

"Well, we don't really know yet," Henderson replied pointedly, "and we probably won't know until, oh, say, about noon. So if you don't mind, I'd appreciate it if you'd cool it a bit."

Arthur closed his eyes for a moment.

"Okay," he said calmly. "I'm sorry: I forgot I was dealing with a bureaucrat. I'll try this again more slowly, so that you can understand what I'm saying. I'd like to know what you're planning to do to get this joker, or bunch of jokers, out of my facility. Or should I be talking to someone who just might know something about what's going on?"

Henderson grabbed a collar of Arthur's expensive suit.

"Come here," hissed Henderson, and he pulled Arthur roughly behind him across the road. He thrust his set of binoculars into the executive's hands.

"There's your god damn plant! Now look at the sulphur block. It's that big yellow thing! Not only is the plant wired to be blown up, but the sulphur block has also been set to go up in flames! Now, he might be bullshitting us, but there's a strong possibility that he's not. Do you want us to take that chance?"

He pointed Arthur in the direction of the plant.

"Go ahead, have a good look," Henderson added. "It's your call. And I want your answer now. If you want me out of here, tell me, because trust me, I've got a lot better things that I could be doing right now."

Arthur's mouth hung open and he looked down at Henderson's hand, which had relaxed its grip on his collar somewhat. He cleared his throat and took the binoculars. He scanned the gas plant.

"No, I don't want you to take any chances," he replied, shaking his head slowly. "Do you know who's in there?"

"Not yet," Henderson lied.

Breukart raised an eyebrow.

Arthur looked at Henderson.

"So what are you planning on doing next?" Arthur asked.

"I'm supposed to phone him again around twelve o'clock. He said that he'll give us his demands then."

"In the meantime," Henderson continued, "I'd really prefer it if you'd wait behind the barricades or in our office in Edmonton."

"The hell I will!" Arthur yelled. "I want to make sure that you people are doing all you can to get that crank out of there!"

Breukart stepped forward.

"Excuse me, Mr. Arthur," he said, "I'm afraid I'm going to have to ask you to leave now, sir. Only authorized personnel are allowed to remain here behind the police barricade. Besides, it's for your own safety: we don't want you to get hurt. If anything further develops, we'll let you know."

"I'm staying!" was the reply. "What's the name of your superior officer?"

Breukart motioned for one of the other police officers.

"If you go with the corporal, he'll provide you with all the details."

Breukart escorted Arthur over to the constable who, with a firm hand on Arthur's arm, led him away from the scene.

"Boy, he is one angry piece of work," Breukart said to Henderson as they watched Arthur being led away.

"He's going to vapour lock if he doesn't relax a bit," Henderson replied. "Say, that was a nice touch about his welfare, but I doubt that Hudson could do anything to him at this distance. Arthur's so stressed he didn't even notice"

"I wasn't thinking about Hudson," Breukart said with a wink. "I was more worried about what you might do to him if I didn't get him the hell out of here. And I think he noticed that."

So, Clint thought to himself. Here we are.

All of us.

Breukart and his boys are over there manning the barricades and directing traffic. Arthur is over there having some sort of conniption on his cell phone. I'm sitting in this truck listening to the radio thinking how great the weather is for this time of year.

And we're all here because of this wacko who we used to consider a colleague.

Well, sort of.

Clint smiled slightly.

Well, this whole thing has certainly added a touch of surrealism to an otherwise beautiful day, he thought.

Was it really Hudson, though, who had made the day seem strange? he wondered. Maybe it's something else. Was it last night, perhaps? I don't get it; maybe it's all moving too fast. Last week, everything was uncluttered, simple. Did I really care if I ever met anyone again? And then, less than 24 hours ago, Renee appears and wham! It's as if every thought I'd ever had about love was a lie.

Am I rushing things? I mean, it's way too soon to tell how far this thing could go. Christ, for all I know, she's sitting there with a major hangover trying to figure out who she'd been with last night.

No, she knew.

Okay, maybe it was just a one-night stand for her.

Henderson leaned back and sighed.

No, she's not like that. No way. She's better than that.

Okay, so say I do go after it. Am I going to get involved with her only because I need to feel that someone has to love me in order for my life to be complete?

But she makes me feel good and admit it, you jerk: you like how you feel. For the first time in years, you haven't noticed that empty feeling.

Maybe it's gone.

Henderson leaned forward and exhaled.

It would be great if she thought the same way, wouldn't it? After all, she seemed pretty sincere, and she seemed to like me for who I am.

Which would be a first, wouldn't it? Actually accepting the fact that someone likes me for who I am.

It would be somewhat difficult, you know. She has a life in Calgary and that means that one of us would have to make a major adjustment. But would leaving the Board's Edmonton office really be that terrible? I'd have to leave Keltner behind, granted, but Pete's a big boy and I'm sure he'd get over it. But is it worth the chance that I'd get over it? We could still visit each other, I guess: it's not like Calgary is that far away.

Still, it would be a big step. I mean, she's got a kid, for Christ's sake. Children are okay, I guess: never really thought about it much. What it does mean, though, is that if you want to pursue this, I'd have to be good enough for two people, not just one. And he may not even accept me. Could I handle that?

It would take a lot of patience on both sides: me with her son, and definitely Renee with me.

So, is this something I really want? Would it be worth the effort?

Well, look on the bright side, he thought, the slight smile reforming on his face. If everything worked out, then perhaps there would be two people in this world who he could love and in return, two people who would need him and could make him feel special. Kind of like two for the price of one.

He shook his head briskly.

Damn it, you think too much, Henderson. Stop complicating things. Just shut up already and start thinking about how it might work, instead of how it might fail.

Although the radio was turned down, Henderson still heard that annoying tone that signalled the start of the twelve o'clock news. With that sound, the slow summer day seemed to come back to life.

The first item on the news was the report of the siege of the gas plant and the announcer warned his listeners to avoid the highway and roads leading into the plant site. As he mentioned the police barricades that had been set up in the area, Breukart walked over to Henderson's truck.

"Time to phone our friend?" he asked Henderson.

Henderson nodded solemnly and the churning in his stomach returned. He depressed the mike switch and when Helen answered, he asked her to dial the phone number of the gas plant. As he heard the distant tones of the number being dialled, the churning increased.

The phone in the control room was answered on the first ring.

"Right on time," the answering voice responded. "That's what I always liked about you, Henderson: you were always so fucking prompt."

"I aim to please," Henderson said dryly.

"Shut up, smartass," Hudson snapped back. "Now, if you've got a piece of paper, and a pen that has some ink, I'll tell you what we want."

Henderson opened the small notebook that he carried, pulled the plastic cover from his pen, and prepared to write.

"Go on," he said into the mike. "I'm ready."

"First of all," Hudson began, "we want six million dollars. You know the routine: small, unmarked bills, nothing larger than a fifty. Just like in the movies. The money is to be in a duffle bag and in our hands by no later than ten o'clock tomorrow morning. Originally, it was to be six o'clock, but I knew that you'd come back whining about an extension because it's impossible to gather the money, and so on and so on. This way, we cut out all the bullshit in between. The point is that in a sense, I've already given you an extension, so there will be no more, got it?"

Henderson sighed.

"I understand. No extensions. What else?"

"You're going to deliver the money personally, Henderson," Hudson continued. "I know that you haven't got the guts to try anything, so tomorrow morning, you'll come through those plant gates, with the money in plain view. You'll drop it off at the back door, the one between the control room and the process building. That way, no one will be tempted to take a shot at me. After you've dropped it off, you leave, calm and slow. Look on the bright side, Henderson: this type of thing will really impress the fucking Board members, and considering what a brown-noser you are, this could really help you make your ass-kissing quota for the year."

Henderson closed his eyes, took a deep breath, and shook his head while he exhaled slowly.

"Are you getting all this, Henderson?"

Henderson hesitated before depressing the transmission switch. He looked at Breukart.

"He's a real charmer, isn't he?" the constable said. "It's a difficult time, I know, but could you ask him about the hostages?"

Henderson nodded. He brought the handset to his mouth and pressed down on the switch.

"Yeah, Gillis, I got it. Now I want to know about the operators."

There was silence from the radio. Henderson looked at Breukart and raised an eyebrow.

After a few seconds, they heard the guarded response.

"What operators?" Hudson asked.

"The ones on shift last night. How are they? I need some assurance that they haven't been harmed."

"Oh them. Oh sorry, but they're tied up right now and can't come to the phone."

Henderson heard Hudson giggle.

"For some reason, I've always wanted to say that. Oh, they're okay, Henderson. You'll have to trust me on that. Mind you, you really don't have much of a choice, you impotent fuck."

Henderson closed his eyes and shook his head slowly.

"Okay, so what happens after I drop off the money?" he asked.

"Everyone out there gets lost for at least twenty four hours. I don't want to see you or the cops during that time. Then, after the twenty four hours is up, the plant is yours again."

"And your escape?"

"Look, Henderson, if I'm going too fast for you, let me know and I'll talk slower and use smaller words. Like I said, you and your police friends disappear for twenty-four hours. We know how we're going to get out of here, but if you think I'm going to tell you, you're nuts."

"All right, Gillis, I understand."

"Finally. Christ, for a while there, I thought that working for the Board had dropped your IQ by at least fifty points."

Henderson lowered the handset and sat for a moment, his chin resting in his other hand. He looked at Breukart, who shrugged.

"I think that's all we're going to get from him, Clint," he said. "He's staying pretty tight-lipped about his plans and the identities of his partners. Look, now we know what they want. Let's hang up and get this to your people."

Henderson nodded and rubbed his eyes with his fingertips. He was just about to speak into the handset when the radio's speaker came to life.

"Yo, Henderson, are you still there?"

"Yes, Gillis, I'm still here," Henderson replied slowly. "Look, I have to pass your demands on. It's going to take some time to raise that much money."

"It shouldn't be too much trouble, Henderson. After all, the government has lots of money to give to all the big oil companies. They'll just have to divert some of it to us little people."

Henderson looked up at Breukart sharply.

"Okay, Gillis, I'll get back to you," he said calmly. He was still looking at Breukart, who returned the look with a puzzled expression on his own face.

"The next time I see you, Henderson, you'd better be carrying a lot of money," said Hudson. "You've got a lot to do in the next twenty-four hours, so fuck off."

Then the phone went dead.

Breukart whistled.

"Well, if this doesn't work out, he could always try for a career in the diplomatic corps," Breukart said. "He's a natural."

He looked at Henderson and his brow furrowed.

"Are you okay?" Breukart asked. "What is it?"

"Hmmm," Henderson replied as he replaced the handset, "hmm, hmm, hmm. I don't know. It's just something that just occurred to me, something that he said. It may be nothing."

"Well, you never know. If it weren't for hunches, I'd still be manning radar traps on Highway 2. Let's hear it."

Henderson sat upright on the edge of the truck's seat.

"It's just a couple of things that he mentioned. Did you notice how tense he seemed to get when I asked him about the operators?"

"He wanted to know which operators," Breukart added.

"Exactly. He should have known that I meant the hostages, unless. . ."

"Unless what?"

"Unless there is some other group of operators in there with him."

"I'm not sure I'm quite following you."

"Okay," Henderson continued, "the other thing he said, right at the end, is that the government should be able to give some of the money it gives to the oil companies to, quote, us little people."

"Uh, sure. What about it?"

"Last week the supervisor of this very plant told me that some of his operators had been laid off in order to cut expenses, so that the company could take advantage of some new government drilling grants. Now, what if Hudson knew that? And what if he managed to convince some of those guys, those that were laid off, to join him in this little scheme of his by telling them that this was their chance to make some money and get back at Western Triassic and the government?"

"I'm not sure I follow…"

"Okay look, you see, Randy, some people, sometimes even me, believe that it's unfair that while the big oil companies are getting government money even when oil prices are sky high, a lot of average working people are still being laid off. There are even a lot of people in this business who are beginning to think like that and, as a result, there's a lot of resentment that's taken root out there. I'm thinking that maybe Hudson was able to find some of it and take advantage of it."

Breukart thought for a moment.

"Which means that the others in there with your friend might be the operators who were laid off out here last week," he said finally.

"Exactly. Or perhaps I'm reading too much into what Hudson said. I've been known to do that. Ask my ex-wife."

Breukart chuckled.

"Maybe," he said, "but like I said before, gut instincts are usually worth checking out. I'll get a list of names from the plant supervisor and have some of my men contact them. If it isn't these guys, maybe they have an idea who it might be. At the very least, we'd eliminate them as suspects."

As Breukart turned and began walking back to his car, Henderson leaned back against the truck seat, his eyes closed.

My God, Gillis, he thought. *What have you got yourself into?*

"That's about it, Al," Henderson said as he finished repeating the last of Hudson's demands to those back at the Edmonton office. The members of the senior Board staff had arrived and were now sitting in Spenser's office. They were listening to the conversation on his speakerphone. Henderson heard a brief silence that ended with a subdued "Wow".

"He's not asking for much, is he?" a distant, echoed voice said. Henderson recognized the voice as that belonging to Simon Rosenthal.

"We'll have to discuss this with someone from Western Triassic," Frank Sears added. "Can I assume that William Arthur is still out there, Clint?"

"Oh yeah," Henderson replied with a sigh. "He's over in his car and I have to admit that I've seen him in a better mood. The R.C.M.P. are keeping him away from the area, but he's as close to the barricade as he can possibly be. He's not a happy camper, I'm afraid."

"No, I imagine he isn't," Rosenthal said, "but then again, he rarely is. On top of everything else, he's not one of our bigger fans and it must really piss him off to know that he needs our help on this. We can get him out of your hair, Clint, but I'm afraid that no matter what we decide to do, we'll need to keep him involved with this and get his input, not to mention his approval. We'd better get him in here. I'll get the number for his cell phone from his office and give him a call right away. Anything else, Clint?"

"Not right now. Most of the media have left. I assume that they've gone back to our office to wait for our man from Communications."

"'e arrived a little while ago," Spenser said. "and 'e's setting up a tea party for the press now."

"Great. All that's left out here are a few camera people. Incidentally, the R.C.M.P. are going to contact those operators who were laid off last week. We have a hunch. Other than that, all I can do right now is sit here, enjoy the sun, and wait for you people to decide how we're going to resolve this."

"Okay, lad," Spenser concluded, "we'll stay in touch. You'll be the first to know if anything develops at this end."

"Thanks, Al. Channel clear. Oh, by the way...."

It was too late. Henderson heard the click of the phone on the other end.

"Shit," he muttered as he replaced the mike in its holder on the side of the mobile phone.

Where the hell is my lunch, he wondered. Damn it, I should have asked that first.

"Again, we understand that verbal contact has been made with somebody inside the gas plant," the young woman in front of the camera read from her notes. "Representatives from the Alberta Energy and Utilities Board are not saying who that person is, only that this individual has indicated that a list of demands will be forwarded to Western Triassic and Board officials sometime this afternoon."

"There have been rumours that the area may be evacuated, Toni," replied the well-dressed anchor with the tousled hair sitting in the newsroom. "Was there any mention of that at the press conference?"

"A question was put to Mr. Richter, the Board spokesman, about the, uh, potential evacuation of area residents. He stated that it is being discussed, but only as a last resort, that there is no danger to the local population at this time. There is a feeling, however, among some of the people here that whoever is in the plant may have specifically warned the Board against evacuating the area residents."

"Thank you, Toni. That was Toni Richmond, reporting live from the E.U.B.'s Edmonton office, where a short time ago a Board spokesman held a press conference to update us on the situation at the Western Triassic Morinville sour gas plant, located northwest of the city. Again, for those who have just joined us, the situation is this: sometime during the night, somebody, at this time we don't know who exactly, entered the gas . . ."

The sharp rapping on the door startled Marie Collins, who clicked the television off with the remote control. Using her crutches as a support, she pulled herself up from the sofa and hobbled to the window. She pulled back the curtain and saw the two police officers standing on the front porch. The sight of them started her heart racing.

Marie turned from the window and looked down the hallway. Behind one of the doors came the muffled shrieks and yells of her children playing. As she went to open the front door, she prayed that her children would stay in their room: she didn't want them to see the policemen in their home.

"Good afternoon," the taller one said with a firm, but kind, smile. "Mrs. Collins?"

She nodded dumbly.

"I'm Constable Baldwin of the R.C.M.P. and this is Constable Leonard. We would like to have a word with your husband."

"I'm, I'm sorry, he's not here right now."

The two police officers looked at each other briefly.

"I see. Can you tell us where he is?" asked Baldwin.

"He's out of, out of town. In, uh, Red Deer. He was laid off at work last week. He had a possible lead on a job, and so he's…"

"I see. Could we ask you a few questions then, ma'am?" Leonard asked.

"Um, sure. Please, come in."

Marie stepped back from the door to allow the two R.C.M.P. officers inside.

"You'll have to excuse me," she apologized. "I broke my leg last month and I'm still having difficulty moving around. In fact, the doctor says that I won't be able to go back to work for another six months."

"I'm sorry to hear that ma'am," Leonard said with a sympathetic smile. "Well, we won't take up too much of your time."

Marie led them into the front room and motioned for them to have a seat.

"Can I offer you anything? A cold drink perhaps?"

"No, thank you, ma'am," Baldwin replied as he took a note pad from his shirt pocket. "You said your husband wasn't here right now. Do you expect him back shortly?"

"He went out this morning to run a few errands and then, like I said, he also had a lead on a job he was going to track down, so he was going to drive down to Red Deer."

"What time did he leave?" Baldwin asked.

"About ten o'clock. He said he hoped to be back before supper."

Again, the two police officers looked at each other.

"Um, could you please tell me what this is all about?" she asked. "Is Steven in some kind of trouble?"

Baldwin snapped his notebook closed.

"At this time, we don't believe so, ma'am. There's been some trouble at the gas plant where he used to work. You may have heard about it on the news."

"No, actually I hadn't," Marie lied.

"Well, we just wanted to ask your husband a few questions about some of his former co-workers."

Baldwin took a business card from his wallet.

"Could you please give this to your husband when he gets home and have him call me? It's very important."

Marie looked at the card and nodded.

"Uh, sure. Yes, I will."

The two officers rose to leave. Marie followed them to the door.

"Sorry to have disturbed you, ma'am," Leonard said. "Thank you for your time."

"I hope you're up and about soon," Baldwin added with a smile. "I know it's not very pleasant to be laid up like this during the summer."

Marie laughed lightly.

"Yeah, if this type of thing has to happen, why can't it be

during the winter?"

Baldwin nodded.

"Thanks again, ma'am".

"Thank you, officers," Marie said at the door. She watched them walk down the sidewalk to their patrol car and stayed at the door until she saw them drive away and turn the corner. Then, shaking, she hobbled over to the easy chair and sank into its plush cushions.

She didn't believe Steven the night before when he told her that he was going on a hunting trip for a couple of days. Normally, he looked forward to his hunting trips and at first, Marie thought that such a trip might ease the depression that her husband had felt since being laid off at the plant.

But this time, the glimmer in his eyes that normally accompanied him on these trips wasn't there.

Then, as he stood at the door in the very early morning, when it was still dark, waiting for his ride to come, he had looked at her with a deep sadness in his eyes. There was a quiver in his voice when he told her that he loved her, a contrast to the yelling and screaming that she had heard constantly over the past week. He kissed her long and passionately. Finally, he looked away to watch for the car that finally arrived in the middle of the night to take him away.

It had all seemed so distant, so final.

And now she knew.

Once again, he was in the plant where he had worked for so long, but this time, she believed that he wouldn't be coming home. With shaking hands, she picked up the phone, and dialled the number she had dialled at least once during every shift he had ever worked at that gas plant.

Henderson was relaxing in the cab of his truck, listening to the radio with his eyes half closed, when the dusty red pickup pulled alongside his. He looked over to see Keltner's face smiling at him and he returned the smile weakly. Then Keltner got out of his truck and walked over. He was carrying a white bag and a can of soda.

"Here you go, mate," he said handing the bag to Henderson. "A double cheeseburger from Seymour's drive-in: no mustard, no pickle, raw onions, extra mayo, just the way you like it. Christ, you're picky."

"Apparently not when it comes to picking my friends," Henderson replied. "Thanks, Pete."

He popped open the can of pop and took a long drink. Then he looked inside the bag and pulled out a foil wrapped bundle. He looked in the bag again.

"Not many fries left," he said, casting a fake glare at his friend.

"What are you accusing me of?" Keltner replied. "I was tasting it for poison. Al's orders. And they were delicious. Bon appetite."

Henderson unwrapped a corner of the cheeseburger and took a bite. His eyes closed as he chewed. Seymour's drive-in was another favourite of the Board inspectors and was known for the best hamburgers in Edmonton.

"Thanks, Pete," he mumbled between bites. "This is great."

"Anytime, my man. Oh, by the way," he added, reaching into his pants pocket. He pulled out a folded piece of paper and handed it to Henderson.

"Someone phoned for you this morning. When Anne told her that you were out, she asked for me. She wanted me to give you a message."

Henderson put the cheeseburger down, wiped his hands and unfolded the note.

When he saw that it was from Renee, his heart leapt.

"Sounds like a pretty nice girl, Clint," Keltner said. "Smart, too. Anyway, she said that she'd be staying over for an extra couple of days and that you could reach her at that number."

"Does she know what's going on out here?" Henderson asked.

"She phoned before we really knew what was happening, but I told her that you were called out to an emergency. She said to phone her whenever you had the chance."

Henderson unhooked the handset. When Helen answered, he asked for the phone number on the note.

"By the way, the burger is on me," Keltner said. "Playing messenger boy is what's going to cost you."

Henderson smiled.

"Uh, huh. And just what're your plans for the afternoon?" he asked while he waited for his call to be placed.

"Nothing in particular," Keltner shrugged. "This thing has sort of thrown the whole office out of whack."

"I could use you out here. You know, moral support."

Keltner nodded.

"Sure, I can do that."

The phone was ringing over the mobile's speaker.

"Uhm, maybe right now, it might be a good idea if I go help the cops direct traffic or something," Keltner said.

Henderson smiled as his friend walked away. The ringing

on the other end of the line ended as the phone was picked up.
"Hello?" a delicate voice answered.
"Hi, Renee, it's me: Clint."

The ringing of the phone shattered the tired, tense stillness of the control room. Hudson, still reclining in the lead operator's chair, lazily plucked it from its cradle.

"Western Triassic," he answered sweetly, "how the hell may we help you?"

His face scrunched up as he listened to the caller. Then he turned and glared at Collins, who looked up at him. Hudson covered the mouthpiece with his hand.

"It's your old lady," he said coldly. "What the hell is she doing phoning here?"

Collins jumped up and grabbed the phone.

"Hi, hon?" he said frantically. "Yeah, I know... I'm sorry, but I didn't want you to worry... I know... Well, it's something that sounded like a good idea. It wasn't supposed to end up like this. It's become a real fucking mess...Yeah, that's what I've been thinking about, too."

Collins's eyes began to well up and a tear fell from his cheek. He wiped it with the back of his hand.

"I know. I'm so sorry," he stammered. His voice began to break and then, after he cleared his throat, its strength returned.

"Sure, hon, I'll do that. For you and the kids. I'll do it right now... I love you too." He paused for a second, and then said in a quieter voice: "I really do... Okay, I'll talk to you later. Bye."

Collins held the phone for a moment and then replaced it gently in its cradle. He stood there facing the main control panel, his back to the rest.

"What's her problem, Collins," Hudson asked. "Does she miss her little Stevie?"

"Shut up, Hudson," Collins replied sternly.

He tapped at one of the pressure controls on the main panel.

"I want out," he said. "This thing was screwed up from the beginning. What am I doing here? I should have known better."

"Oh, somehow, I don't think so," Hudson chuckled. "Sorry, but you're in this for keeps, Collins."

Hudson swung the chair around.

"Relax, okay?" Hudson said. "It's like I had promised you: when we get the money, you leave. It'll be dark, so no one will see you. No one will ever know it was you."

Collins turned around. He buried his face in his hands and then, with his eyes closed, he ran his fingers through his hair and breathed deeply. He locked his hands behind his head. His eyes were still closed.

"No, Gillis," he replied calmly, "I made a mistake, a huge mistake, and I want out. I'm going to give myself up."

Hudson laughed.

"Are you out of your mind?" he said with disbelief. "Do you have any idea what they'll do to you? They'll throw you in prison for the rest of your life, assuming, that is, that they don't shoot you as you walk across the parking lot."

Collins looked at him.

"I don't care. I'll take my chances."

Hudson shook his head in disgust. As he did so, he looked away from Collins.

"You're crazy, man," he said.

"No, I was crazy," Collins replied. "Actually, now I'm tired. And I'm fed up. You know, I must have been fucking nuts to get involved with this."

Michaels stood up and grabbed Collins's arms.

"Come on, Steve: lighten up," he said. "Hey, this is a good way to get back at the company, to get some money out of them. This is your chance to show them that you're somebody that they can't treat like dirt, somebody with pride!"

"I had pride, Warren," Collins said flatly, "and my family was proud of me. I should have realized that before I got involved with this horseshit."

He shook himself free of Michaels' grip.

"I've always done things honestly. I may not have a job, but I have my dignity, and I have a family that loves me, and I love them. Look, nobody has been hurt yet. Like I said, I'll take my chances, tell them that it was a big mistake."

"You're a fool, Collins," Hudson said quietly.

"I'm just tired, Hudson. I just want to go home. I want to see my family."

Hudson stared coldly into Collins's bloodshot eyes.

"All right, Collins. Have it your way."

"Look, I promise I'll keep my mouth shut," Collins said. "Nobody out there will know who else is in here."

Hudson nodded, again looking away from Collins, as did the others. Although they all watched him, no one would look him in the eye as he walked toward the door. They were all tired and although he didn't show it, Phillips began to think that Collins was right. Maybe they would be better off surrendering now, before anyone got hurt. Simpson just stared at Collins as his friend, and the man upon whom he depended for so much, began to leave.

Phillips was looking at the floor and was about to say something, but the ear-splitting report of a gun made him shut his mouth.

Because they had all been watching Collins, no one saw Hudson slowly lift his pistol, casually aim it in the direction of Collins's back, and then pull the trigger.

The impact of the bullet sent Collins flying forward and there was a dull slap as his body hit the tile floor.

    Henderson had explained the situation at the gas plant to Renee and promised that he would see her when it was all over. She had promised to stay; she needed to see him again, she had said, and if it was all right with him, her parents were going to bring Sean up for the weekend to meet him. Henderson had agreed at once and now, suddenly, realized that he was really looking forward to seeing Renee again and meeting her son.

    Henderson had just set down the handset and he could tell that he had a major grin on his face because it was actually making itself felt in his jaw muscles.

    That's when he heard what sounded like a muffled gunshot and he dropped down under the dash of the truck. Keltner and Breukart came running over to him and, after crawling out from the cab, Henderson huddled down with them behind the safety of the truck's metal sides.

    "Christ, what was that?" Henderson yelled.

    "Sounded like a shot," Breukart said. "It was too muffled for an explosion."

    "Unless it came from inside the process building," suggested Henderson.

    Breukart scanned the gas plant through the binoculars.

    "I don't see any smoke. Well, whatever it was, I don't

think it's anything I want to be hearing."

"Lord, me neither," added Keltner quietly. "Ever."

They waited for a few minutes before they stood up and peered cautiously over the edge of the truck bed. Breukart looked over at the rest of his men and motioned for them to move the barricade further down the road.

Henderson reached into the truck and grabbed the handset.

"QJ3379 to base," he said frantically, "Al, are you there?"

"He's downstairs right now, Clint," said the responding voice.

It was Mills.

"He's in a meeting with Rosenthal, Sears, and a group from the County of Morinville," Mills added.

"Get him on the radio now!" Henderson ordered.

"Yeah, yeah. Hang on, Clint."

A few seconds later, Spenser's voice came over the speaker.

"What's 'appening, Clint?"

"It sounded like there was a gunshot from the plant."

"Oh, good God. Are you okay?"

"We're all fine. Nobody out here has been hurt. There's no smoke from the process building, so we've ruled out an explosion. The shot sounded muffled, so we'd like to think that it probably wasn't directed out here."

Henderson looked at Breukart, who nodded agreement.

"My god, the 'ostages!" Spenser exclaimed. "What's the situation out there now?"

"It's quiet. There was only the one shot."

There was a pause.

"All right, lad. Look, try phoning 'udson. We 'ave to find out what's 'appened. It could just be a mistake."

"I'll use Pete's mobile. I'd like you to stay on this line."

Henderson gave the handset to Keltner and opened the passenger door to the red pickup. He dialled channel two on the mobile and had Helen ring the gas plant.

"Please, Gillis," Henderson prayed as he heard the phone

ring, "tell me everything is all right, that if it was a gun, it was fired by accident."

After the fifteenth ring, Henderson slammed the handset onto its mounting bracket.

"Shit!" he mumbled. "Shit, shit, shit."

He scrambled back to his own vehicle.

"Al, there's no answer."

"Okay. Pete's out there with you?"

"Yeah, he is."

"I want you and the constable in charge to get back to the office 'ere. Leave Keltner in charge. We've got senior R.C.M.P. officials in 'ere, and I think we decided that it's time we do something about this mess. I'd like you to be part of the discussion."

"Right, Al. We'll be there as soon as we can. Channel clear."

The pungent, sharp, sulphurous reek of burnt cordite mixed with grey smoke and hung in the control room just below the ceiling. The ears of everyone in the room were ringing. The fluorescent lights in the ceiling receded and the room had become a tunnel. They all stood there motionless.

Then Hudson sat back down in the chair. Gently, he swivelled back and forth in it. It continued to creak as it moved. He ignored the telephone, which had just started to ring.

Phillips was the first to react. He leapt to the side of his fallen friend.

"You bastard!" he screamed. "You sick bastard!"

He turned Collins over on his back. Fired at such close range, the bullet had gone through the body and blood was streaming from the double wound, quickly forming a slick pool on the smooth floor. Although he hadn't really aimed carefully, Hudson had managed to put the bullet through the heart. Collins had died just after he realized he had been shot and right before his body had hit the floor.

The hostages, bound and gagged on the floor, stared in wide-eyed horror at the scene before them. Each of them knew that if it happened again, one of them would probably be next.

Michaels, stunned, looked at Collins's body and then at

Hudson.

"You're crazy," he whispered. "You're really crazy! You've fuckin' lost it, you know!"

The telephone stopped ringing.

Hudson jumped out of the chair. He grabbed Michaels's shirt collar with one hand and shoved his pistol into the soft skin on the underside of his jaw.

"Shut up!" he yelled, and then, looking at the others, "all of you, just shut up! I told you before: I'm not afraid to see this whole plant get blown sky high, with us in it if necessary! He knew better! He fucking well knew better! Now, if any of the rest of you want out, let me know right now and I'll put you out!"

Hudson pushed Michaels back against the main control panel and sat down, his chest heaving and his eyes on fire. He kept his pistol ready while his eyes darted around the room.

"Now, we're going to see this thing through to the end," he said evenly. "By this time tomorrow night, you'll be rich and I'll be dead. So let's all try to get along in the meantime. Dump that useless carcass out back. I don't want it stinking up the room."

They stood there, silent.

"Now!" Hudson screamed.

Michaels shook his head and stepped over to the body. Phillips was still holding it. Michaels rested a hand on his back. Simpson, who had been on the verge of tears, was more lost and confused than ever before. He wobbled slightly and glanced frenetically between Collins's body and Hudson as he came over to help.

"The retard stays here!" Hudson said, gesturing with the gun.

Michaels stood up.

"He's not retarded," he spat, fixing a glare at Hudson. "Steve was his friend and helped him more than anyone else. If Terry wants to help him now, he can. If you want to stop me, you'll have to shoot me too."

"Oh man, don't tempt me," Hudson said as he returned the glare.

Michaels continued to stare him down. Finally, Hudson

looked down at the floor for an instant.

"All right, he can help," said Hudson, "but I'll be watching you. If any of you try to make a break for it, I'll blow this place to hell and believe me, you won't have time to make it far enough away from here for it to matter!"

Michaels gestured at the other two. They lifted their dead colleague to their shoulders and carried him to the door leading out to the process building. Blood continued to pour from the wounds and it left a spotted burgundy trail along the bright white tile floor.

They stepped into the late afternoon air and Michaels took a deep breath. They found a secluded spot behind the control room and gently laid Collins on the gravel. Simpson found a plastic tarp that had been used to cover some chemical barrels and brought it over. He covered the body and looked up at Michaels; the gentle, proud smile on his face before had changed to one of sadness.

"Why?" he asked quietly. His brown eyes were bright and full.

"Oh, Christ, man. I don't know." Michaels took him in his arms.

As he held the young man, Michaels felt Simpson sobbing. Phillips stood there, stunned, still shaking his head.

"That motherfucker is crazy," he said quietly.

He looked at Michaels.

"You know he's going to kill us, don't you?"

"No, he won't," replied Michaels, still holding Simpson. "We won't let him. We're going to stop him."

"What can we really do about it now, Warren?" Phillips asked.

"I'm not going to just sit here. We have to do something, anything, even if it's letting the cops know that we want out."

"What are you thinking?"

"Oh shit, I don't know. Something to get their attention…."

Michaels patted Phillips on the arm.

"I've got an idea. I don't know if it'll do any good, but I

need you to distract Hudson for a few minutes."

"Yeah, well I hope you know what the hell you're doing, Michaels. I should never have listened to you in the first place."

Michaels nodded grimly.

"Me neither," he whispered. "Me neither."

The three of them came back into the control room. Hudson was still reclining in his chair.

"Took you long enough," he said.

"Shut up, Hudson," replied Phillips. Michaels noticed that Phillips had moved to the far side of the room and that Hudson had turned his chair to follow him.

"Oh my, aren't we tough all of a sudden."

"Look it, asshole," continued Phillips, "we may have to stick this out to the end with you, but I still don't have to like you. In fact, if you're serious about going up with this place, and I for one don't think you have the guts to actually do it, then I'll be the first one to laugh over your stinking grave. In fact, if they ever find whatever's left of it, I'll bet they'll just stuff the pieces into a green garbage bag and dump it in the nearest landfill they can find. Provided the local city council isn't adverse to having a toxic piece of shit like you pollute their town and lets them do it."

Hudson laughed.

"You know, guys like you, Phillips," he said, "will never, ever amount to anything. After this is all done, it'll be my name that they'll remember. That, to me, is worth more than the sick, pathetically useless life you'll go on to lead."

"You're wasted, man," Phillips concluded, shaking his head.

"Maybe," replied Hudson with a smirk on his face, "but at least I'm not a waste."

There had been enough time to allow Michaels to adjust a dial on the control panel without Hudson noticing him.

This particular dial controlled the amount of fuel gas that was being added to the flare stack to help the hydrogen sulphide burn more completely. Michaels turned the dial to the right as far as it could go. At that moment, he knew that the flare at the top of the flare stack had grown from a small, greenish pinpoint of light to an impressive bright yellow flame.

Michaels scanned the strip chart to the right of the dial. The blue and red pens had begun to move to the left as they recorded the increase in the volume of fuel gas being sent to the stack. So far, Hudson had not appeared to be all that familiar with the operation of a gas plant and Michaels was betting, and was almost sure, that Hudson wouldn't pay any attention to the strip chart. In about an hour, it wouldn't matter as the section of the chart that showed the jump would have scrolled behind the top edge of the recorder and two straight lines would be all that would be visible.

Michaels turned from the panel.

"Knock it off, you two," he said. "If I'm going to be stuck in here for the next day or so, I don't want to listen to you two assholes bicker and gripe at each other. I'm going to the kitchen to make something to eat. Anybody else want anything?"

Henderson and Breukart drove back to the office in a police cruiser, its lights flashing and the siren wailing. As a result, they were pulling into the crowded parking lot of the Board's Edmonton office within thirty minutes of leaving the plant site. Henderson led Breukart up to the conference room through the back staircase, paying particular attention to avoid the area that he knew would have been reserved for the press.

In the conference room, there were still two empty chairs at the large table. Spenser, Rosenthal, and Sears were there. There were also three, apparently senior, R.C.M.P. officers who acknowledged Breukart, and three other men and a woman. Henderson assumed these people represented the county.

And there, seated at one corner of the table, was William Arthur. He looked quiet, but it was obvious to Henderson that he was still extremely upset and impatient.

Breukart and Henderson sat down. Spenser closed the door to the room and returned to his seat.

"Ah, gentlemen, good to have you with us," Rosenthal said. "Perhaps you could fill us in on the latest development from the scene."

"Well, about forty-five minutes ago, at approximately 2:30 pm," Breukart began, "Mr. Henderson and I heard what sounded like a muffled gunshot from within gas plant area. R.C.M.P. officers from the Morinville detachment have the area sealed off. We are assuming that the gunshot originated from inside the control room. We don't know if there were any casualties or who fired the shot."

"I made an attempt to contact Gillis Hudson inside the plant," Henderson added. "Now, whenever I tried phoning him before, he was pretty quick to answer. This time, there was no answer."

"Do we have any idea at all yet who else might be in there with him?" Frank Sears asked.

"Mr. Henderson and I followed up on an idea that we had," Breukart said. "We thought that it might be possible that some members of a group of operators who were laid off at the plant last week might be involved. Officers from the detachment went to the homes of these men to question them. In all cases, the men were not home. Attempts to talk to the family members of these individuals did not provide much additional information. One man is a bachelor and has no family in the area."

"Another still lives with his mother," he continued. "She said that one of the men who used to work with him had told her that he and few other men who worked at the plant were going to take her son on a hunting trip with them. The man who told her that is currently separated from his wife, and she had no idea where he was."

"Don't eat any of that, Elmer," Spenser muttered quietly. "Smells like 'orseshit to me."

"At this point, it would seem that they're the most likely suspects," Rosenthal observed.

"Oh, bullshit," Arthur said quietly.

"You have something to share with the rest of the class, Mr. Arthur?" Rosenthal said, more of a command than a question.

"I know these men," he muttered. "None of them are capable of being involved with anything like this."

"The wife of the fourth man said that he had been home at ten o'clock this morning," Breukart continued. "She also said that she believed that he would be home before evening."

"There you go," Arthur blurted. "That proves that those men don't have anything to do with it."

"Unless he's not involved," Sears said.

"Or she's lying," Henderson added.

"Look, it doesn't matter who the hell is in that plant!" Arthur yelled. "This is all useless trivia and has nothing to do with the immediate matter at hand! I want them out, do you hear me? I want to know what the hell you are going to do to get them out of there!"

He had directed the question at Rosenthal.

"First of all, we're trying to determine exactly what we're dealing with here," Rosenthal replied calmly. "Any solution that we come up with will depend upon whether we are facing a group of professional criminals or a group of amateurs."

"They're amateurs," Arthur concluded angrily, "so just go in and get them out."

"The problem we have if they're amateurs," said one of the senior R.C.M.P. officials, "is that although there's a better chance that they may be easier to subdue, they will be more likely to press the switch which will blow up the facility, especially if they're tired and scared. On the other hand, if they're professionals, we'll have to be more cautious in settling this with force. It may be better to pay the ransom and try to catch them later."

"Perhaps someone from the county has an opinion," Rosenthal said.

"Well, I think it goes without saying that we are very, very concerned about the results of that sulphur block being set on fire," the woman noted. "The devastation to the residents and farmland would be, to say the least, horrific. I'd also like to point out that although the previous council went on record at the original hearing as being in favour of this facility, some of us were greatly opposed to the construction of this plant from the very beginning."

"And, as you said, most of you weren't," interjected Arthur. "May I remind the counsellor of exactly how much tax revenue the county has received from my company as a result of this facility?"

"Okay now," Rosenthal said, a touch of anger in his voice. "Let's not rehash the original hearing. We can do that later after we sort the whole thing out. The point is that right now, we have a very serious situation here. If we don't resolve it, one way or the other, by ten o'clock tomorrow morning, then we're facing some serious consequences, consequences neither the county nor Western Triassic will be able to avoid. Now, as I see it, we have two alternatives: we either pay the ransom or we take the plant by force. I need to know the position of each of the concerned parties. What's the official position of the county?"

The four representatives held a brief, whispered discussion among themselves.

"This had been discussed by a quorum of the council this morning, when we first received the news," the woman said. "We feel that the R.C.M.P. and the Board have the best means of assessing the situation and arriving at a solution. I realize that it sounds like we are sitting on the fence, but the county will accept and support whatever decision the Board and the police make."

"Thank you. Mr. Arthur, what is the position of Western Triassic?"

Arthur sat back in his chair and threw his pen on the table.

"I don't care what you do. Just get them the hell out of there."

"I'll record that as an abstention," said Rosenthal to one of the R.C.M.P. officials, "which means that the decision has been left in our hands. In that case, I'd like to thank the representatives of the county and Western Triassic for their time and their opinions. Mr. Arthur, will you please keep yourself available? If we have to make a move on the plant, we'll need your permission."

"Leave me out of it. You know what you have to do."

"May I remind you, Mr. Arthur, that we're talking about your plant? Legally, we'll need your approval before we can make any kind of move on the plant."

"The hell with that noise. I've washed my hands of the whole thing."

"Which means what, exactly?" asked Rosenthal.

Arthur gathered up the papers he had on the table, tossed them into his briefcase, and flashed Rosenthal a bright, if brief, smile. From the lid of the briefcase, he fished out another two sets of folded papers and threw them across the table to Rosenthal. Arthur then closed and locked his briefcase, and then stormed out of the room.

"Well," Rosenthal said as he reached over to pick up the papers, "as gracious and charming as ever, I see. As for the rest of us, gentlemen, I suggest we take a coffee break and reconvene back in this room in, oh say, fifteen minutes to discuss our options."

Spenser joined Henderson and Breukart in the coffee room as Rosenthal and Sears shook hands with the county officials before they left.

"Looks like it could be a long night," Henderson said as he handed Spenser a cup of coffee.

"And then some, lad" Spenser replied. "It's times like this that 'elped me appreciate a taste for single malt."

Rosenthal and Sears came in and poured themselves each a cup of coffee. Rosenthal was shaking his head.

"Isn't that Arthur something?" Rosenthal asked as he handed Spenser the papers that Arthur had thrown at him. "Are you ready for this?"

"Oh, aye," Spenser asked as opened the papers, "what's all this then?"

Rosenthal added cream to his coffee and was still shaking his head as Spenser read the papers. Slowly, Spenser's head started moving back and forth as well.

"Oh bloody 'ell," said Spenser quietly.

"What?" Henderson asked.

"'e's sold the plant to another company, a numbered company. Christ, 'e must have been on the phone to the bloody lawyers before 'e even thought about calling us this morning."

Rosenthal tasted his coffee.

"It gets better," he said. "Have a look at the other one."

Spenser handed the first set back to Rosenthal and opened the second set.

"Sweet mother of ...," Spenser said after reading it. "Can 'e do this? Are these even legal?"

Rosenthal shrugged.

"Well, probably not, but let's face it: we really don't have the time to sort this out in the courts first, Al. I'd say that this is Mr. Arthur's way of walking away from this thing. We could go after him, but he knows that something has to be done right now. He's content to let us deal with it, whatever happens, and then fight it out in court later."

"What is it?" asked Henderson, losing patience.

Spenser handed him the second set of papers.

"Our friend's numbered company, the new owner of the plant, has declared bankruptcy," he said, "so as of right now, we have to proceed under the assumption that the plant has no owner."

"But aren't we're going to need Arthur and his company to help us get the plant back?"

"No, not really, Clint," Spenser replied. "Although there is no formal contingency plan for dealing with a situation like this one, there 'as been some discussion behind closed doors, between the Board and the R.C.M.P. We also met with the R.C.M.P. earlier on today, before Arthur and the county people arrived. The truth is that we already 'ave a tentative plan worked out."

"Well, let's look on the bright side," said Rosenthal. "At the moment, Arthur's left this for us to handle. He'll answer for it eventually, but right now, we can take comfort in the fact that he won't get in the way. Shall we return to the conference room, gentlemen? By the way, where do you keep the sugar?"

The atmosphere around the table was more relaxed this time. Rosenthal sat at the end of the table, his hands behind his head, chewing on the little plastic stick he had used to stir his coffee.

He briefed the others on the latest action that had been taken by William Arthur.

"From the comments we received from the representatives of the county," he concluded, "and of course, those both verbal and, most recently, written in triplicate, from the ever gracious and eloquent Bill Arthur, I would say that we have the authority to proceed with our plan. Although most of us here were present when we discussed our various alternatives, I think we should recap for Mr. Henderson and Constable Breukart. Frank?"

"Under no circumstances can we afford to pay the ransom," Sears said. "As with every other place where this type of thing has happened, we just can't allow the possibility of this ever repeating itself in our province. There are just too many unprotected gas plants and other facilities out there that could be taken hostage if it were assumed that we would pay a ransom for them. For economic and political reasons, we can not be seen to be paying a ransom."

"That leaves us with one option: we have to take the plant back and capture those who are holding it."

"The R.C.M.P. have a team on standby who are ready to seize the plant," said one of the R.C.M.P. officials. "They just need to be told when to move. We just have one problem, which is the one we discussed this morning and for which we don't have a solution."

"And that is?" Breukart asked.

"To be blunt, our people do not understand gas plants," another of the R.C.M.P. officials replied. "We can go in and take these guys out, but we need somebody who understands the plant, can shut it down properly, and ensure that there is no immediate danger once the criminals have been apprehended."

"And we can't count on anyone from Western Triassic, I assume?" Spenser asked.

"Arthur's taken care of that," Rosenthal answered. "He doesn't want himself or any of his people involved. He's worried about liability and that's why he's pulled a stunt like this. That's fine. We can get somebody from our legal department onto this and settle up with Western Triassic when the time is right. I'm sure that eventually, we'll beat him in court and we can deal with him and his company at that point. Right now, though, we can't force him to cooperate and we haven't got the time to play around with this. We have to proceed on the basis that the plant is an orphan."

"Well, there is only one answer then," Spenser said quietly. "It 'as to be someone from the Board who knows gas plants. And unfortunately most of our gas department staff are either on 'olidays, out in the field…"

He took a deep breath and looked at Henderson.

"Or are otherwise not people who, how do I say this, well, I don't feel comfortable putting them out in the field for something as risky as this."

Rosenthal threw his pen down onto the table in front of him.

"Christ, I hate the thought of putting any of our people in that type of situation," he muttered. "There has to be another way, but I'll be damned if…"

"But it has to be done, right?" interrupted Henderson. "And I'm the only one available right now who understands the situation and understands gas plants, especially this particular plant."

"What are you suggesting, lad?" asked Al after a second's pause.

Henderson looked at him.

"Well, you've all said it yourselves," he said, "there is no other option. I guess it has to be me, then, doesn't it?"

There was silence around the table. Al looked at Rosenthal, who looked back with a slight shrug. Al leaned forward to face Clint.

"You don't 'ave to do this, Clint," he said. "I'm sure that we can come up with another solution."

"Like what?"

Now Al leaned back, tossed his own pen down on the table, and rubbed his eyes.

"Christ, I 'ave no idea."

There was a brief silence from the table.

"We won't tell you that you won't be in any danger, Clint," the first R.C.M.P. official said finally, "but we'll do our damnedest to ensure your safety and make sure that you won't get hurt. We need you to follow our people in, and shut down the plant and check it out after they're finished."

"The only thing is that I'm not a hundred percent confident that I can do it all by myself," added Henderson. "I'd like somebody else to go in with me."

"Anybody in mind?" Spenser asked.

"I know who I would like to go in with me," replied Henderson.

He closed his eyes.

"I've given him some training that I'm sure that he'd be able to help me. Anything he's not comfortable with, well, he's willing to follow my directions. Plus it's more an issue of trust than anything else. I really need someone I can trust and he's the only one that I think I could count on for something like this. Whether he's willing to do it or not is another question. I'll have to talk it over with him."

"I take it you mean Pete?" asked Al.

Henderson nodded, his eyes still closed.

"Oh great. It's not like the two of you don't get into enough trouble when you're out there in the field together."

Henderson opened his eyes. Spenser was looking straight at him, sternly, although buried inside his frown there was a glimmer of a grin.

Rosenthal nodded and looked at his watch. It was now four thirty.

"Clint, why don't you talk it over with Pete over dinner and let us know what he says. If he says no and you feel that, for whatever reason, you don't want to do it, we'll understand. In the meantime, we'll see what we can do to work out an alternative."

"I'd like someone from the R.C.M.P. there to help me explain the plan," said Henderson. "To be honest, I think I need to hear it again as well. I need to be real sure I know exactly what I'm volunteering for."

"I'll have the team leader join you," the official said.

"Okay. Have him meet us at the plant site at half past five," added Henderson. "Tell you what: why don't we discuss it over dinner? I know a great place."

Rosenthal looked around the table.

"Okay, if that's all, gentlemen, I say we get busy," he said.

Spenser came over to Henderson as they were breaking up and put his hand on his shoulder.

"Part of me was 'oping that you would volunteer, lad," he said. "Rosenthal agrees with me that you are the best one, probably the only one, 'oo can do this, but we didn't want to put any pressure on you. Thanks for coming through."

"Yeah, well, tell me how you did it," Henderson replied with a slight grin. "Maybe it'll work on Pete, too."

Keltner had been waiting anxiously for Henderson's return. He was pacing between his truck and the R.C.M.P. barricade, his binoculars still bobbing up and down in his hand. He had just checked his watch for the fifth time in two minutes when the barricades by the highway were pulled aside and he saw the flashing lights of the police cruiser swing around from the main highway and come toward him. He was by the side of the car before it had even come to a stop.

Henderson could see through the car window that Keltner was excited about something.

Keltner handed the binoculars to Henderson as soon as he was out of the car. Breukart joined them.

"What is it?" Henderson asked, taking the binoculars.

"I'm not sure," replied Keltner, leading him to the edge of the brush, "but I think it's something, all right."

Henderson trained the binoculars on the plant site and began scanning it.

"Look at the flare stack," Keltner said.

Henderson re-focused the binoculars to just the right of centre so that he was looking at the thin vertical red and white pipe. He saw the bright yellow flame that flickered from the top.

"It happened about an hour ago," continued Keltner. "I

noticed the change when I was looking at the plant. It went from almost nothing to that."

"Son of a bitch," Henderson muttered. "Hmmm, hmm, hmm, hmm." Then, a bit louder, he added, "It changed fairly quickly, did it?"

"Just like that," Keltner said, snapping his fingers.

"What is it?" Breukart asked.

Henderson handed him the binoculars.

"The acid gas flare stack," he explained, "the one used to dispose of the hydrogen sulphide that isn't converted to sulphur. Normally, the flare should be just barely visible. If it can be seen at all, it should be a light blue. You may notice that the flare is now a good size yellow flame. What that means is that for some reason, there's been an increase in the volume of fuel gas being burned with the acid gas."

"Perhaps it's a problem with the plant," Breukart shrugged. He handed the binoculars back to Henderson. "Maybe it really was an explosion, not a gunshot, that we heard before. Could it be related to that?"

"Nah, I can't see it," countered Henderson. "If there was a problem with the plant, residue gas would be dumped from the emergency stack, the silver one on the left. No, it's something else."

Henderson peered through the binoculars at the flame from the acid gas stack again.

"According to a very reliable source, by which I mean Pete, this flame has been like that for about an hour now," Henderson added. "That, plus the fact that you can hear that the plant is still running, means that someone has added a lot of fuel gas to the acid gas stream. That's what results in a flame like that. The question is why would someone do it?"

"Think it could have been done on purpose?" asked Keltner.

"A signal perhaps?" suggested Breukart.

Now Henderson shrugged.

"Okay," he said, "maybe. But for what?"

"Let's suppose for a minute that whoever is in there

doesn't know how to operate the plant," replied Breukart, "and is relying upon the hostage operators to run it. Maybe one of the hostages has had a chance to try sending us a signal."

"Perhaps, but what if the people in there do know how to run the plant?" Henderson said. "We still haven't ruled that out."

"Maybe it's a signal from one of the terrorists," volunteered Keltner. "Maybe there's been a problem and they can't communicate with us."

"Sure, maybe some of them want to contact us and the others don't," Henderson added. "Whatever, is it safe to assume that someone inside that plant is trying to communicate with us and is either unwilling or unable to use the phone?"

"If that were the case, what do we do about it?" Keltner asked.

Henderson put his hand on Keltner's shoulder.

"Pete, my boy," he said, "that is an excellent question. So far, I've been very impressed with your training and I knew you'd learn something if you hung around with me long enough. Anyway, I'm really glad that you're the one who brought that question up. Let's go for dinner and we'll discuss it."

"Discuss what?"

"We have reservations at 'The Sand Bar' to talk about exactly that. Don't worry, though: it's not as if you'll be buying."

"Oh, right," replied Keltner, "why am I not impressed to hear that?"

"Evening, gentlemen," said Sarah.
"And me," replied Keltner.
"And you. Does your wife know that you're out?"
"Who do you think sent me here?"
"Ah, I see. So what can I get you two?"
"Glass of white, please," said Henderson.
"Done. Pete?"
"Club soda, please dear."
Sarah looked at him.

"You sure that's not too much for you?" she asked. "Maybe you'd better think about pacing yourself."

Keltner was looking into the flame of the candle that that she had lit just a minute before and which was now flickering from the table top in front of them.

"Yeah, you're probably right," he drawled.

He looked up at her and smiled.

"Maybe you should cut it with a couple of shots of vodka."

"Ah," replied Sarah. "Sounds like you've had one of those days."

"I have a feeling it's about to become one."

His gaze returned to the candle.

She looked at Clint, who just nodded briefly.

"We're expecting a few others in a bit," he said. "I believe we have one of the private rooms booked."

"Hmm, yeah, okay, now I seem to remember your name on the sheet," Sarah replied. "Amanda will be looking after you tonight. Should I let you know when the others arrive?"

"If you wouldn't mind, please, Sarah," Henderson replied. Then he added in a whisper, "In the meantime, I'll get whatever Pete would like."

"Done."

She turned to Keltner and cleared her throat.

"So. Kathy kicked you out, did she?" Sarah said.

Keltner stared up at her.

"Yep. I told her that Clint here needed a hand with something and she thought I should be here to provide him with…"

Keltner looked over at Henderson. He raised his hands from his lap and wiggled both forefingers in the classic gesture of quotation marks.

"Moral support," he added.

Henderson cleared his throat.

"Man, I would love to meet someone like your wife," he said with a nervous chuckle.

"From what I heard from Amanda about your date last

night," Sarah interrupted with a wink, "it sounds like you did."

"Oh yeah?" asked Keltner, raising an eyebrow at Sarah.

"Oh yeah," was her reply as she turned and walked away from their table.

Keltner waited until she was at the bar before he looked up. Then he sat back in his chair and clasped his hands behind his head.

"You know, I would really like to hear more about that, I really would," he said, staring Henderson in the eye, "but right now, there are other things I think I'd rather discuss."

"Such as?"

"Are you going to tell me what's going on?" Keltner asked. "You know. Why we're here? Who we're waiting for?"

Henderson looked around the room and focused his gaze on the main door.

"A couple of members of the local R.C.M.P.," he said.

"The cops!?" blurted Keltner.

"Yeah, the cops," replied Henderson, "and if it's okay with you, I'd really prefer to wait until they got here before I tell you any more. They'll be able to fill in the details a lot better than I can."

When he looked back at Keltner, he saw that his friend's eyes were wide and his mouth was slightly agape.

That's when Sarah arrived back at their table and put their drinks down in front of them.

"Ah, thanks my dear," Henderson said.

He cleared his throat, picked up his glass and, after taking a sip, added "So: did you ever wonder why they call this place 'The Sand Bar'?"

Keltner took a long drink, swirled the glass to shake the ice inside, and then took another drink.

"Uh, no, not really," Keltner replied as he bit into an ice-cube. He shrugged. "This is the bar I always come to when I'm told to go pound sand. Do you think that's a coincidence?"

"Now who'd tell you to do a thing like that? Nobody from the Board, I trust."

Keltner looked up.

"Your insight is amazing," he said.

Henderson took a sip of his wine. "Anyone I know?"

"You'll figure it out soon enough," replied Keltner, "as I sense that he wants a big favour from me."

Henderson frowned at him.

"Does he now?" he said. "You should be careful about assuming things like that, you know. You can go home, if you'd like. I won't stop you, I promise."

Keltner laughed.

"Oh come on, Clint. I know that this has something to do with Hudson and the situation at the Triassic plant. Whatever's going on, I'm not going to hold it against you. I know you well enough to know that you have a good reason for it. I also know that you probably have a good reason to be waiting to tell me. I don't really think that you're just trying to get me drunk, either. I know that you know that I'm onto you and that I'm not that easy, despite what Kathy says."

"Look, it's like when we get stuck out in the boonies," he continued, "trying to find some piece of gas well hocus-pocus to inspect. You're not intentionally trying to screw up my day when you get us stuck. Hudson has now planted us in the middle of one hell of a mess. I may not be happy about it, but I'll still do whatever I can to help dig us out of it."

Henderson looked into his wine glass.

Is that a trace of a lump forming in my throat? he wondered. He shook his head and coughed to get rid of it.

"Would it make you feel worse to know that I drove us here, then?" he asked.

Keltner took a sip from his vodka and soda and bit into another ice-cube as he put his glass down. He shrugged.

"Like I said, I'm sure that you had a good reason for bringing me here."

As he chewed on the ice, he looked at Henderson again and smiled.

"Doesn't mean that you owe me any less," he added. "I do need to know if you'll be driving us back to the office, though. With all the media attention we have on us right now, I don't think it would look very good for the Board if you get us stuck somewhere."

Henderson saw Breukart enter the lounge. Sarah met him at the door and she walked him over to their table. Henderson and Keltner both rose from their chairs.

"Evening, Randy," Henderson said as he shook Breukart's hand. Breukart then turned to shake Keltner's and introduce himself.

"I understand that there will be a fourth individual joining you gentlemen," Sarah asked.

"And me," replied Keltner. "I'm not going to tell you again."

"It's no wonder that your wife kicks you out of the house." Sarah added as she nudged Keltner in the ribs with her elbow.

"Yes, there will be a fourth," Henderson said.

"Okay. I thought I'd let you know that my colleague Amanda is awaiting your presence in the back room. No hurry, but shall I inform her that you shall be making an appearance now or after the remaining member of your party has arrived?"

Sarah concluded by blinking her eyes at them twice. This was followed by a few seconds of silence.

"Wow," Keltner said finally, "she's good. Isn't she good, Clint?"

"How can anyone refuse an offer like that?" replied Henderson. He pulled his wallet from his back pocket and fished a twenty-dollar bill from it.

"No, he'll be here soon," he added as he handed the bill to Sarah. He finished the last of the wine from his glass. "Well, we might as well go get settled."

They were sitting in a private, reserved room located in the back of 'The Sand Bar'. Henderson, Keltner, and Breukart were there and shortly after they had moved into that room from the main lounge, a tall, trim man joined them. His name was Dennis

Becker. Dressed in clean blue jeans and a light cotton shirt, the reserved young gentleman didn't look like the leader of a police assault team.

Becker had just finished explaining the basic outline of the proposed plan, including the follow-up role of the EUB staff, when Keltner presented his thoughts on the matter.

"Whoa, whoa, now!" he exclaimed. "Say what? Are you all out of your freaking minds?"

Henderson shrugged.

"It doesn't seem all that bad," he said.

"Ha! Yeah, right."

"We go in after the assault team to shut the plant down. It's as simple as that. I can't do it myself; I need help. There's no one else around who can do it, and to be honest," Henderson looked Keltner in the eye, "there's no one else I would trust doing it with."

"Is this an order from Spenser?" Keltner asked Henderson.

Henderson shook his head.

"No, not at all," he said, "although they did sort of hint at who they would like to have go in. I volunteered. You're being given the same chance. I'll understand if you don't want to do it."

"Why did you say yes?"

"I like my paycheque."

Keltner put his hand on Henderson's arm.

"No, no. Come on man. I'm serious now. What in the world would prompt you to volunteer for something as crazy as this?"

Henderson thought for a moment.

"Look, Pete, I've been involved with this thing right from the beginning and I'd like to see it through. But the main reason is that, well, when it comes right down to it, somebody has to do it. As I see it, the Board allowed that plant to be built."

"Yeah, but you didn't approve that plant, Clint! Christ, you didn't even want it built here. I remember you saying so at the time! Why don't some of those jerks from head office get their asses out here and do it?"

Henderson took a deep breath and exhaled. He was looking at the tabletop and his right hand was flipping a small spoon over and over in his fingers.

"It doesn't matter who approved it, Pete. Right now, we all work for the same organization. Maybe after this is all done, they'll be more careful the next time. At the very least, I'm willing to bet that our opinion will be taken more seriously."

"Ha," Keltner said, "I'll believe that when I see it."

"If Hudson follows through with his threats," Henderson continued, "well, I don't even want to think about it. The bottom line is that somebody has to do it. No one else in the Edmonton office knows that plant like I do, or can go in there to shut the son of a bitch in after the cops have finished their job."

"And let's face it," he added, "I've been griping for ages about making a difference and actually doing something about changing this industry. I figured that it was time to do something about it or shut up. That's why I said yes."

Henderson looked at Keltner.

"And I'm asking you because I'll need some help and I don't know who else I can count on."

Keltner sat back in the booth. He was shaking his head.

"I don't believe this. This is all because I phoned you early Monday morning, isn't it, Clint?"

Henderson smiled.

"I told you I owed you one," replied Henderson.

"Yeah, you sure did."

Keltner sighed, and then sat upright again.

"Well, who knows? Maybe they'll make a movie about it. Think of the millions we'll make selling EUB action figures, with their plastic hard hats and clipboards. Okay, let's hear the details of this plan again. Specifically, I want to hear that part about how my cute little behind is not going to get shot off."

"Considering it makes quite a target," Henderson said, "it's the one I'd be shooting at."

Keltner looked at him.

"Don't forget, I could still say no, you know. But if I wasn't there, they'd be shooting at you, and let's face it: with your scrawny butt, you're not much of a trophy."

Becker pulled out his working copy of a map of the plant site. The rest cleared the dishes and plates from the table to make room for it. Amanda closed the door to the small dining room; the lounge management had guaranteed their privacy.

"The assault team will consist of four members of the R.C.M.P.," Becker began, "and you two. We'll be going in after dark."

"I think that it's obvious that we can't go in through the front. That would be suicide. Therefore, we'll have to surprise them from the back. In about an hour, when it begins to get dark, we'll arrange to have the headlights of the police vehicles, as well as some additional floodlights, trained on the front of the control room. The purpose of this is to keep the attention of our friends on the front area of the plant."

"We'll be in the back of the van and we'll approach the plant from the road immediately to the east of the site. We want to stay dark, so we won't be able to drive along this road with the headlights on and we'll have disconnected the brake lights as well. At the south end of the road, the bush will have been cleared and a red light, with blinders attached and aimed to the north, will be set up to guide the driver of the van. Once he's turned onto that road and heading south, all he has to do is aim for that light. It will guide him along the road."

"When we get to this point here," Becker pointed to a spot located southeast of the plant, "the van will slow down and we jump out. The stretch of road along that point is covered to the west by a small clump of birch trees. From this spot, we will move across the field to the northwest, following this route."

Becker ran his finger along a jagged path.

"This will allow us to take advantage of natural cover and avoid a couple of small sloughs. We will arrive at the plant site boundary here."

Becker pointed to the extreme southeast edge of the plant site.

"We cut the chain link fence and once we're into the plant site, we'll move north along the fence, past the sulphur block and the incinerator, to the LPG tanks. After we've determined the location of any explosives which might be there, we head west to the process building by passing through the middle of these tanks."

"From there, we go into the process building through the southeast door, work our way through the building and meet here, inside the process building, by the northwest door. At that point, we'll regroup, finalize the actual assault on the control room, and then take it."

Becker looked over at Henderson and Keltner.

"You two will wait outside until we give the signal that everything is secure. Then you come in and do whatever it is you have to do to shut down the plant. Once that's completed, our bomb disposal people will dismantle the explosives that these guys have planted."

"What will you be armed with?" Henderson asked.

"My assistant squad leader and myself will be equipped with revolvers," answered Becker. "The other two will have high powered rifles."

Henderson shook his head.

"Wrong. God forbid, if you do have to use them, you don't want bullets piercing any of the process equipment. It's a long shot, granted: most of the process vessels are made of thick metal and covered in insulation, but there's a chance that a stray bullet would do Hudson's work for him."

"Yeah, that's a good point," Breukart said. "The last thing we want is any uncontrolled gunfire inside the plant site."

Becker was nodding and massaging his chin with his right hand.

"Well, I don't know then," he said. "Let me think, let me think,...hmmm."

Henderson noticed from the corner of his eye that Becker's left foot was tapping the floor anxiously.

"Okay," Becker said finally, "this is going to sound a bit silly, but what if we went with crossbows?"

"Crossbows?" Henderson responded.

"You mean like Robin Hood and all that?" asked Keltner.

"Well, not quite," Becker said with a smile. "Believe it or not, a couple of my guys have been trained on crossbows. We can get them from the Fish & Wildlife people."

Henderson looked at Breukart, who nodded briefly, and then at Keltner, whose eyes widened for brief second before he rolled them.

"Okay," Henderson said, "works for me."

"Anything else we should be concerned about, then?" Becker asked.

Keltner leaned over the table and pointed to the square that marked the process building.

"You won't be able to meet inside the northwest door," Keltner said, "at least not if you want to discuss any final plans or anything. It'll be too noisy"

"Pete's right," Henderson added. "With the plant running at full blast, the noise in the process building will be too much. The best bet is to regroup outside the southeast door before we go inside the process building."

He looked across the table at Keltner.

"I'm impressed. You really have been paying attention."

Keltner stuck his tongue out at him.

"What about going around the south side of the process building?" Breukart asked.

Becker shook his head.

"The sulphur plant is located on the south side," he said. "If we were to go all the way around, we'd be outside too long. Besides, there's a window on the south control room wall, which, as we understand it, offers a pretty good view of the south process area. The risk of being seen from there is too great. The current route offers us cover pretty well all the way to the back door of the control room."

"What time do we go in?" Keltner asked.

Becker looked at his watch.

"It's now six-thirty," he said. "Dusk should be falling in about two hours, but thanks to the long evening, it won't be dark until at least nine-thirty. I had anticipated loading up the van about eleven and hitting the control room around quarter to twelve.

That will give us forty five minutes to get the van around the back of the plant and for us to cross the field to the plant site."

"Okay, now I've been trying to be real cooperative here," Keltner said, "but I want to know how safe it will really be for my friend and me. Seeing as how he's too polite to ask."

"Well, I'm going to be right up front with you, Pete," Becker responded seriously, "there is some risk, as you've figured out. You won't be armed. However, you will not have to enter the control room until we have given you the signal that everything is secure and the room has been cleared for you to come in. As well, like the rest of the assault team, you will be provided with bullet-proof vests to wear."

With the words 'bullet-proof vests', Henderson swallowed hard. An urgent voice told him to back out now, to go back to the hotel and find Renee, and forget about the whole thing. Let somebody else do it, the voice told him.

But there was nobody else, as he had insisted so many times earlier in the day. Henderson knew that. So did Keltner, who was in it because of him. He would have to rely on the soft-spoken police officer's assurances that everything would be done to prevent them from being hurt. There didn't seem to be anything artificial about those assurances. Despite everything else that could be done, Becker had been completely honest when he said that there would be some risk. However, in its own way, even that honesty was reassuring somehow.

Keltner, however, had a lot more at stake, Henderson realized. At least Henderson was familiar with the plant and knew how it operated. Keltner wasn't completely trained in gas plant operations and he would be relying completely on Henderson to guide him through the plant shut down. As well, he had his wife to worry about.

And yet, Keltner had agreed to do it, mainly to help him. In the Edmonton office, most of the staff liked each other and worked well together, but really, they could only be considered to be, at best, acquaintances. Keltner was doing this for him, Henderson knew: not for the Board. Henderson swore a silent oath not to let him down once they were inside the control room.

It was then that Keltner looked over at him and jabbed his finger into Henderson's chest.

"Don't you ever," he said slowly, with a barely perceptible glimmer of that familiar grin on his face, "tell Kathy I went along with this hare-brained, cock-a-mamy scheme willingly. She'd kill me if she thought I was actually stupid enough to volunteer for this."

Hudson yawned again, and rubbed his eyes. His stomach growled. They had ransacked the refrigerator in the small kitchen located next to the control room, but not having eaten in over twenty four hours, a bologna sandwich and a piece of cheese didn't really fill any kind of spot tagged by hunger. Hudson sat forward in his chair.

"What the hell is the matter with you guys?" Hudson spat. "Don't any of you have a wife that can put together a decent lunch?"

The hostages were still on the floor, bound and gagged. Hungry and weary as well, they had finally resigned themselves to the fact that they would be staying where they were until the situation resolved itself. That process had not been easy, though. A puddle had formed on the floor under one of hostages. Even through that, he had laid there quietly and motionless, praying for the nightmare to end.

The other men in the room, Hudson's now reluctant partners, were also quiet. Hudson was still sitting in the lead operator's chair, but now he found himself having to stay awake to watch the other three. It had become an uneasy truce and Hudson kept his pistol ready all the time. He had also made sure that the other weapons were located away from the reach of the others.

Phillips had put Simpson to sleep on the cot in the first aid area, which was located behind the main control panel. Phillips looked into the slow, bright eyes of the young man who now stayed so close to him. With a half-hearted smile and a tussle of his hair, Phillips now regretted deeply agreeing to the inclusion of Simpson in the plan. It was bad enough that Collins was dead, but he had understood completely what he was getting involved in and was aware of the risks. Simpson had come along for the same reason that he always had: he just wanted to be part of a group, any group, to feel as though he belonged somewhere. Collins and Phillips had made him part of their group right from the beginning and so of course, he had still wanted to be with his friends.

Phillips liked this young man and he knew that Collins had as well. Others had complimented them on the effect that they had on Simpson, bringing him out of the shell he had lived in for almost twenty years and making him feel useful and wanted. Simpson's mother always said that she could never thank them enough for the change they had made to her son's life.

Now it appeared as if it would all be for nothing. The change doesn't get much bigger than this, Phillips thought to himself. We were good people before. Now look us.

It was all screwed up: the plan, his life. All the result of a little greed, a lot of resentment, and the promise of revenge, he thought. Those had been the reasons for it.

And what were the results so far?

Collins was dead and Phillips knew that if Hudson didn't blow them all up first, then he would be going to jail for a long time.

For the first time since he was a kid, Gordon Phillips felt as though he was going to cry and, for whatever reason, he actually wanted the tears to come, even if only to prove to himself that he could still be the good person he had always thought he was.

Hudson stretched and he waved his arms slowly above his head. He peered through the curtain at the front of the plant.

"It's awfully goddamn bright out there," he murmured. "I wonder if they have enough cops. They've probably got a radar trap set up so that they can give you a speeding ticket when you leave."

He laughed at his joke.

There was no answer. Hudson closed the curtain again.

"What time is it?" he yawned.

Michaels, who was sitting in one of the other chairs with his feet up on the desk edge of the control panel, looked lazily at his watch.

"Quarter to eleven," he muttered quietly.

"What did you say?"

"I said a quarter to fucking eleven!"

Hudson attempted a smile, but a sneer appeared instead.

"Just a few more hours to go," he said. "Just a few more hours."

"Are you two lads okay?" Spenser asked.

"I think so, Al. Thanks. Pete?"

"Oh sure."

The vest felt heavy, foreign, and Henderson thumped the front of it with his fingers.

"Oh, it's you, Clint, definitely you," Keltner said as he fiddled with the straps on the side of his own vest, "but not with those shoes."

"Do you really think that these things work?" Henderson asked Keltner.

"Not a chance," was Keltner's reply. The adjustment complete, he pulled on the straps to tighten the vest to his chest. "If someone shoots you in one of these things and you're wounded, they tell you it saved your life. If the bullet makes it through and kills you, you won't know any different. Either way, you don't complain and the manufacturer never has to refund your money."

Spenser chuckled and patted Keltner on the back.

"Well, you two take it easy, and I'll see you when it's all over, okay?" Spenser said.

Becker, who had been talking to Breukart and the other members of the team by the van, walked over to them.

"And how are you two doing?" he asked in a friendly voice. "You guys set?"

Henderson looked at Keltner.

"I suppose," Henderson said. "Actually, I'm kind of anxious to get going. The longer we wait, the more nervous I'm getting."

"That's the way this job is," Becker added. "The tense part is always the waiting. Once you get going, you don't have time to notice."

"Sergeant," Spenser interrupted, "could I 'ave a word with you in private?"

"Uh, sure."

They walked around back of the van, where it was dark and quiet.

"What's up?" asked Becker.

Spenser turned to face him.

"I just wanted a wee chat with you before you set out," Spenser said quietly. "Now, my lads 'ave volunteered for this operation because they believe it's the right thing to do. I still 'ave my reservations about it, but quite frankly, you and I both know that there's no one else 'oo can do the job that they're expected to do tonight."

"Yes sir. I agree a hundred percent and appreciate what they're doing."

"Aye, then I need for you to do me a favour. Now, we both know that individuals in both of our professions can experience a wee boost of testosterone in situations like this one."

"Uh, yes sir," replied Becker, "I think I know what you mean. But, if you don't mind me asking, what does that have to do with the operation?"

Spenser closed his eyes, and then smiled and nodded his head before opening them again.

"The point is that they're here to 'elp you with a rather specialized part of this operation," he continued. "Your boys are not familiar with gas plant operations and my lads, well, although they're the best at what they do, they're not trained for this type of thing, and 'ave never been involved with anything quite like this before, unlike your people. Furthermore, they don't 'ave to do this. Because Clint and Pete are volunteering for this, I've given them my word that nobody on your team is going to get all gung-ho and macho, and call them down for what they do for a living. Not everyone is trained as a member of an elite assault unit and I expect that your people will understand and respect that."

"I just wanted to let you know that I've given Clint and Pete the option of refusing to go into that plant site tonight if they feel that they can't count on the members of your team to see them through this the best they can. And they'll have my full backing on it."

"I can assure you, sir, that they can count on the members of my team."

"Thank you, Sergeant. I'd also like to add that what would 'elp matters immensely, and I'll admit that this is sounding pretty anal on my part, is if your people didn't 'arass them in any way about their lack of special operations experience, if you get what I mean."

Becker held out his hand for Spenser, who took it, and Becker shook Spenser's hand with a tight grip.

"I think I understand what you mean, sir," Becker said. "I appreciate very much the situation that they're in and I appreciate what they're facing. You have my word that your men will be treated with the respect that they deserve. I'll look after them."

"Aye, thank you Sergeant."

They walked over to the van. The other three members of the team were already sitting on the cloth benches that ran lengthwise down the far side of the van. Breukart offered his hand to Henderson as the driver started the van.

"Good luck, Clint," he said. Even in the darkness, his eyes twinkled and the smile under his moustache comforted Henderson.

"We'll see you in a couple of hours," he added.

"You bet, Randy," Henderson replied. "Thanks for your help."

Henderson stepped into the van and sat on the bench seat across from the assault team. Keltner crawled in and sat next to him.

"Well?" Henderson asked Keltner after they were both settled.

"Hell, no. Does it look like I want to be here?"

With a thud that seemed to rock the van, Breukart closed the sliding side door. Then the van pulled away from the scene and headed north.

As soon as they were away from the police barricades, the interior of the van plunged into darkness. It felt strange to Henderson for the highway, normally so busy at this time of year, to be deserted, and the absence of headlights coming from the opposite direction added to the eerie atmosphere.

"Can I ask you a question, Pete?"

A pair of eyes looked at him through the darkness in the van. Light from the outside passed over the rest of his face in irregular streaks.

"You know you can."

"Do you think I'd make a halfway decent father?"

"Do you want to be a father?"

"Never thought about it before."

"And now you do?"

"Yeah," Henderson sighed, "now I think I may have to."

"Okay. Do you want to be a good father?"

Henderson thought for a moment, compressing all of his thoughts from the afternoon into a few seconds.

"Yeah, I think I do."

"Then you will."

Henderson looked up at Keltner, who winked at him.

"We both would," Keltner added quietly.

Henderson patted his friend's knee firmly.

"Thanks man."

"You got it, mate."

"Can I ask you another question?" asked Henderson.

"Okay. Just this once."

"Do you think gas plant inspector action man will be a hit?"

"Well, the way I see it," Keltner replied slowly, "is that

Barbie is going to want to kick Ken out of the house for a few hours when she hears that rig inspector action man is back in town, if you know what I mean. That's where gas plant inspector action man comes in. He'll have to keep Ken busy until she lets him come home again."

Henderson blinked.

"Is there absolutely nothing sacred to you?" he asked.

"No, not really," replied Keltner with a grin.

The van moved slowly along the empty road. When it reached the intersection with the first crossroad, the driver turned right.

Henderson turned his head to the left. In the distance, he could see the police staging area, bathed in bright lights, and the gas plant, also bathed in light and now about two miles to the south. It all seemed so far away.

The van picked up speed as it headed east. They were behind a row of tall hedges and the light from the plant area flickered between the thin branches of the thick shrub. It was as if the plant was fizzling out, much like a dying sparkler, but Henderson knew that they would be back there soon enough.

A mile down the road, the van slowed again. They were now approaching the road that would take them along the backside of the plant. The driver turned right onto this road and stopped. He then doused the headlights and waited for his eyes to adjust to the darkness.

Henderson turned to Keltner.

"Scared?" he asked his friend quietly.

Keltner looked at him with the familiar grin.

"You bet your ass I am," he replied. "I haven't been this scared since my wedding night."

"Oh, for Christ sake," muttered one of the members of the assault team, "where'd we get these two pussies? The pet store?"

"Thompson!" snapped Becker.

"Sir!" the member replied.

"Do you have even the slightest idea how that gas plant works?"

"No sir…"

"Then I can't count on you to shut it in and make sure it's done right, is that correct?"

"Uh, that would be correct, sir."

"Then back off!"

"Yes sir!"

He turned to Henderson and Keltner.

"Yeah," Keltner added, "what he said."

"Sorry, guys," Thompson added.

Keltner nodded.

"Apology accepted. But you can buy the drinks afterward."

Everyone in the van was looking forward now. As their pupils widened, they could vaguely make out a small, but highly defined red light straight ahead. As long as the driver aimed for that light, they would stay on the road.

The van moved forward again, slowly at first so as to avoid spitting gravel and rocks from under the wheels. The van accelerated to a crawling speed. As they moved slowly south along the road, the glow from the plant, which was now coming back into view, seemed to brighten the interior of the van and it painted the faces of the assault team a ghostly pale white.

Now they were alongside of the plant. It stood west of the van, about three quarters of a mile away, but still the van moved. It wasn't until they were behind the birch trees that the vehicle stopped.

Becker jumped across the floor of the van and opened the sliding door. The hot summer night air, cool compared to the heat generated by the nervous occupants of the van, chilled the sweat which ran down Henderson's back. He was the last one out, after Keltner, and no sooner had his feet touched the dirt on the road than the van slowly pulled away, the side door still open.

Henderson looked for a second at the retreating vehicle, part of him wishing that he were still on it, headed for the safety of the far end of the road.

Without a word, Becker stepped off the road, through the shallow ditch that ran along side, and onto the field. The others followed, with Henderson and Keltner taking up the rear.

Becker used the lights of the police vehicles and the gas plant as markers to guide the group along the path that he had laid out. They moved in a kind of run, bent at the waist to allow as little of them to be seen as possible from the plant. Stubble from the harvested area of the field crunched under their feet. Henderson knew that they were hidden in complete darkness, well beyond the glare of the plant, and could not be seen from the control room. Still, he wished he could crouch lower. Now he knew what those gophers out in the fields at Keltner's father's farm felt like during the spring.

Behind a haystack, they stopped. They were now less than two hundred feet from the southeast corner of the plant.

Henderson noticed that the assault team members, although in much better physical shape than either of the men from the EUB, were breathing heavily as well.

At least I'm not the only one, Henderson thought.

Becker looked around the edge of the haystack and then turned to face the rest of the group.

"This is the last stretch," he said in a hushed whisper. "Next stop is the perimeter fence. Everybody ready? If you're not, we'll wait. I don't want anyone slowing down on the open field."

Henderson held up his hand.

"Hang on for a minute," he panted.

Becker smiled and nodded.

"Relax, Clint," he whispered, "this isn't a contest. We'll take as much time as you need."

Henderson looked around the haystack again. After about a minute, he felt his breath return. He looked at Keltner, who was alert and ready to move.

"Okay," Henderson whispered, "I'm ready."

Becker motioned for them to follow and the six men ran across the open field to the apparent safety of the chain link fence. When they first stepped from behind the haystack, the plant seemed so far away, as if they were still looking at it from the van. As they approached the plant, it seemed to grow before them and the lights seemed to bathe them. Henderson was sure that they could be seen.

He had been to this plant so many times before. Now he was approaching it from a different angle, running to it like a moth to its bright lights. All of this, combined with the mixture of terror and excitement that he felt within, made the plant into something completely different, something he'd never seen before and with all honesty, never wanted to see again.

It was bathed in light, crystallized and brilliant before them. Clouds of steam streamed for the sky, disappearing into the darkness above. The plant bellowed and roared, and underlying all of that, there was a constant rumble. Occasionally, there was a breath from it, a breath that smelled of chemicals, and oil, and of sharp, pungent sulphur.

And it didn't stop. It continued to process the oil and gas that came from deep below the earth upon which it sat. It kept on spewing out the products, the stripped gas, condensate, and sulphur, for which it was built. Its life persisted, unconcerned with the activities of the humans inside its walls or outside its fence.

They approached the chain link fence at what was for Henderson a fierce speed. For the first time since they had stepped onto the field, Henderson noticed the huge sulphur block behind the fence. It loomed out of the darkness and the side facing them was pitch black, as it was in the shadow of the bright lights behind it. He had only imagined before the sight of the big yellow block with a condensate moat and explosives wired to blow it up. As he looked upon it now, he could see the dirty brown liquid that surrounded the block almost peacefully and which, under the bright lights that towered above the ground, seemed so still and quiet. Then he saw the explosives placed at intervals along the chalky sides of the block.

They were at the fence. Again they stopped, but not for long as one of the members pulled out the wire cutters and snipped the thin strands of the chain link fence. He worked with precision and caution. They couldn't take the chance of being seen from the control room and so they took the time necessary to cut the hole big enough to allow the assault team to get through safely.

Now they were inside the plant grounds, along with those who were in the control room. Henderson wondered what Hudson was thinking and doing at that moment, and what he would do if he knew that he and his partners were not alone. A chill ran down his spine.

They moved northward, along the eastern edge of the sulphur block, past the incinerator, to the giant silver bullets that contained the propane and butane. Each of the R.C.M.P. members searched the vessels for the explosives that Hudson claimed he had set. Henderson was amazed at how quickly, efficiently, and quietly the team members moved around and through the plant compound.

As each of the team members reappeared from the vessel they had inspected, they used hand signals to report any discovery they had made.

They had found them. There had been one explosive on every other vessel, four in all, but that was enough.

Becker extracted a small can of bright red spray paint from his backpack and on the side of each processing vessel where an explosive had been found, he painted a bright, gaudy arrow to the location of the device.

Once again, silently, they were on the move, but this time they stopped after only a few feet. They were next to the southeast door of the process building. Becker motioned them to stop and they all crouched down around him.

"I don't have to tell you that, well, this is it," he whispered breathlessly. "Clint, I want you and Pete to stay well behind us, but please make sure that you keep up. Mike, you and Ray will kick open the door to the control room. Make sure it's a bloody good kick; we'll only have one chance at it, so hammer the thing like it's locked. Cy and I will be the first ones through. We'll give them a chance to surrender while we're moving. But if they try anything, anything at all, whether they go for the explosives or even show that they're thinking about scratching their balls, take them."

Then, turning to Henderson, he added:

"Once we have the control room secure, I'll yell for you

two. While you're shutting the plant in, we'll be calling for backup. Any questions?"

They all looked at each other. No one had any questions. The assault team members used this opportunity to place a single, solid thin arrow in each of their powerful crossbows.

"Well, let's go then," Becker said with a tense smile and he opened the door to the process building.

The roar that filled their ears when they entered the process building made them feel like they had been dropped into the middle of a high-powered rock concert that had no melody. The treble was provide by the high pitched scream that was whistled by millions of cubic metres of natural gas flowing through the plant, the bass by the loud rumble of the equipment used to process that gas.

The process vessels in the plant, the stars of the concert, wore their bright silver insulation almost proudly. Above and round the assault team, pipes painted brilliant greens, oranges, reds, and blues, each colour identifying a different product, ran indifferently through the building as if resigned to the fact that the building was where they would stay forever, or at least until their usefulness had ended and the facility torn down.

As the team moved cautiously through the building, sidestepping the process vessels, pumps, and other equipment, the harsh light of the overhead mercury-vapour lamps cast strange shadows on the dull grey cement floor.

They entered by the de-ethanizer, the vessel used to strip lighter vapours from the gas stream. Then they turned to the right and moved diagonally to the northwest, under the overhead platform used by the operators to take measurements from instruments located high on the taller vessels. Crossing a clear section of the floor in the centre of the building, they then headed for the door between the gas compressors that would lead them to the rear of the control room.

They walked in single file quickly. In less than a minute, they were by the northwest door and in position to take the control room. They exited the building and now it was the turn of the silence to engulf them. They stopped for just a moment. For the majority of the team it was a final opportunity to gather their thoughts. Becker scanned the back of the control room, searching for anything, any small sign at all, that might force a change in the overall plan. Then one of the team members saw the muddy brown boot sticking out from under the tarp. He signalled to Becker, motioning him over to investigate. Becker then signalled for Henderson and Keltner to join him.

They all sensed what it was before the tarp was pulled back to expose the dead man's face to the night air. The body's eyes were half-closed and there was a dried trickle of blood from the nose. Henderson looked away from it. He had never seen a dead body before, but what made it worse was that he recognized the face from previous visits he had made to the plant. He looked over at Keltner, who had his hand against his forehead, as if he were blocking out the lights from above. Whatever he was feeling was hidden behind an emotionless face.

Becker tapped Henderson on the shoulder.

"So I guess that's what the gunshot was about," Becker whispered when Henderson turned to face him.

Henderson stared at Becker and nodded, his eyes wide.

Becker replaced the tarp over the dead man's face.

"Right: we hit it on three," he ordered the team with a whisper.

Each of the men checked their crossbows. Henderson and Keltner moved back, retreating further into the darkness of the shadow behind the control room. That's where they would stay until Becker confirmed that everything was all right.

Becker looked at the back wall. In the middle was the door through which they would enter the control room. To the left was a window located high on the wall. The angle to that window was too sharp to see anybody on the inside.

Becker pointed to the door and two of the team members took up a position on either side. Becker and his assistant moved back slightly so that they were centred on the steps leading up to the building. They looked at each other and then Becker nodded to the men by the door.

Becker held up his hand with three fingers and slowly lowered each digit in turn until his hand was a fist, which he brought quickly down to his side. With that, the two men on either side of the door braced themselves against the railing behind them and fired their feet at the door in unison.

The door crashed in with a loud bang, the cheap lock giving away instantly. Henderson and Keltner barely saw the two other men launch themselves into the control room.

Becker was first into the room.

"Get down!" he screamed, his crossbow trained on the first man he saw move. It was Hudson who, because of his weariness, barely had time to get halfway out of his chair before he stopped moving.

Becker's second-in-command was right behind his leader and he trained his weapon on Michaels, who froze where he stood, his only movement then being his mouth dropping open. He turned pale and began to tremble.

The other two members of the assault team had followed their colleagues into the control room and, while the team leaders kept their weapons trained on Hudson and Michaels, they moved quickly through the rest of the building, grabbing the rifles and Hudson's pistol.

Phillips appeared from behind the control panel, where he had been sitting with Simpson. He put his hands up when he saw the police officers. One of the assault team members grabbed him and threw him to the floor. The other member of the team forced Hudson and Michaels to the floor as well while Becker searched the control room. He found Simpson and dragged him off the cot. For a brief moment, he felt some sympathy for the young man who had such terror in his eyes, but then he dragged Simpson into the brightness cast by the fluorescent lights overhead.

Within seconds and without any additional words, the assault team had regained control of the control room.

"Look for the triggers," Becker ordered one of his men quietly.

While the search for the triggers for the explosive devices began, Phillips burst forth with the tears he had wanted to shed earlier.

The other two members of the assault team stood watch over the now subdued group of amateur terrorists lying prostrate on the floor as Becker went back to the rear door.

"Okay, it's clear," he announced briskly.

Henderson and Keltner stepped out of the darkness of the shadow and into the glare of the fluorescent lights of the control room. Henderson led Keltner to the control panel. Hudson's eyes hit Henderson as soon as he came through the door.

"Henderson, you bloody faggot," he spat from the floor, "I should have known, you fucking ass kisser."

"Quiet," one of the assault team members guarding them said as he nudged Hudson with his boot.

"Just like your boyfriend, Keltner," Hudson was able to add before the assault team member grabbed the hair on the back of his head and shoved his face to the floor.

"Yeah, yeah, yeah," muttered Keltner as he scanned the control panel. "Well it's not like I'm the one getting all intimate with the tiling."

Henderson found the emergency shut down switch, a prominent button coloured red, and pushed it.

For a second there was silence. The humming of the process equipment, until now an integral part of the gas plant's atmosphere, stopped. Then, from a distance came the muffled sound of the plant's siren that indicated that the gas plant was about to shut down.

Outside, the emergency flare stack roared to life. The tall, bright flame from this stack, coupled with the siren, would be the first signal to those outside of the plant gate that the plant was now under the control of the assault team.

"Watch the inlet pressure," Henderson cautioned Keltner. "Make sure that it's dropping. That'll tell you if the emergency shut down valve at the front end of the plant has closed properly."

Keltner found the inlet pressure gauge and watched it for a few seconds.

"Okay," he said finally, "it's coming down."

"Good. Get on the refrigeration system, would you? "

Henderson was watching the other pressure gauges, making sure that the equipment was being depressurised as quickly, but safely, as possible.

Behind them, one of the members of the assault team was taking care of the hostage operators. They were untied and helped to their feet. One of them came over to help Henderson and Keltner manipulate the controls to bleed off pressure in the plant. For a second, Henderson shifted his eyes from the control panel to the unkempt man on his left. The man smiled at him briefly before his attention was drawn back to the panel.

"Uh oh," the operator said suddenly, "looks like we have a pretty high level in the sales gas compressor suction scrubbers."

Henderson looked over. What the operator meant was that the hydrocarbon liquids that were dropping from the gas as it screamed for release from the emergency flare stack were reaching a critical level in the compressor suction scrubbers. These were vessels designed to remove any liquid from the gas stream before it reached the compressors.

"Can you open the dump valve any more?" Henderson asked.

The operator shook his head.

"It's fully open," he replied calmly. "The valve was designed for a gas stream that was a lot leaner. We've had this problem before. Tying in those rich oil wells last year have really raised havoc with the shut down system."

"I don't remember seeing that mentioned in the application to expand the plant," Henderson said with a smirk.

The operator looked at him a bit sheepishly.

"Sorry, man," he said, "not my department. I only help run the place."

"So what do we do about it?" Henderson asked.

"We've piped in another dump line," was the reply, "but the other valve has to be opened by hand."

"Okay," Henderson sighed, "I'll do it. Where is it?"

"Next to the scrubbers," replied the operator. "While you're out there, would you mind checking on the amine circulation pumps as well? I don't trust this readout."

"Sure," Henderson answered. Then he turned to Keltner, who was busy monitoring the refrigeration system.

"How are you doing, Pete?"

"So far, I'm okay, chief. Doing just like you said."

Henderson scanned the gauges and dials that Keltner had been monitoring.

"Okay, keep up the good work. I'll be back in a few minutes."

"I'll be here."

Henderson stepped out of the control room and breathed in the evening air. He looked up: the flame from the emergency flare stack lit up the sky. He could see bats circling around it, eating the bugs that were attracted to the bright light.

He opened the door to the process building. The noise had subsided a bit by now, but there was still a lot of gas flowing through the pipes. Henderson was closest to the amine system, so he sprinted over to the pumps located by the amine regenerator. He bent down and put his hand on the motor housing. It was warm and he could feel vibration. Then he repeated this with each of the pumps in turn. All of them were operating properly.

Henderson had a cursory look at the rest of the major equipment in the building. The compressors had stopped, so there was no noise from them, but the rest of the equipment seemed to be in fine condition and doing what it was supposed to do during shut down. Henderson noticed that pressures were gradually falling off and the noise in the building was decreasing as the plant slowly ran out of gas.

The suction scrubbers were located at the south end of the building. Evidence of the high levels in these vessels was found in the sight glasses mounted on the side of each of the three vessels.

There was only a small clear spot at the top of the sight glass attached to the vessel with the highest pressure.

"Well, that's cutting it a bit too close," he thought to himself.

Henderson found the valve and tried turning the handle. It was tight and he couldn't budge it. He began to look around.

"There has to be one around here somewhere," he muttered.

He finally found what he was looking for: a three-foot length of thick pipe. To the layman, it was just that, a piece of pipe, but to anyone acquainted with a gas plant, it was a snipe: a piece of pipe that provides extra leverage to swing pipe wrenches and turn the levers on stuck valves.

Applying the pipe to the lever, Henderson was able to crack the valve, after which it opened with relative ease. The liquid level in the vessel began to drop. Henderson knew that it would be flowing into the tanks located at the north end of the plant.

Inside the control room, the newly released operator and Keltner monitored the condition of the plant while the members of the R.C.M.P. assault team were securing Hudson and his partners. Each had been dragged to his feet and was in the process of being handcuffed.

When Michaels's arms were pulled behind his back, he jerked forward.

"I'm the one who sent you guys the signal!" he yelled while he struggled uselessly against the burly police officer.

"Shut-up," was the response from the officer, who pulled Michaels's arms down to get the cuffs onto his wrists.

Becker turned toward them, grabbed Michaels by the collar, and swung him around.

"What signal?" he asked.

"You know, the flare," Michaels gasped. "I'm the one who put the extra gas to the flare stack. You must have seen it!"

"You did what?" Hudson seethed, swivelling his head around to face his former partner. Although his arms were being held tightly by one of the assault team members, the handcuffs on Hudson had not yet been latched onto both wrists.

"You asshole!" he yelled and lunged at Michaels.

"Hey, hey, cool it," ordered the police officer holding Hudson. He tried to pull Hudson back.

Hudson was still struggling for a grip on Michaels when the third police officer came in from the kitchen holding a medium sized wooden box with three switches on it. An antenna protruded from the top.

"I think I found the trigger mechanism," he reported. "It looks like it's been converted from a remote control airplane set."

The other officers turned to look.

That's the type of distraction that Hudson needed. He inhaled deeply and brought his arms first up, and then down. This broke the hold of the police officer. Then Hudson snatched his pistol from the desk where the officers had piled the weapons and jumped through the control room door.

"After him," Becker said, slapping one of the officers on the back.

"And get those three cuffed now!" he ordered the other two before following his man outside.

Hudson had landed on the ground in a lump after jumping over the steps. Then he rolled to his feet and punched open the door to the process building with both hands.

Henderson was on the other side of that door when it flew open. It hit him in the face and he flew backwards. Then he saw Hudson jump over him.

Hudson recognized the man he had bowled over and turned, aiming his pistol at Henderson.

"You son of a bitch, Henderson!" he screamed.

Henderson saw Hudson through the cloudiness of a burning nose and rolled over at the same instant that Hudson squeezed the trigger.

Becker cracked the door open just as the bullet slammed into it. He and his partner retreated slightly and jumped to either side of the doorframe on the outside. Hudson leapt over to kick the door closed. Henderson used this opportunity to scramble to safety behind the large amine contactor vessel.

Seeing the police officers at the door frightened Hudson.

He turned, ran across the floor of the process building to a ladder that led to the overhead platform, and then he began to climb. He was about halfway up to the platform when he saw the door open again and he stopped. He fired another shot that ricocheted off the floor, kicking up sharp pieces of cement shrapnel. Then he continued with his climb to the top. Once there he began running along the overhead platform, back toward the end of the building where he had left Henderson.

By now the plant was almost completely depressurised. There was still a hint of gas blowing through the pipe, but for the most part, the building was still.

Again, Becker opened the door a crack.

"Henderson!" he called out.

"What?!" Henderson yelled back.

"Are you okay?"

Henderson huddled close to the vessel and shook his head.

You've got to be joking, he thought.

"For now!" he called back. "Get him off my back, will you!"

Two shots were fired in quick succession. The first hit the glass pane window in the door, while the second struck the door just below the window frame.

"Forget what I said!" Henderson called to Becker. "Stay where you are! There's still gas in the pipes. We can't risk him hitting one!"

Another shot. This one whistled by Henderson and struck the floor to his left.

"Christ!" Henderson yelled.

A sharp piece of cement had struck him in the side of the face. Henderson slapped his hand over the wound and felt blood in his palm.

"That's it, Clint," Becker said, this time more calmly. "He's out of bullets. We're coming in."

"Okay, but be careful," Henderson warned. "He could still do a lot of damage in here!"

Henderson stood up, his back still welded to the contactor

vessel. Suddenly he heard the clanking of Hudson's boots on the metal platform above.

Henderson closed his eyes and took a deep breath.

"What the HELL am I doing here?" he muttered to himself.

Hudson had stopped running. In the background, Henderson could hear the slow, consistent, echoed click of a methanol pump. Water was dripping somewhere. Other than that, and his own deep breathing, Henderson heard nothing.

He opened his eyes. Becker and his partner had entered the building now and were looking up at the platform. Both men had their crossbows drawn. Their rubber soled boots scraped along the cement as they slowly stalked along the western edge of the building. Their eyes scanned the overhead platform in search of Hudson.

To Henderson it seemed like forever, but finally the R.C.M.P. officers were at the south end of the plant.

Henderson inched his way to his right, away from where the bullet had struck, still clutching the vessel behind him.

While his partner covered him, Becker climbed slowly up the same ladder that Hudson had climbed. Other than the steady, regular sound of the pump in the background, the building was silent.

Henderson continued to move to his right. He knew that there was another door at the far northeast corner of the building, behind the inlet separator.

I'll go for that, he thought, and leave Hudson to the professionals.

As he turned to look for the door, he found himself staring directly into the hatred of Hudson's eyes.

"Oh, Jesus," Henderson mumbled.

"You ugly little motherfucker," Hudson said quietly. "You realize that I'm going to kill you, don't you? Right now. In fact, if you don't scream, I'll even make it quick so you don't feel anything."

Henderson then realized that Hudson must have come back down to the building floor by the other ladder that provided access to the platform, the ladder that was right by the same door he had wanted to use to get out. He also saw that Hudson had found a sledgehammer.

Hudson heaved the huge hammer behind him, its weight slowing his swing. Then he brought it down in front of him. Henderson fell backwards and the hammer smashed into the insulation covering the amine contactor. Small, fine pieces of blue fibreglass fell from the open wound on the side of the process vessel.

Henderson pulled himself backward along the floor. Hudson extracted the sledgehammer from the tin metal covering the insulation around the vessel, turned, and swung again.

Henderson rolled to his left, still pulling himself backwards, his feet kicking and scrambling, desperate to get enough time and traction to stand up and run.

The hammer struck the floor to the right of Henderson's head. Above him, Henderson could hear the police officers running along the platform to the north end of the building, looking for him.

Meanwhile, Henderson was pulling himself in the opposite direction.

"Where are you, Clint?" Becker yelled.

"I'm down here, damn it!" he screamed back.

Hudson had swung again and this time, he barely missed the side of Henderson's head

"Get him away from me!" yelled Henderson.

"We can't get a clear shot!" Becker called back. The process vessels between them muffled his voice.

Henderson was just able to scuttle away from yet another swing. Hudson was blind with rage, concentrating only on Henderson. He barely noticed the thin, black arrow that cut through the air behind him, just grazing the back of his scalp. Becker's partner had been able to take advantage of a brief second in which he was able to see Hudson clearly in his sights.

Henderson found his footing and took a chance. He stood up to run. That's when Hudson swung the sledgehammer sideways.

The heavy steel head smashed into Henderson's right knee. The momentum of the swing propelled him backward and to the side, and he fell to the floor in a heap.

Henderson screamed.

He was almost at the south end of the building now and he could hear the two police officers running back toward him on the overhead platform above.

But Hudson was closer and Henderson couldn't see the door through the tears that were now welling up in his eyes. All he could see were spots and a rapidly building darkness. Through that, he could see Hudson moving toward him, slowly raising the sledgehammer above his left shoulder.

Henderson was almost blind with pain now. He could feel pieces of bone falling from the knee as they grated and cut into the surrounding muscle and tendons of his leg. Anxiously, he looked around with blurred eyesight for something, anything that would allow him to escape from Hudson.

With a quick look behind him, Henderson caught a wet glimpse of the valve that he had originally come out to close. He reached for it with his right hand. The pipe was there, just as he had left it, and his trembling fingers closed around it. He pulled it off the valve lever and tightened his grip.

Hudson was almost right over him now.

Henderson wrapped his other hand around the base of the pipe so that he had a tight batter's hold on his own weapon.

"You're going to die, you piece of shit," Hudson hissed. The sledgehammer was above his head and he was about to put all of his energy into one final swing.

Henderson closed his eyes and swung first. It wasn't a graceful arc, but Henderson used the weight of the pipe to follow through. It caught Hudson on the side of the head and the blow knocked him to the right. The hammer slipped out of his hands and Hudson fell, landing in a crumpled heap.

The police officers were scrambling down the ladder now. At the same time, Keltner entered the building through the northwest door. He ran over to Henderson, arriving there at the same time as Becker and his partner.

Henderson tried to pull himself up on his elbows, but the pain conquered him, and he screamed and collapsed back onto the floor. Keltner put his arm under Henderson's neck and pulled him gently upward.

"What the hell do you think you were doing?" Keltner asked patiently as he put one of Henderson's arms around his own shoulder.

"Oh damned if I know," panted Henderson. "I didn't have too many choices and it really seemed like the right thing to do at the time. Oh Christ, it hurts!"

Another member of the assault team had entered the building. A paramedic accompanied him.

"Well, it's over now," said Keltner quietly. "The plant is all shut in and they've called in the cavalry."

After making sure that Henderson was all right, Becker and his partner checked on Hudson.

"How is he?" Henderson asked, his voice shaky.

"He's not dead," Becker said, "but he'll be out for awhile

yet. And he'll have a hell of a headache when he comes to. Fortunately for him, we have lots of Advil at the station."

Becker stood up, shook his head, and whistled.

"Man, you really did a number on him."

He and the other two police officers picked up Hudson's unconscious body and, after locking his hands together in front of him with handcuffs, they carried him out of the building.

The paramedic had cut away the denim material around Henderson's right knee. He removed the cloth to reveal a hideously swollen lump of bluish-green flesh. The paramedic applied a splint to either side of the knee and wrapped a tight bandage around it to secure it. Henderson winced as the bandage was being wrapped.

"Man, that really fucking hurts!" he said through clenched teeth.

"I know," Keltner muttered as he assessed the bandage on Henderson's leg. "You said that already. Except that this time you added a bad word."

The paramedic looked up at him when he was done.

"There's an ambulance outside," he said, "but we won't be able to get a stretcher through those doors."

"I'll help him out," Keltner said. "Come on, Clint. Let's call it a night."

He moved his arm under Henderson's back and, with the paramedic, helped Henderson to his feet. Henderson tried to stand on his own, but he would have collapsed if Keltner hadn't been supporting him. Henderson felt faint. He saw the process building through a dark red tunnel and he wobbled slightly.

Keltner stood with him for a moment, his arm under Henderson's shoulder.

"That's okay, mate," he said gently. "Take your time. We're not in any hurry."

Henderson closed his eyes and waited for a few seconds. Then he nodded.

"Okay, let's go," he said quietly.

With Keltner and the paramedic supporting him, Henderson staggered to the door on one leg.

"Christ, there goes my promising hockey career," he said through clenched teeth. Even he could tell that his voice was wavering and weak.

"Well, look on the bright side," Keltner replied quietly. "Now you won't have to learn how to skate, so think of all the money you'll save on lessons. Okay, take it easy here. Whoopsy daisy."

Keltner and the paramedic helped him over the doorsill.

The hard glare of the lights in the process building gave way to the soft glow associated with the plant site at night. Henderson could see the flashing lights of the police cars and two ambulances. They were in the parking lot now, and the familiar feel of the plant site's gravel being crushed softly under his feet was reassuringly comforting.

It's over, Henderson thought. It's finally over.

Christ, how can you get to the point where you want to forget a whole evening? he wondered.

He breathed in the gentle early morning air. Although it was still August, Henderson thought he could detect a slight crispness, an edge that was usually associated with an early fall. The air was cool, but pleasant, and it seemed a touch damp, as though the morning dew was just about to arrive.

As they approached the edge of the plant site, Henderson could see the open door of an ambulance waiting for him. He also saw three police cars pulling out, those carrying Michaels, Phillips, and Simpson. There was no sign of Hudson. Henderson assumed that he had already been taken away to hospital under police escort.

Henderson saw Spenser get out of another police car and walk over to them.

"Oh aye," he said. "What did I say about you two getting into trouble?"

Spenser patted Henderson lightly on the shoulder.

"Good work, lad, good work."

Spenser turned to Keltner and held out his hand to shake Keltner's. He pulled it back when he saw that Keltner was supporting Henderson with both arms.

"And you, too, Pete," Spenser continued. "I'm very proud of the both of you. Look, I 'ave to get back to the office for the press conference, but I just wanted you both to know that you've each earned an extra day off. Maybe even two."

Spenser smiled at the two of them.

"I'll catch up with you later and we'll talk," he added with a wink. Then he returned to the police car.

"Uh oh," Keltner said suddenly. "I'm in shit."

"Why?" Henderson asked. He squinted his eyes. "What is it?"

Concentrating on the pain in his leg, he had difficulty focusing on the scene in front of him.

"My wife is here," was the response. "You know, I told you that if she ever found out that I'd volunteered for something like this, she'd kill me."

"I'm sorry to hear that," Henderson said slowly. "Don't worry. I'm sure we'll find someone to deliver a sparkling eulogy."

"Well, if I were you, I wouldn't speak too soon."

"Why? Ow!" Henderson breathed in sharply, closed his eyes, and groaned as a twinge of pain shot through his leg again. "What do you mean?"

"Because Renee is with her."

Henderson opened his eyes and looked in front of him. There she was, standing next to Kathy behind the police barricade. Renee ducked under a policeman's arms and ran towards him.

Ah, now I get it, Henderson realized. Then there are the evenings that you never want to forget.

Like the one last night.

Keltner and the paramedic stopped as Renee approached. She hesitated for a minute when she was right in front of him and then gingerly, she put her arms around his neck and hugged him tightly.

Henderson lifted his hand from the paramedic's shoulder and put it around her. He squeezed as hard as he could, but found that he could only manage a gentle hug.

Renee put her head back. She looked at his face and into

his eyes. With a dusty hand, Henderson stroked a spot of blood from her face. He realized that it had come from the wound on his cheek. As he tried to rub away the sticky fluid that had come from his own body, she looked at his fingers and then at him.

"I'm sorry," Henderson said. "I'm getting your face dirty."

Renee shook her head. There were tears on her face, but she found a smile and hugged him tightly again.

"Look, we have to get your leg looked at," the paramedic interrupted, and he and Keltner began to lead Henderson again gently toward the waiting ambulance.

Renee stayed by his side. As they approached the waiting vehicle, with its red light flashing in the night, they saw Kathy waiting for them. She stepped forward as they approached. Her arms were crossed on her chest and she was shaking her head.

She stopped in front of Keltner.

"What the hell do you think you were doing?" she asked.

Keltner looked puzzled.

"Uh, when?" he asked.

"Tonight!"

A second or two passed in silence, as Keltner appeared to think about the question for a bit.

"I can't really say for sure," he said. "What time?"

Kathy smacked him very lightly on his left temple.

"You two are really something," she said sternly. "I can't leave you alone for five minutes. I said 'moral support', not 'go out and get yourselves killed'."

"Oh that," Keltner said. He took the hand that had been supporting Henderson's stomach and quickly used it to point at him, before returning it to his waist. "I was with him."

Henderson grimaced and inhaled sharply.

"It's true, Kathy" he gasped, "Pete was with me."

Kathy began to laugh and she wrapped her arms around her husband. Henderson noticed that she was crying too.

"It was all his idea," added Keltner.

"You're such a liar," she said quietly, and stood up to kiss Keltner on the lips. She pushed aside a strand of his hair that had fallen on his forehead. "And a fair bit of a fool, too. What am I ever going to do with someone like you?"

"Personally, I think that taking me home and putting me to bed would be a really good idea right now. Hang on a second, hon."

Keltner let go of his wife while he escorted Henderson over to the ambulance. The stretcher had been brought over and the paramedic and Keltner laid Henderson on it gently. It was put into the back of the ambulance. Renee jumped in after him.

"Pete!" Henderson called out.

Keltner's face appeared in the rear door of the ambulance.

"What?" he asked.

"Thanks," Henderson said quietly.

"We're even now," Keltner replied. "Just you remember that."

"Think the kids would buy gas plant inspector action man now?" Henderson asked as he closed his eyes.

Keltner smiled and patted the foot on Henderson's healthy leg.

"Well, I know I would. See you at the hospital."

Then the door was closed behind them.

Renee sat beside him and took Henderson's hand in hers. With the other hand she stroked his forehead. Her touch was cool and gentle.

"I think I could really fall in love with you," she said quietly, the occasional tear still trickling off her cheek. She laughed softly. "Can you believe that? I really never thought I'd say that again."

Henderson looked into her warm eyes and felt a growing sense of warmth in his heart.

"I think I'm already in love with you," he mumbled.

Feeling comfortable for perhaps the first time in years, Henderson drifted into unconsciousness as he felt the squeeze of her hand.

The phone rang twice. Henderson grabbed it before the third ring.

"Gas Department. Clint Henderson here."

"Hallo? This is Frederick Montague with Mitec Explorations here. I wish to complain about your fascist regulations, which I find to be extremely oppressive and wordy."

"Well, Mr. Montague," Henderson replied, "you should know that we're shutting your operation in, you freak. And that goes for your sick friend, Pete Keltner, too."

Henderson heard a laugh at the other end of the phone.

"Hey, my man, how are you doing?" Keltner asked. "How's the leg?"

"It aches sometimes, especially if I sit in one place for too long. I'm still using a cane. Makes me look rather distinguished, I think. Plus it's one of those that has the little flask inside the handle, which helps kill the pain a bit at coffee break."

"I'm sure. I bet the onset of winter isn't helping at all."

"We've had a nice little Chinook blow in, so it's not too bad right now. Heard you're having a bit of a cold snap, though."

"Well, we're discovering just how strong Alexandria's bladder is, that's for sure. She does not like going out in this weather one bit."

"Uh huh. How are you doing?"

"Do you want the good news first or the bad news?"

"Uh oh. You'd better give me the bad news first."

"My attempt to make amends with Kathy's brother kind of went down the toilet."

Henderson closed his eyes, leaned his head back, and sighed.

"Do you want to tell me about it?" he asked.

"Well, it's his birthday coming up and we were going to have them over for dinner. Kathy's been busy lately, pulling some extra shifts, so I said that I'd look after the cake."

"And?"

"Well, I went down to Rosie's, you remember Rosie's?"

"Yeah. Awesome sausage rolls."

"That's them. Anyway, I'd ordered a double layer, German chocolate cake, with white chocolate icing. I was going to have 'Happy birthday, Lawrence' written in bright red lettering on top, which costs a mint, but you know how he prefers to be called 'Lawrence'."

"Sounds great. What happened? What did you do?"

"Why does everyone assume that it's my fault? It's not fair."

"Come on, Pete…"

"Look, I figured that everybody would only pay attention to what was written on the top of the cake. After the putz blows out the candles, the cake gets sliced up and what's inside the cake gets all mushed together. Nobody would have seen or known."

"Seen or known what?"

"That I'd had the words 'Drop dead, Larry' written in icing on top of the first layer."

"Oh, Pete."

"No one was supposed to know! It was all supposed to be covered by the second layer."

"So how were you found out?"

"Kathy was in the bakery getting croissants for our breakfast and Alex, you know Alex?"

"Yeah. He's Rosie's son."

"Well, he was doing the cake and he'd finished the first layer just as Kathy came in. So he showed it to her and asked her if it was all right."

"I don't believe it. And she gave you shit, I trust."

"Nah, I think that she would have gone for it. Of course, though, it had to be the day that her sister-in-law was with her."

Henderson shook his head.

"Oops," he said. "Okay, then: what's the good news?"

"I'm going to be a daddy."

"Oh, you're kidding! Wow! That's terrific! How's Kathy?"

"Great. The doctor figures that it looks pretty good this time provided she takes it easy, so I've convinced her to stop working. She says she's more excited than me, but don't you believe that for a second."

"I'm really glad to hear that. Are you hoping for a boy or girl?"

"The doctor has told her, but I don't want to know. I don't care."

"Well, regardless, I hope it has her looks."

"Just between you and me, so do I."

"Give my love to her will you?"

"I'll do that. Say, how are you and Renee getting along?"

"Great. Wonderful. Stupendous."

"I take it things are going well?"

"They really are. The kid's just great, he really is. He gets a little confused once in a while. Occasionally, he really misses his father and he ignores me. I've got to admit that it bothers me sometimes, but hey, he is only two and a bit. Renee has been helping me deal with it."

"She sounds like a great gal."

"I couldn't ask for any better."

"Good. It looks like things are finally going your way. Oh, by the way, remember that kid Simpson?"

"Yeah, the boy they said was retarded. What about him?"

"My dad's hired him to work on the farm. He'll get room and board, and the whole bit. I guess he's a natural with the cattle. Dad thinks he'll really do well on the farm."

"It was pretty decent of Phillips to stand up for him at the trial."

"You can't help but agree with him, though. There's no way Simpson belongs in jail. I still can't believe that the others dragged him into it the way they did. It's disgusting."

"Neither can I. How about the rest?"

"Sentencing is next week."

"Boy, that was a bitch of trial, wasn't it?"

"I must say you were pretty cool on the stand."

"Thanks, but after that night in the plant, it was pretty easy, I'll tell you."

"You can say that again. So, to change the subject: how's the Calgary office treating you?"

"Pretty good. I enjoy the job. It's fairly challenging, although I miss not being able to get out in the field."

"Much chance to get up this way once in a while?"

"It's funny you should say that. I was just about to phone you as a matter of fact. I have to review a site for a proposed gas plant, just south of Slave Lake. Interested in taking me out there?"

"Sure. Who am I to miss seeing you do some real work again? When?"

"I'll be flying into Edmonton next Tuesday night. We could go up on Wednesday."

"Yeah, okay. Stay with us on Tuesday night."

"Are you going to cook?"

"Me and the brand spanking new hundred gazillion BTU propane flame broiler extraordinaire."

"Is it safe?"

"Hey, you taught me everything there is to know about gas stuff."

"I guess that it would save the Board a few bucks."

"Plus give me a chance to whip you in chess."

"That too."

"Okay, then. I guess I'll see you at the airport on Tuesday night. It'll be good to get out in the field with you again."

"I'm looking forward to it. Oh, and Pete?"

"Yeah?"

There was a pause.
"You will bring a jack with you, won't you?